CAPTAIN GREY'S GAMBIT

Also by J. H. Gelernter

Hold Fast

J. H. GELERNTER

CAPTAIN GREY'S GAMBIT

· *A Novel* ·

W. W. NORTON & COMPANY

Independent Publishers Since 1923

Captain Grey's Gambit is a work of fiction. Names, characters, places, and incidents are the products of the author's imagination or are used fictitiously. Any resemblance to actual events, locales, or persons, living or dead, is entirely coincidental.

Copyright © 2022 by J. H. Gelernter

Printed in the United States of America
First Edition

For information about permission to reproduce selections from this book, write to Permissions, W. W. Norton & Company, Inc., 500 Fifth Avenue, New York, NY 10110

For information about special discounts for bulk purchases, please contact W. W. Norton Special Sales at specialsales@wwnorton.com or 800-233-4830

Manufacturing by Lake Book Manufacturing
Book design by Brooke Koven
Production manager: Anna Oler

Library of Congress Cataloging-in-Publication Data

Names: Gelernter, J. H., author.
Title: Captain grey's gambit : a novel / J. H. Gelernter.
Description: First Edition. | New York, NY : W. W. Norton & Company, [2022]
Identifiers: LCCN 2021038218 | ISBN 9780393867060 (hardcover) | ISBN 9780393867077 (epub)
Subjects: GSAFD: Historical fiction.
Classification: LCC PS3607.E417 C37 2022 | DDC 813/.6—dc23
LC record available at https://lccn.loc.gov/2021038218

W. W. Norton & Company, Inc.
500 Fifth Avenue, New York, N.Y. 10110
www.wwnorton.com

W. W. Norton & Company Ltd.
15 Carlisle Street, London W1D 3BS

1 2 3 4 5 6 7 8 9 0

This book is respectfully dedicated to

Yusaku Maezawa

In hopes someone will let him know that I am available for a
moon flight on short notice

CAPTAIN GREY'S GAMBIT

I

November the 22nd, 1803
At Thineh, on the North Coast of the Sinai

T O TRAVEL FROM England to India, one takes a ship round the
southern tip of Africa, and spends four months at sea, if the
winds are with you, and six months if they are not.

If you haven't six months to spare, or even four, you can chance
an overland crossing at the Isthmus of Suez.

Provided you can find ships to carry you to one end and away from
the other, and that you're lucky, and that you meet no Barbary slavers
along Egypt's ill-defined eastern frontier, you might shorten the journey from Britain to the British Raj by half—a two months' trip was
not unheard of. Under orders from His Majesty's Office of the Admiralty and Marine Affairs, it was the overland route that had taken
Thomas Grey, with urgent dispatch, to India. He had been pressed
into service as a royal postman, carrying letters from His Majesty's
Secret Service, in London, to His Majesty's Major-General Wesley,
somewhere east of Bombay, at the head of an Anglo-Indian army.

Grey caught up with Wesley at Assaye, and—after some minor
confusion arising from the general having changed his name, unac-
countably, from Arthur *Wesley* to Arthur *Wellesley*—the letters were

delivered. Now Grey was on his way home, carrying a response and report by Wellesley, to Whitehall. Grey traveled by the same over-land isthmus route, reversed. And finally he was approaching the final leg of the trip.

Having crossed from the Red Sea to the Mediterranean—from the port of Suez, through the Sinai Desert, to the coast town of Thineh—Grey was seated comfortably on a beach, less than a mile east of the eastmost branch of the Nile Delta. The sand was warm, and the surf gentle; Grey was eating flatbread dipped in date honey, and watching His Majesty's frigate *Juno*, thirty-two, drop anchor a hundred yards offshore. Grey finished his breakfast as *Juno* finished lowering her stern jolly boat. It was early morning, just after dawn on the appointed day, at the appointed hour, of the first scheduled rendezvous attempt of HMS *Juno* and Mr. Grey. There would have been a second attempt in a week's time, and a third a week after that. But, much to his own satisfaction—Grey being a man who enjoyed a race—he had beaten *Juno* to Thineh by almost two days.

At Suez, he'd purchased a pair of camels—the second to carry Grey's Bedouin guide—and crossed the isthmus in the wonderfully expeditious time of three nights and two days. Four days was stan-dard, but the weather was unseasonably cool, which meant the men were able to ride not only by night, but throughout the day, barring the hour before noon and the two hours after. Each day as the sun approached its zenith, Grey and his guide spread a shade awning and slept the few hours, with the camels beside them. It was childish, perhaps, but sleeping camels never failed to amuse Grey—choosing, as they do, to repose with their serpentine necks and their spin-dly legs splayed out in arbitrary directions, as if they were rag dolls dropped from the top of a tall building . . . In any case, the short stops had helped Grey to Thineh with two days to spare. In thanks, he'd made a gift of the camels to the Bedouin—who, though unable to take credit for the cool weather, was a most amiable fellow, who'd kept Grey entertained throughout the journey with stories of French archaeological digs: one of his cousins had been with Napoleon's expedition, as a translator (the Bedouin spoke no English, but his

French, like Grey's, was perfect). This cousin had been present at Rosetta when the great stone had been discovered; this was of particular interest to Grey. When he'd left London four months earlier, the stone had been the invariable topic of conversation at every club and coffeehouse; the first translation of the stone's Greek portion had just been published.

Grey wondered if, during his time away, anyone had deciphered the hieroglyphics. In the offices of the secret intelligence service—at Admiralty House, beside the Horse Guards Parade—there was scarcely a man to be found without a homemade brass rubbing of the stone on his desk, and a Greek dictionary open beside it. Grey's good friend Aaron Willys—chief of staff to the chief of naval intelligence, Sir Edward Banks—had been forced to make a new career of confiscating the things and ordering secret servicemen back to their work. Willys had personally burned Grey's rubbing (which Grey had rubbed himself, at the Montagu House museum) with a cheroot. As it burned, Willys had dangled the flimsy sheet from his thumb and forefinger and bellowed the question at Grey, did the gentleman know there was a f——g war on?

Grey smiled at the memory. In any case, he'd given the camels to the Bedouin guide, who reciprocated by inviting Grey to wait out his time till *Juno* arrived at the family camp, where his tribe was stopped for the season—on the banks of the Nile, a few miles to Thineh's southwest. Grey had gratefully accepted, and spent part of one day and all of one night enjoying some superb Bedouin hospitality.

He smiled at that memory too.

The jolly boat, an eighteen-foot cutter with six oarsmen pulling together against the tide, was just crossing the breakers. Grey stood, rolled up his trouser legs, and—with his boots stowed and his dunnage over his shoulder—waded out to meet it.

"Are you Mr. Grey, sir?" said a young lieutenant at the boat's stern, while two of the oarsmen stood in the surf, holding the boat in place for Grey's approach.

"I am, sir," said Grey, tossing his bag to one of the dry-footed oarsmen and pulling himself out of waist-deep water, over the gunwales.

"I'm Hopper, sir," said the lieutenant, and then, to the oarsmen in the surf, "Shove off there."

"A pleasure to make your acquaintance, Mr. Hopper," said Grey. The two men in the surf pushed the jolly boat back out over the breakers and were pulled aboard by their mates, and then, all together, they pulled for HMS *Juno*. The whole operation was splendidly efficient, and Grey had only just enough time to put on his jacket and make himself halfway presentable before oars were pulled up at the accommodation ladder. Grey climbed the accommodation with the ease of a man who'd spent many years at sea—the first volume of his working life had been as one of the red-coated marines who round out the complement of all British warships.

Having been recruited to naval intelligence from the marine officers' corps, Grey retained a courtesy rank of captain, but it was a title he seldom used—discretion being the better part of spying. So traveling as he normally did, as Mr. Grey, he eschewed saluting the quarterdeck, and instead shook hands with *Juno*'s captain, who greeted him at the gangway.

"A pleasure to have you aboard, Mr. Grey. I hope we didn't keep you waiting."

"On the contrary, Captain Crowther, your punctuality is impeccable. I appreciate your taking me off."

"Certainly, Mr. Grey. Can I offer you tea?"

"Thank you, yes," said Grey.

"Mr. Burnes," said Crowther to a young lieutenant on the quarterdeck, "when the jolly boat's hauled up, weigh and set a course north till we sink the land, then west-by-north. You have the deck."

Captain Crowther led Grey into the great cabin, which occupied the entire width of the sternmost fifteen feet of gundeck, and was, on any warship, the only interior space that might be described as spacious. Even if *Juno*'s required Grey and Crowther both to stoop slightly.

"Please to be seated," said Crowther, sitting himself on the stern lockers. "My table and chairs had to be struck below last night when it came on to blow. They should be up with the tea."

So they were, and as Captain Crowther repopulated his desk with maps and papers, Grey sipped tea and regretted a final cup of coffee not drunk before parting from his Bedouin hosts.

"So I gather——" started Crowther, as he was cut off by a knock on his cabin door. "Come," he said.

"Beg pardon, sir," said a midshipman of about twelve, "and Mr. Solomon reports all of the red grain is dry and only one of white damp and Mr. Bibble reports down to six inches in the well."

"Very good, Mr. Matthews; when she's cleared, have Mr. Burnes send the hands at the pumps to breakfast. And tell Walpole he may light the fires and serve hot."

"Yes, sir; thank you, sir."

"Though you'll never go wrong erring on the side of good discipline and good manners," said Crowther to his young midshipman, "in these cases, the 'yes, sir' will suffice alone."

"Yes sir. Thank you, sir."

The boy blushed and the captain half smiled. "Now cut along, there's work to do."

"Yes sir."

Crowther poured himself a second cup of tea and sat down opposite Grey. "It's his first time at sea and he's still tolerably nervous. He needs more beef. In any case . . . where was I?"

"You had gathered something," said Grey.

"Ah yes: I gather from my orders that you are carrying dispatches, but they—my orders—leave it an open question as to whether these are official dispatches. That is to say, I must know if I should order all hails be met with a signal of 'carrying dispatches.' "

It was normal for two king's ships that encountered one another at sea to make their numbers and establish the seniority of their captains. It was not uncommon, in those cases, for the senior officer then to invite—that is to say, order—his junior to come across with any news he might have, to compare chronometers and to collect mail. The only circumstance in which a ship of the Royal Navy could ignore such an order (or any order a senior captain might make) was if she were carrying dispatches. Then, a sloop might refuse the command of a three-decker beneath a pair of admirals. Naturally, it was a signal captains enjoyed having at hand.

Grey thought for a moment, took a slow sip of tea. "Yes," he said. "I believe you would be justified."

"Very good," said Crowther. "MR. WINTHROP," he called, and the cabin door was opened by the marine standing outside it.

"Yes, sir?"

"Pass the word for Mr. Hopper."

"Yes, sir," said the marine, closing the door again.

THE LETTERS that Grey carried from Wellesley pertained to the efforts of Napoleon's France to break the stalemate in its war with Britain. After subduing the rest of Europe, France had expected a swift victory over the United Kingdom—and why not? Having raised armies in response to the Jacobin Terror, the Allies had swiftly lost Belgium, the Netherlands, Piedmont, Switzerland, and Italy; the First and Second Coalitions had each been smashed to pieces, and only Napoleon's decision to point the French army inward, replacing the Jacobins' dictatorship with one of his own, had kept guillotines out of Vienna and Berlin. Europe east of the Rhine had accepted a French empire west of the Rhine, provided it stay there. Only the United Kingdom of Britain and Ireland refused to yield and kiss the ground before young Bonaparte's feet.

For the time being, the British Isles stood alone—the last great power that refused to believe the short Corsican intended to confine himself behind the river Rhine, and that wasn't prepared to accept a world under his rule. Fortunately, word of a French invasion fleet had reached England before the fleet itself—and now it faced a south coast heavily fortified—covered with Martello tower batteries that His Majesty's engineers seemed to put up in matters of hours, and behind which stood a new home army of fifty thousand reservists.

Still, the towers and soldiers could only hold if, as it had since 1066, the Royal Navy controlled the English Channel. Britain could only win on the beaches if she kept control of the seas. The Corsican himself had become quite open about this, proclaiming to his

"Armée of England," anxiously waiting to board their armada of landing craft, "Let us be masters of the Channel for six hours and we are masters of the world."

But the Royal Navy couldn't be moved. And now Napoleon was trying to move it by setting fires elsewhere in the world that Britain would have to spend time and treasure extinguishing. Wellesley and his Indian allies had General Pierre Cuillier-Perron and the Maratha Empire under control, for the moment. Parliament was preserving a peace with the United States, even as Napoleon sold Louisiana to the Americans, and sold with it a considerable amount of North America that Britain claimed. Even so, it was only a matter of time. Either Britain would find allies who would enable its opening a second front—a land war, on the continent—or one day soon, a storm would blow the Channel squadron far enough off its blockade course for the French invasion fleet to slip out of port. Then the invasion would begin, and Britain would be forced to fight an ugly, costly, defensive war, on the beaches and the landing grounds—in the fields and in the streets—in the hills, until the kingdom was either subjugated and starving, or the winner of a bloody, bloody pyrrhic victory.

It was only a matter of time. Unless Britain could form a Third Coalition, and make it Napoleon who was forced to fight a defensive war.

"Sir?" said Lieutenant Hopper, opening the door to the great cabin.

"Tell Mr. Burnes to answer any signal with the reply 'carrying dispatches' and to keep to this course. As soon as we veer west, spread all plain sail and prepare to bend studding sails as well."

"Very good, sir."

"Capital," said Crowther to Grey once Hopper had withdrawn. "Capital. We ought to make splendid time back to the Rock, and to England then. Can I offer you some breakfast?"

2

THE VOYAGE WEST through the Mediterranean was fast and smooth; the levanter that had shaken up *Juno* just before Grey's embarking her proved to be the last big blow she'd see east of Gibraltar. She touched just briefly at the Rock, to water and replace some lime juice of a suspect nature, and then was out into the Atlantic, rounding Cape Trafalgar and heading north against an indifferent current, making better than ten knots with the westerlies blowing one point abaft the beam.

England was perhaps a week away, and Grey's eagerness for hearth and home was tempered only slightly by the regret he always felt at the end of a sea voyage. Having spent so many of his formative years at sea, he found it easy to fall back into a naval routine and less easy to step out of it. With the sailing smooth, the decks were free for the marines to drill, and Grey had indulged them (or, it would perhaps be more accurate to say, they had indulged him) with joining in exercising the cutlasses—fencing and sparring on the forecastle— and in running out the Baker rifles. Afterwards, Grey had retired to the quarterdeck, where he leant on the taffrail and read *On the Flora of Lapland, and the Soil On Which It Grows,* by a botanist of Grey's acquaintance named Kefauver. Grey had just finished a lengthy chapter on *Cladonia rangiferina,* the "reindeer moss"—in truth, said the book, a *lichen*—upon which the tundra ungulates principally sustain themselves. He was advancing to a discussion of the phosphoretic soils that sustain this lichen when a call came down from the foretop, "On deck there! Sail on the starboard beam!"

All eyes turned east, towards the Bay of Biscay and France— though neither France nor indeed the horizon hiding it was visible. About ten miles away and close over the water was a thick fog topped by a rank of thunderheads. The weather in the bay was, as a matter of tradition, terrible, so this surprised no one—however, the sight of a sail headed due west out of the storm put the same idea in the mind of every man on the *Juno*: she must be a blockade-runner slipped out of Rochefort, doubtless a smuggler packed to the gunwales with wine and cognac, and wasn't it just her godless Jacobin luck to run out of a storm and into a British man-o'-war.

A second thought, though, entered the minds of the officers walking *Juno*'s quarterdeck: they were, evidently, carrying dispatches. Did that give them leeway to snap up a smuggler?

"Mr. Grey: a word if you please," said Captain Crowther, who was standing at the leeward rail. As Grey stepped forward to join him, the other officers retreated to windward to give the illusion of privacy.

"My standing orders," said Crowther to Grey, "require me to take or sink any blockade-runner I encounter. However, my orders, in this case, are made subject to yours. If it is your belief that the letters you carry can't risk a sea fight or a day's delay, you must say so now."

"Might I borrow your glass, Captain?"

"Certainly."

Grey brought the spyglass to his eye and took a close look at the French ship, which was perhaps six miles to leeward and not very much clearer in refraction than it had been to the naked eye. Still, Grey could make out two masts and square rigging.

"A brig-rigged sloop, sir?"

"So I believe, Mr. Grey." That would make her rather a lavish smuggler. Of course, there was the other possibility:

"A sloop of war, sir?"

"Possibly, Mr. Grey."

"Perhaps carrying dispatches of her own?"

"The thought occurs, Mr. Grey." Grey looked a moment longer, then closed the glass and handed it back to the captain.

"In that case, Captain Crowther," said Grey, "let us have her."

Crowther smiled and couldn't resist the familiarity of patting Grey on the shoulder. He turned to his windward officers, all of whom had been straining to eavesdrop on the deliberations.

"We shall beat to quarters, Mr. Burnes. Clear for action."

Now Burnes smiled. "Very good, sir." He turned to the boatswain at the break of the quarterdeck and bellowed—"WE SHALL BEAT TO QUARTERS."

The boatswain repeated the call, the marine at his side beat a drumroll calling the ship to action, and every hand set quickly to his work. No doubt the same was true aboard the Frenchman, though their officers were facing a more difficult decision. Rochefort is a harbor with an uneasy approach even in clear weather; as a lee shore in fog, it is mortal. That taken with a British blockade to pass through for a second time, there could be no retreat for the sloop. The only question left to her was whether to run south or north. Grey felt sure that, at the moment, her officers were debating the *Juno*'s sailing qualities: whether she would be relatively swifter with the wind afore or abaft the beam; whether north or south would offer the better chance of escape.

But she seemed to be taking her sweet pastoral time about it— still she was on her original course, straight at HMS *Juno*. Could she be contemplating a fight? Certainly not, said Grey to himself. If she were a sloop of war, she might ship ten or twelve or even fourteen guns, none of them heavier than four pounds, for a total broadside of a mere two stone. *Juno* threw a weight of metal more than eight times that. Including carronades on the quarterdeck and forecastle, her broadside was something in the way of two hundred and thirty pounds. Two hundred and thirty to twenty-eight. And more than ten score men against fewer than ninety. No, for the Frenchman, a fight would be suicide.

But still she came onward. At no great speed—perhaps five knots. But all the same, she came onward. Soon she was close enough for some detail to appear in a spyglass. "Batavian colors, sir," said Lieutenant Hopper, who was officer of the deck and had his own glass trained on the sloop.

"Very good," said Crowther. Beyond the break of the quarterdeck, a landsman waister was lifting a chicken coop down the companionway; Grey heard him loudly observe—in case it hadn't occurred to his mates—"We ain't at war with the Dutch, though."

"Shut your mouth, Nibley," answered a boatswain's mate. "Her colors don't signify; get them damned birds below before I start you down myself."

Indeed her colors didn't signify—any ship might legitimately fly a false flag in hopes of confusing an enemy, so long as she hoisted her true colors before firing a shot. It was commonplace; soon the flag of Batavia would come down and the Tricolore would go up.

And so they did:

"Batavian colors struck, sir. French colors running up."

The Frenchman was still coming on. Grey squinted to get a clear look at it.

"Sir . . ." said Hopper a moment later. "I wasn't—that is to say, I am not quite certain—but I believe—at first I thought it was just the wind blowing it back on itself—but I believe, sir, that her ensign's inverted—red to the in and blue to the out."

In two steps Captain Crowther was beside him, saving time by appropriating the lieutenant's spyglass—"By your leave, Mr. Hopper"—peering, squinting through the lenses . . .

"You're right, Lieutenant." He returned the glass and turned to Grey, clasping his hands behind his back, looking just moderately disappointed. "Well, at least we shall still make a prize of her, but no fight today, Mr. Grey. She flies a distress signal."

He turned to the helmsman. "Keep to this course. Straight at her."

Reaching the distressed French sloop took not much more than half an hour—Crowther kept the *Juno* flying as fast as she could go, trimming and retrimming the sails to get every bit of speed out of the brisk westerly breeze. No seaman worth his salt would ever treat the case of a ship in distress as less urgent than the prospect of prize money. Grey reflected on the strange rules of honor at sea—it was a navy man's duty, and often his pleasure, to fight, and often to kill, any enemy he might encounter. However, that same enemy had only to ask for help, and he would be helped with the zeal of a sister nurse, who knew nothing of flags and wars; only that all men were brothers.

As the *Juno* closed with the Frenchman, they could start to see the source of her distress: her sails were all ahoo; clew lines were snapped and sheets were flapping. Her rigging was tangled and loose, and her decks—which, from a distance, had looked curiously bare—could be seen packed with bodies laid flat, and with a man presumed to be the French surgeon moving among them. When the ships were within hailing range—about ten yards apart, parallel and each showing her starboard broadside, Crowther shouted across—

"Ahoy, *le sloop française . . . Que-est-que le . . . trouble. Avec vous.*"

On the French sloop, it was a warrant officer—the sailing master, Grey guessed—who answered.

"Monsieur, we were terribly thrown about during the storm, the wind coming off the land making the very short sea, and the cross sea. We could not get our head to the waves, monsieur, and were tossed. Grievously tossed. The commander and the lieutenant are not able to stand, are not awake. The cadet is mortal. With broken hands and legs, we have not enough men to work the ship."

"We will put across our surgeon and a prize crew," said Crowther. "We will make fast to you fore and aft; throw your lines."

The crew of the *Juno* were still at their battle stations; the guns were still run out, and the decks still cleared for action. Crowther now gave the order to secure from quarters and fasten the French sloop. *Juno*'s waisters and forecastlemen caught monkey fists thrown by some of the few French crewmen still standing; used them to haul across heavy French bowlines, which were fed, one at a time, into *Juno*'s capstan. The waisters got to work turning the capstan, pulling the ships together as the lines tightened, finally making the bowlines fast to *Juno*'s bits with the two ships only ten feet apart.

The French sloop—whose name had now been given: she was the *Marianne*—being a much smaller ship, reached her quarterdeck only slightly higher than the *Juno*'s gundeck; a gangway was laid from her main deck to *Juno*'s gundeck entry port. Lieutenant Hopper and a handful of marines preceding them, the *Juno*'s surgeon and his mates and a skeleton crew began to cross over from the English ship to the French.

Hopper was to take command; with the incapacity of the French officers, it was the sailing master (for so he was; the Frenchman in charge) who would present Hopper with the captain's sword—the ceremony that formalized the French surrender.

The sailing master removed the sword from its sheath and held it out, laid across his two open palms, for Hopper to accept. Hopper stuck the pistol he carried into his belt and reached out to take the sword. As he did, the French sailing master turned his right hand palm-down onto the sword's hilt, gripped it, and drove it into Hopper's gut. As he did, hell broke loose.

The wounded French who scattered the main deck rose from their *extremis*, miraculously healed; a dozen or so bore muskets and pistols, which they fired at the prize crew on the gangplank, and the marines at *Marianne*'s gangway, and *Juno*'s officers on her quarterdeck. Some of the invalids ran to the *Marianne*'s cannon, which were evidently primed and loaded—they were quickly aimed and fired, directly into *Juno*'s own gunports, dismounting seven of her thirteen starboard guns and killing, in a stroke, perhaps thirty men of the gun crews. Aboard *Juno*, with the men having for the most part departed their battle quarters, there was chaos—some men running back to their stations, others to the arms lockers, still others grabbing handspikes and belaying pins and rushing to fend off the boarders who were now rushing up the gangplank and flooding into *Juno*'s gundeck.

The *Marianne*'s gun crews raced to reload as the *Juno*'s gun crews raced back to their guns, or to guns that could still be fired. *Juno*'s first shots, fired from the forecastle and the quarterdeck, and followed shortly thereafter by a single twelve-pounder on the gundeck, crashed down into *Marianne*. The volley was returned by the surviving *Marianne* gun crews, who dismounted three more of the *Juno's* main cannon.

These were the last shots *Marianne* fired; *Juno* poured three more volleys into her—making pig iron and matchsticks of her guns and forecastle—before it became clear that but little crew remained aboard the Frenchman. The fighting was man-to-man and on *Juno's* gundeck.

And it was bloody. Despite being grossly outnumbered, the French had the great advantage of surprise; the swords, pikes, and axes of the first Mariannes across the gangway hacked up a score of Junos before they'd recovered their wits, and a dozen more before they'd been able to arm themselves. The odds in *Juno's* favor had diminished from two-to-one to three-to-two, and were still falling as the French pressed home a well-planned and utterly criminal ambush.

For Grey's part, he'd been with the *Juno's* officers on her quarterdeck, watching Hopper accept the French surrender. As Hopper was killed—as the French barrage started—Grey reached for his sword—which he wasn't wearing, having been nominally a guest on Crowther's quarterdeck, and not in uniform. He turned to the break of the deck, where a small arms chest sat before the helm. What he saw was *Juno's* marine sergeant bleeding from a shot to the neck and unconscious. Grey grabbed the cutlass from the sergeant's limp hand and turned back to the rail. The French boarding crew, which had been primed for action, was already for the most part across. Grey grabbed the mizzen shrouds, pulled himself up onto the rail, and leapt, five feet to his left and ten feet down, onto the cross-ship gangplank.

He crashed down among the final dozen French boarders, knocking one off the plank and into the water as he landed, almost following the man in, grabbing a second Frenchman by the shirtfront to steady himself, then hurling that man over the side into his friend's wake. Now Grey brought the cutlass to bear—the match of an experienced swordsman with a gang of overstimulated seamen was not a fair one. Grey stabbed easily into the belly of the first man he faced, who came on swinging wildly with a boat hook. As he fell into the water, Grey ran the next man through; he, falling, pulled Grey's sword with him, forcing Grey to pull it back at an angle and strike the next man with his backhand, taking the head cleanly from the shoulders.

The next Frenchman in line carried a long pike that he lanced forward at Grey. Grey leaned away from it, almost fell backward into the sea, grabbed the shaft of the lance, and yanked towards the *Juno*, steadying himself and pulling the Frenchman awkwardly forward. Grey clutched the lance to his side with his elbow and torqued the man into the water. That was the last boarder crossing from the *Marianne*. Grey turned to the backs of the men who'd crossed already. He drew back his sword to perforate the one closest to him, of the men forcing their way along the plank and into *Juno*'s gundeck—but finding himself unable to stab a man in the back—even a man who could use a distress signal as a ruse, something *so far beneath contempt that it might be presumed to exist only in the infernal regions*—he instead grabbed the man by his collar and twisted him off the plank. Another man into the water; another, and another—one detected something behind him; heard Grey, amidst the cacophony of shouts, the shouts of his comrades falling into the sea between the ships, or maybe the screams as they struggled for handholds or debris to cling to, or carrion to cling to—few European seamen knew how to swim—as they tried to keep from being swept under either bobbing ship, or worse, pulped between them. This next French boarder turned and raised an ax; Grey sliced off the arm holding it, on the upswing, and on the downswing swept the man into the sea.

Grey was up at the *Juno*'s gangway now, with all the Frenchmen ahead of him inboard; he heard shouting from above, from the quarterdeck; he slipped the sword into his belt, grabbed the stern chains, and hoisted himself up, feet slipping against the ship's side, dangling beneath him as he pulled himself up hand over hand—pulled himself onto the chains, up to the rail and over, back onto the quarterdeck. Some of the French had come up the afterhatch and were pressing an attack on the few men still about the helm; Lieutenant Burnes, sword in hand, was lunging and thrusting and parrying like a madman, holding half a dozen Mariannes at bay; behind him a fragment of a gun crew was trying to bring one of the aft carronades to bear forward.

Grey joined Burnes, and the helmsman turned from the wheel to club a Marianne that had clambered up from the waist. In an instant, a voice behind them was shouting "DOWN, DOWN" and Burnes grabbed the helmsman by his belt and pulled him to the deck. Grey dropped flat beside them, and over their heads, chain shot tore a bloody hole through the French assault, tearing through chests, tearing off legs and arms and heads.

One horribly disfigured man stumbled, in agony, back towards the rail nearest his ship, an instinctive move towards the barest comfort. Grey followed him and put him out of his misery; at the same time, a cry came from somewhere beneath them—an English rallying cry—some kind of maddened huzzah—and Grey felt a stitch in his chest: perhaps the tide was beginning to turn. With Burnes at his heels, Grey followed a trail of gore down the afterhatch and plunged into the diminishing crowd of Frenchmen. They were now clustered afore the gangway, abaft the mainmast, and seemed to know they were fighting a losing battle. Another long pike stabbed out towards Grey—again he stepped away from it and pulled it forward by the shaft. The piker came with it, and Burnes stabbed him twice about the lungs. As the man spit blood, a French officer broke away from the throng of his men and loped towards the gangway, clutching a deep wound in his belly. Grey stepped forward to chase after him; at the same time, a man grabbed Grey from behind and yanked him backward, pulled him spinning onto a bloody coil of rope. It was Burnes that grabbed him—the French had cut a cannon free and it charged past, leaving a track of crushed bodies behind it. A roll in the ship slowed the loose cannon enough for a dozen Englishmen to tackle it and throw it onto its side, before it was able to crash through a hatch and down through the hold and through *Juno*'s bottom.

Burnes pulled Grey back to his feet. "Thank you," said Grey, before running out the entrance port and onto the gangplank, crossing over to the French ship. The escaped French officer was leaving a thick trail of blood behind him that Grey could follow even amongst the piles of plank and tackle made by the *Juno*'s cannon and carronades. The trail led up onto the *Marianne*'s quarterdeck, towards her poop—past the body of Lieutenant Hopper—and into the *Marianne*'s great cabin. And there was the officer, on his hands and knees, scrabbling through the wreckage of a desk, looking for something.

Grey could see now that the officer was the French captain. Grey couldn't help but be pleased with the destruction that had rained down on his home, his private cabin. He'd had a desperately weak hand and had tried to win with it by cheating. He'd gotten what he deserved. A doubtless beautiful sweep of stern windows had been atomized. About a third of the roof had collapsed—or rather, about a third of the poop deck had fallen into the great cabin. Cannonballs rolled in an almost serene cycle of port to starboard, starboard to port, something like the pendulum of a giant clock. Or a box of giant's marbles. Grey stepped carefully through undulating tide of balls, towards the captain, who continued to search through the wreckage of his desk.

Grey had his sword half-raised. Menacing rather than threatening.

"Mr. Captain," he said in French, "you will understand that your turpitude will prevent me from accepting your word of surrender, so I must ask you to put your hands on your head and accompany me back to His Majesty's ship *Juno*."

The captain ignored him; was elbow deep in his former desk, feeling for something. Grey put the edge of his sword at the captain's throat.

"*Monsieur le capitaine,*" he said again. "*Que cherches-tu?*"

The captain stopped his search and looked up at Grey.

"*Tes bras,*" said Grey. The captain slowly withdrew his arms from the remains of his desk. Using his left elbow, he lifted part of a heavy oaken drawer out of the way so his right arm could pull something with it.

Grey pressed the cutlass blade lightly into the captain's throat. "*Doucement.*"

Slower now, the captain continued to withdraw his arms. Grey expected the captain's right hand to emerge clutching a pistol or a dagger. Instead it appeared pulling a wide, flat canvas bag. A bag the size and shape of a large quarto.

ALL MEN-O'-WAR—BRITISH, French, or otherwise—ship a wax-sealed, lead-weighted canvas bag containing a book of private signals. The signals allow warships to tell friend from foe; the wax kept it from water damage; the lead was to sink it if capture seemed imminent. In the French captain's place, Grey should have dropped it overboard before heaving-to to surrender. But of course they had not intended genuinely to surrender.

"Drop it," said Grey, pushing the sword edge harder into the captain's neck. The captain simultaneously spit at Grey and threw the canvas bag out the gaping hole at the cabin's rear.

In a single motion, Grey slit the captain's throat and dropped the cutlass. He plucked a rolling cannonball off the ground, took three steps towards *Marianne*'s shattered stern, and dove into the sea.

ITALIAN ASTRONOMERS notwithstanding, water is not air, and in it, heavier objects fall faster. The cannonball, and Grey's encompassing hands, hit the water first; the rest of him followed, and the twelve-pound iron ball began pulling him down at a startling, and increasing, speed.

Grey blinked his eyes, trying to bring them into submerged focus; the water was clear and the sun was high overhead—it illuminated the white canvas twenty, maybe twenty-five feet below him.

Its lead covers pulled it down. Grey's lead ball pulled him down faster. And he was getting closer. But now the light was dwindling— the bag was darkening to a blue smudge on a black background. Grey let go the ball with one hand; his body was pulled taut now in a straight line from the lead in his left hand through his awkwardly twisted hips to his trailing right foot. With his right hand he reached out for the bag . . .

It was dark now, dark as pitch. Grey's hand swept a field of water where he felt the bag ought to be . . . just beyond his fingertips . . . had he gone past it? Has he missed it? Black and black, no light, very disorienting . . .

He felt something brush against the webbing of his thumb. He snapped his fingers closed on it. It was the signal bag. Instantly he dropped the cannonball. The lead in the bag wasn't much to pull him down . . . but it seemed to be enough to keep him from floating back up . . . which way was up? He swiveled his head . . . there was a cool glow before him, like a sky before dawn . . . in the middle of it, a pinprick of light. That was the surface. He put the bag in his teeth—felt his teeth sink into the wax—began to search with his fingers for the collars of his shirt and jacket—pulled them over his head—kicked off his boots—pulled off his trousers—he felt his body push ever so slightly towards the prick of light—he was lighter now—he kicked, pushed with his arms, deep, long strokes. The prick of light turned into a fish-eye, and with a minute or so having passed, Grey's head broke the surface.

Instinctively he gasped for breath; dropped the bag out of his mouth and caught it gingerly with both hands. He let himself float a moment, canted backward.

There was cheering behind him. He turned. It wasn't for him, but for the French colors—the inverted French colors—being hauled down on the *Marianne*. How strange—he'd almost forgot the battle. With a long, easy stroke, he swam to the *Marianne*'s port accommodation ladder and began to climb up it—slipped with his stockinged feet unable to get purchase on the wood—pulled off the socks and resumed climbing, and hoisted himself up onto *Marianne*'s deck with the French bag in his teeth and otherwise as unencumbered as the day he was born.

This was not the first time Grey had emerged from deep water with somewhat fewer clothes than he'd gone into it with. Nakedness was no cause for comment among men who spent years on end sleeping shoulder to shoulder, each with fourteen inches to sling a hammock, and notions of privacy so far gone they might as well have belonged to other lives. Grey walked to the nearest, cleanest dead Frenchman and—saying a quick prayer for the dead; disliking the idea of seeming to rifle a man for loot—recovered a mostly blood-less jacket, which he tied around his waist. Among the throng of Englishmen now wandering, somewhat disorganized, on the deck of the *Marianne*, he caught the eye of the youngster Matthews and waved him over.

"Raise the sail room and fetch a shirt and trousers out of my duck bag, won't you? And tell me where I might find Captain Crowther."

Young Matthews saluted Grey and said, "The great cabin, sir."

"Which?"

"The French, sir, begging your pardon."

"Thank you, Matthews. Bear a hand." Matthews ran off towards the plank to *Juno*, and Grey returned to the shattered French cabin.

Captain Crowther—whose uniform was badly torn and blood-ied, but whose face and limbs seemed all to be in working order—was standing over the body of the French captain. Lieutenant Burnes was feeling for a pulse.

"None, sir," said Burnes, after a moment.

"Gentlemen," said Grey, introducing himself to the conversation. Burnes and Crowther looked at him, briefly considered his poverty of clothes, and then turned back to the body. Burnes, thought Grey, had the ghost of an amused smirk. Grey continued:

"I was obliged to kill him, I'm afraid, in an effort to preserve these." Grey held up the canvas bag. Crowther nodded.

"Just as well, Mr. Grey," he said. "If he had lived, I would have hanged him for a pirate." The English captain shook his head—"In all my life . . ."—and then trailed off. He was looking at the dead man, with contempt, but more, with bewilderment.

3

Three weeks later, in London

G REY SAT AT HIS DESK in his office in the Old Admiralty Building, as it was rapidly becoming known. Much of the naval establishment had decamped to a new home at Somerset House, and now, besides maintaining apartments and meeting rooms for the lords of the Admiralty; boardrooms for the navy boards, the Old Admiralty Building—Admiralty House—was more and more a private concern of naval intelligence.

Grey had time to reflect on the gradual change in London's distribution of government offices because he had nothing else to do. This was not an oversight. Five days earlier he had returned to London bearing not only letters from Wellesley (né Wesley), but a new French signal book (worth five hundred times its weight in gold, for the havoc it could cause among the enemy) and coded dispatches that had been secreted with the signal book in its waxed-canvas bag. Upon their delivery, Grey had been told to hold himself over for a new assignment, which was in the offing. He had attended to a four-month backlog of correspondence, and now was deciding if he should wander down to the Admiralty's dowel library, where he could catch up on four months of British, American, and continental newspapers. Or if he might perhaps chance another trip to the Rosetta stone for a new rubbing.

He considered too calling it a day and setting off for Marsh Downs, his home in Sheerness. It was December the 24th, and Westminster had already a certain holiday sleepiness to it, and it was quite a long ride into Kent. Believing he'd hit on a sound approach, Grey was devising a plan of action wherein he would set off for the Downs after an attempt, for Christmas Day, to borrow some of the library's past-date *Timeses*—perhaps leaving his new watch as security (his former Breguet, which had been much admired by the records' secretary, had perished in the Bay of Biscay). His devising was cut off by chief of staff Aaron Willys appearing in his doorway.

"I've come to send you home, Tom," he said to Grey, with admirable timing. "And I come with news. Those French dispatches you took—the cipher men are still about them, not much progress yet—but they have concluded that the seal and signature are, in fact, just what they appear to be. That those are letters from the desk of Bonaparte, written in his own little Corsican hand. I bring you Sir Edward's compliments for bringing them off."

Sir Edward Banks: chief of naval intelligence. Grey had not had an audience since returning to London, which surprised him. Sir Edward was not a warm man, by and large, but he had a fondness for Grey that made Grey wonder at Willys's employment as a go-between.

"Along with his compliments, I come bearing an assignment: Go home for Christmas and get some rest. Real rest. Mind and body. Spend a week at the Downs, and then present yourself next Sunday morning at eight, at Number 10 Downing Street."

"Next Sunday, is it?" said Grey. "I don't mistake that it will be New Year's Day?"

"You do not. But they don't close up government for a holiday, Tom. I'll be here tomorrow."

"Well, that ought not bother you, Aaron."

Willys yawned and shrugged. "In any case, Tom, these are orders from Sir Edward—be well rested and at the prime minister's door at eight on January first. And have a happy Christmas, and my best to Mrs. Hubble and Canfield."

"Brother, you can't mean not to tell me what I'm sent to Number 10 for."

"I'm afraid so. But you'll learn soon enough."

THE LORD HIGH newspaper-keeper could not be induced to part with a single issuance—it had begun raining, and he dared not contemplate seeing his collection puckered. Grey had been staying at Buttle's, a club that was very nearly home to his friend and man of business Pater. Stopping there on his way out of the city, Grey was able to induce Mathers, the porter, to part with part of the club's *Times* collection, through which Grey had been reading since his return to London. Mathers absolutely declined to accept security— Breguet or otherwise—saying only that he relied, as always, on Grey's discretion in the matter . . . though would Mr. Grey perhaps prefer Mathers to get him a chaise to take him east to Sheerness? . . . it was a long way to ride in the rain. Grey thanked Mathers and declined, asked that a room be held for him New Year's Eve, if one could be arranged. It could, said Mathers, and Grey took his leave, with the *Times*es folded in his undershirt and his modest luggage in saddlebags. Most of his things were already, or rather, permanently, at Marsh Downs, because Grey refused to concede having a place in town, or that the ride's length required one.

At all events, Grey enjoyed a ride and was a good rider—though he found the new horse Canfield had picked out for him too clever by half and consequently prone to declining Grey's rein and choosing his own route through the metropolitan traffic. Canfield would train him out of it, but in the meantime Grey wondered if he oughtn't just nap in the saddle and let the animal navigate home himself. And if they ended up in Gloucestershire, wouldn't the horse feel silly. Well, no, perhaps he wouldn't.

It was dusk when they arrived at Marsh Downs. Though he'd owned the Downs since the turn of the century, this would be his first Christmas there. It would be his second Christmas without his wife, and he got a sharp pain in the chest thinking how her love for the house had made buying it among the happiest moments he could remember.

Grey barely noticed Canfield taking hold of the halter.

"Good evening, Mr. Grey, and you're earlier than we'd expected—Mrs. Hubble will be so pleased—she's been worried sick all day long that you wouldn't make it home ever, not in time for Christmas; that those slave drivers, as she calls the administrators in Whitehall, sir, would make you work through the eve and the day and never set you free for the honest pleasures entitled to every decent Englishman, which was her thinking. How was Casca, sir?"

Canfield said that changing a horse's name was said to be bad luck; therefore, it was pagan folderol to be ignored. He took it upon himself to rename any young horse bought for the Downs that hadn't learned to answer to one yet. Casca was so named, Canfield said, because—him being a bold horse, and Grey recently having lent Canfield a copy of *Julius Caesar*—he would set that foot of his as far as who goes farthest.

"Very determined," said Grey.

"Yes indeed, sir—he has a noble luster in his eyes, hasn't he? I'll take him in, sir; you must go in before Mrs. Canfield comes to remonstrate over the lightness of your coat."

The house was lively as Grey entered—much to Grey's surprise, during the moment it took him to remember that he had insisted Mrs. Hubble have her father and young sister and her sister's children come for the holiday. Mrs. Hubble's sister, Mrs. Boothe, had been widowed these past three years, since her husband had been killed at Copenhagen, working the guns aboard HMS *Elephant*. Grey neither liked nor disliked children, but he was sufficiently attached to Mrs. Hubble to feel certain that any children connected with her must be a cut above the average sort. In any case, with Grey now to spend Christmas in England as if it were old times, Mrs. Hubble could not—despite Grey's sincere efforts—by any means be detached from her duties at the Downs. Grey didn't like to see her family the worse for it, and so they had compacted a treaty whereby Mrs. Hubble could work on Christmas provided her family would join them as

Grey's guests. Grey made the same offer to Canfield, who likewise had refused to abandon his action station on Christmas. Canfield, however, was northern, and said his family wouldn't understand a southern Christmas, and in any case, they were well provided with clootie pudding where they were.

"Oh, Mr. Grey, you've made it!" said Mrs. Hubble, who had observed Grey's arrival from her kitchen and was awaiting his entrance with a cup of hot cider in one hand and a cloth in the other. "Please to dry your hair, sir. I was terribly afeared they wouldn't let you go, what with the continent the way it is. So many of the local boys, you know, are spending Christmas at the Martello towers, with poor Captain Austen, who I don't suppose has had so much as a decent warm English meal this Advent, the poor soul. I mean to have Angela bring him a duff at the Fencibles house when she leaves for home—you know Mr. Boothe served under him in the nineties, and he's been so terribly kind to her.

"But enough of that, I will present you my family"—in an undertone: "I *do* hope they won't incommode you any, Mr. Grey.

"This is my father, Mr. Hubble."

Grey bowed courteously; Mr. Hubble, who had been many years at sea as a master's mate, and later, the sailing master of a whaler, began to raise a knuckle to his forehead before thinking better of it and bowing instead. He was dressed in a high-collared brown coat, and despite a grizzle to him, gave off the air of a well-heeled gentleman farmer. In point of fact, he was a seaman's innkeeper on the road to Canterbury, and though Grey would never pry into Mrs. Hubble's private affairs, he gathered her father was doing quite well.

"Mr. Hubble," said Grey, "it's a pleasure to make your acquaintance after so many years in your daughter's indispensable charge."

"You're most kind, Mr. Grey, sir, to say so, and to have us to your home for Yuletide."

"I'm glad of the opportunity, sir."

"And this is my sister," said Mrs. Hubble, "Mrs. Angela Boothe."

"Mrs. Boothe," said Grey to the rose-cheeked younger sister of his housekeeper. "It is kind of you to move your Christmas here to save me the privation of your sister's absence." Rose-cheeked she was, and younger than Mrs. Hubble by perhaps twenty years—they had different mothers, both dead before their time—but she had nothing of the youthful naïf in her face. No doubt it had been eradicated when she became the widowed mother of two. Though perhaps the rose did contain an element of shy blush to it.

"Mr. Grey, you're so very kind to have us, sir, and I do hope we won't be in your way. Do please not to hesitate to tell us if we are—and my daughters and I will do our best to help with the housework in the kitchen, as it were, so that we won't be too much underfoot."

Grey smiled and raised his hand in a gentle contradiction: "I'm quite certain neither you nor your daughters will be the least inconvenience; it will be a pleasure to have some life to the house. Are your children asleep?"

"Yes, sir, they are. My sister has seen us to rooms, very lovely rooms."

"Well, that's fine, Mrs. Boothe, and I look forward to meeting them."

"Come along now, Angie, and let us finish dinner—" They were all of them standing in an awkward circle in the foyer, with Mr. Hubble having come from the sitting room and Mrs. Boothe having followed her sister out of the kitchen. Angela Boothe curtsied and followed her sister back to the kitchen—as they went, Grey said, "Mrs. Hubble, when Canfield returns from the stable, will you remind him to join us?" and then led the ladies' father back to his seat by the fire.

"Mr. Hubble, can I offer you a drink of sherry? Please to be seated."

"Thank you, Mr. Grey," he said, looking modestly uncomfortable to be sitting while his daughter's employer stood. "I understand, sir, from my daughter, that you were a captain of the marines."

"I was, sir," said Grey, offering Hubble his drink and taking a seat in his particular wingback chair, opposite Hubble's and with a short couch interposed between them. "I understand from your daughter that you were a whaler and a navy man."

"I was, sir; man-o'-war's man until I was paid off a few years into the American war, and then fished Greenland and the south seas until the middle nineties."

"How I should love to sail the southern ocean," said Grey. "I've only dipped in my toe in the passage round Cape Horn."

"It can be remarkable, Mr. Grey, quite remarkable—I'm afraid at Cape Horn you got the worst of it, down near the sixties. The roaring sixties are enough and enough; we took many a fine fish southeast of the Cape, around the Crozets and Kerguelens. The richest waters you ever did see, sir, and seals and penguins thick enough to walk to New Holland."

He took a sip of sherry and shook his head.

"Of course, no English whalers there now, with the French b——s coming south out of the Mauritius. Oh, I beg your pardon." Grey waved him off.

"They being the reason I retired to my public house, Mr. Grey. You can imagine the man who's spent three years out in the forties and fifties and's ready to come home to his share from the company, and ends up taken by a French brig that tosses him onto the beach at Rodrigues, with nothing but debt for three years' food and board and maybe a chance to work his way home on an American. Sodomites. I beg your pardon."

Grey removed a cigar case from his jacket and offered it to Hubble.

"Thank you, sir, but I will smoke my pipe, if I may."

"Please do, Mr. Hubble."

Hubble continued:

"No, there's nothing in it with the seaborne frogs, I tell you—though I'm sure I don't need to, Mr. Grey. Perhaps you saw the new gazette been issued yesterday, with an account by a Captain Crowther of a French sloop which signaled distress as bait in a mantrap? Murdered several of his officers and scores of his men—I've never in a long life heard of so blatant an act, of anything so hard against the laws of war and seamanship. The laws of manhood, even—of most basic civilization. The sodding barbarians. I tell you, Mr. Grey, if it was up to me, there would be no prison hulk for any of them, but a gibbet—and a gibbet still too good for them. No, sir, I was in the American war and I tell you the Americans—and I tell you even at Christmas, when they might cross a river to kill you—no, the Americans would never do such a thing. It takes a Frenchman."

"Never to contradict you, sir," said Grey, "but I may observe that even for the French it is deeply atypical. I quite agree, though, in the main. Most shocking to read of."

"And I imagine, Mr. Grey, that you know more of it than I. You are, as I think—if I am right—in the Foreign Office?"

"I am, sir."

"It must be a most interesting line of work, Mr. Grey."

"It is, on occasion, Mr. Hubble. Though more often than not it is bureaucratic drudgery of the lowest sort—account books from the West Indies and the like. Requests to be moved from a cold colonial office to a warm one, or from a hot one to a cool one. Seniority disputes." He shook his head and smiled like an overworked calculator. "If I may ask, do you enjoy your work?"

"I do," said Mr. Hubble. "Even from the beginning it was a great deal easier than fishing or fighting, I daresay, especially once I realized that I'd gotten too old to pass from warrant to commission, and found myself in the high latitudes. Still, in the beginning it was all hands, watch and watch, never a moment to spare. But it's a good spot on the road to Canterbury, and once I got a few old messmates to spread the word a bit, I was able to put on some landsmen, if you smoke me, and now with Angela to help keep them in line, and doing the accounts too—I taught her when I was studying for my warrant onshore when she was just a girl—they say you don't know the trigonometry 'less you can teach it, you know, so I taught it, and so she knows her numbers right well. But pardon me, what was I saying? Oh yes, with a crew of barmen and Angela as boatswain—ha ha—I've been able to have some ease, spend most of my time filling and refilling and telling stories with old messmates and singing the old songs. I am very fortunate to have been able to obtain a rather lovely square Broadwood of five octaves—I mention this principally out of admiration for your exceptional Érard. May I ask, Mr. Grey, is it a fortepiano or a piano?"

"A piano, sir."

"A most admirable instrument. I mean yours, sir, beyond the admiration owed pianos as a general company. Beautiful. Mr. Harrison, who owned the whaler I shipped on, had one very much like it at his home in Portland, and I had the pleasure of hearing it play on three or four occasions. I was most covetous—I was a fiddler at sea, and always dreamed of deeper playing; finally getting a knockabout for the public house, and then the Broadwood, and now I'm teaching my granddaughters, ha ha, to be sure I really know it. Do you play, sir?"

"It was primarily the domain of my late wife; she made efforts to teach me, but I'm afraid I was never able to obtain anything like true proficiency with it. Too much time away from home, perhaps. Now I believe it's only by the grace of Mrs. Hubble that it remains in tune; she has a man from the village come in. Or at least she did—I must confess I have not touched it in months."

Mr. Hubble's eyes were full of the instrument, but his manners prevented his asking about it further. Barring an invitation from Grey, of course.

"I would be most gratified to hear you play it, if you choose," said Grey, feeling he had to. Truth be told, the Érard remained an object of persistent sadness for him, inasmuch as it reminded him of his dear Paulette. He would just as soon have seen his guests give it a wide berth—but this was Christmas, and he felt obliged to fulfill his duties as host.

"Well, I say, if you're certain you wouldn't object," said Hubble, getting to his feet. "I should hate to bring disharmony to your home, ha ha." Grey silenced his objections with a raised hand and a smile.

"Well then, if I may." He stepped to the piano and, after briefly examining the contents of a sheath of scores atop it, sat down and began to play. It was the prelude from elder Bach's fourth English suite, an exceptionally light, playful, joyful piece. Grey stared at the drink in his hand.

When the prelude concluded, Hubble turned smoothly to the *allemande* and continued. It was less sprightly, but equally filled with joy. As Mr. Hubble played, Canfield entered the room, wear-

ing his Sunday best and looking uncomfortable to find himself there
socially, rather than at his work. He didn't wish to take a seat without first thanking Grey for the invitation. And he wouldn't speak
while Hubble played. He could hardly be recognized as the entirely
self-possessed man who'd met Grey's horse a half hour earlier.

Grey tried to put him at his ease by pointing to an easy chair and
gesturing for Canfield to sit. Canfield gestured that he was uncer-
tain of this seating choice. Grey pointed again, decisively. Canfield
perched uncomfortably atop its cushion, seeming to will his body
weight not fully to compress it. Grey shook his head, with a small
grin on it. He stood up, filled a glass of sherry, sliced a cigar, and presented both to Canfield, who after a moment's hesitation accepted
them. Grey lit Canfield's cigar while Hubble, who had played
through the brief *courante*, moved on to the slow center of the suite,
the *sarabande*. Grey resumed his seat and let the light, slow, deep
but unserious music flow over him. He had subsisted for some time
on songs fiddled atop a capstan: songs for hauling and sheeting. He
enjoyed those, but they weren't Bach. Elder Bach, Christian Bach,
Haydn, Handel, Mozart—how did the Germans produce such superior composers? Perhaps it came from the chaos of a people united
by language, divided into three hundred tiny, absurd little countries,
kingdoms, principalities, and city-states. Perhaps the freedom that
comes from the absence of a strong government stimulates the art-
ist's imagination. The Italians, who were exceeded in the quality
of their composers only by the Germans, were likewise exceeded
only by the Germans in chaotic national disunity. Was there something in this? If so, Napoleon's ongoing war of political pressure—
his "mediatization" of the Germans he'd crushed in the War of the
Second Coalition; his forcing free states to reorganize according to
his wishes—would be a great blow to music. Though of course it
would be a great boon to Britain, if the Germans were pushed too
far, forced to repossess some part of their *Menschlichkeit*. Unfortunately all of the manhood east of the Rhine had been annexed to
France under the terms of Campo Formio and Lunéville.

Hubble was on to the minuets: the palate cleanser before the suite's big finale. Hubble played very well, thought Grey, though he claimed no great judgment in the virtuosity of pianists. Still, there was an earnest joy in the playing that complemented the joy of the music very well. Grey had picked up from Mrs. Hubble, over the years, some parts of her father's history—the son of a dairy farmer who had gone to sea, had worked his way up through the ranks before the mast, from landsman to master's mate, paying a large share of his small salary to his ship's schoolmaster along the way. Some men made it from afore the mast to the officers' mess, but Hubble had not been one of them, despite coming quite close. It must have been a bitter disappointment, but he showed no signs of embitterment. Grey greatly admired this. It was the same strength of character possessed by Mrs. Hubble, his daughter—"Mrs." only by virtue of her place as housekeeper, which carried the honorific by tradition. She had been engaged, Grey knew; the engagement's failure, of which Grey knew nothing, had prompted her to enter service. But disappointment never seemed to darken her moods; she was indefatigable.

Hubble began the *gigue*: the jig with which Bach's fourth English suite concluded. It had the energy of a chaise-and-four pulled at full gallop, and Grey couldn't keep himself from beating the time as it built to its rousing, antiphonal conclusion.

Hubble hit the final note—which he was able to sustain with the Érard's new patent striking mechanism—and Grey slapped the arm of his chair, only dimly aware of the change in his mood.

"Well done, sir, very well done. What did you mean keeping your lamp under a bushel? You should have laid a course for the piano the moment you arrived."

Hubble nodded modestly. "You're much too kind—the quality of your instrument far exceeds the quality of my playing."

"Nonsense," said Grey, standing. "But allow me to present my groundskeeper, Canfield—though I suspect you are acquainted."

"We are, sir," said Hubble, who, with Canfield, had followed Grey to his feet.

"Please don't let me intrude," said Canfield, who was looking uncomfortable again. "I've interrupted you."

"You've done nothing of the sort, Canfield," said Grey, energetically. "For the dear's sake, man, it's Christmas. I shouldn't like to compel you to enjoy yourself—but confide that if I must, I will." Canfield laughed.

"There's a good chap. Now perhaps we can impose on Mr. Hubble to play us something further, while I refill your cups. A glass of sherry with you, Mr. Hubble?"

"With all my heart, sir."

"And with you, Canfield?"

"With pleasure, sir."

After a healthy sip, and relighting his pipe, Hubble resumed leafing through sheet music, furrowing his brow as he considered the appropriate encore. And then his face lit up.

"Oh! Mr. Grey, if I might desire you to join me, I have never had the pleasure of 'Jesu, Joy' for four hands—indeed, I don't believe I've heard it before, rendered on a piano."

Grey chuckled. "Ah no. I think not; I am not in the vein."

"Oh *do*, sir," said Canfield, who—when Grey turned to him— seemed surprised by the vehemence with which he'd spoken. It was, however, his favorite hymn. It was everyone's favorite hymn. No more beautiful melody had ever been written.

Grey hesitated, then set down his glass. "Oh, well, why not indeed. If you both resolve never to repeat to anyone the sum of false notes I play."

With his cigar clutched in his teeth, Grey sat down beside Hubble, to his left, intending to play the less difficult bass line while Hubble grappled the complex intertwining harmonies of the treble.

Grey looked at Hubble; Hubble, facing the score, nodded his head: one, two, three, and began to play.

The beauty of the piece, which began with several bars of Hubble playing alone, slowly suffused the room. Truly, Grey thought, it was the most beautiful piece of music ever written.

Now Grey joined in, with the principal ascending melody, and was captivated by it. The beautiful swell of the song wrapped around him and flooded through the house. And then, without warning, a pure, full voice began to sing. Instinctively, Grey peeked back over his shoulder. Mrs. Hubble had been drawn from the kitchen by the sound of the hymn; Mrs. Boothe had come with her, and begun to sing:

Jesu, joy all joys excelling,
Lord divine, to earth come down;
Fix in us thy humble dwelling;
All thy faithful mercies crown.

Jesu, joy is thy creation,
Pure unbounded love thy art;
Visit us with thy salvation,
Enter every trembling heart.

Jesu, joyful we endeavor
That our words be heard above,
Let our hearts for now and ever,
Glory in thy perfect love.

How perfectly true was Angela's voice! Grey felt the hairs on his neck stand.

Jesu, joyous, we adore thee,
Lo, we cast our hearts before thee,
Songs of grace and mercy raise,
Lost in wonder, love, and praise.

Grey turned to look at Angela Boothe. Beside her, her sister was crying and smiling. Fearing Canfield might have had the same reaction, Grey was careful, for the next few minutes, not to meet his eye.

4

O N HIS TRIPS to and from India, Grey had allowed himself
to slack off his routine of physical exercise. Besides the
periodic drilling with the marines and his regular climb-
ings of the foremast in pursuit of the relative cool and quiet provided
by the crosstrees, he had confined himself to the role of nondescript
courier, and felt, in consequence, somewhat fat and fulsome. So for
the five days succeeding Christmas, he had swum an hour at dawn
and another hour in the middle afternoon. His home had the name
Marsh Downs from its northern edge, where a maze of tall grass and
sandy rivulets terminated in a beach on the Thames estuary, where
the water was brackish from mixing with the North Sea.

The water was incredibly cold, and though Grey insisted it wasn't
necessary, during the duration of each swim Canfield lit a fire on the
beach to warm and dry Grey when he emerged, and to warm the
dry clothes he would put on for the walk back up to the house. On
the first day it also dried Fred, Grey's (or perhaps Canfield's) superb
Irish setter, who had briefly joined in the swimming, before a swift
change of heart. On succeeding days, he chose instead to pace Grey's
progress by running up and down the beach, and then to offer some
body heat when Grey returned indoors. Exercise notwithstanding,
Willys had told Grey to rest, and the rest of his time he spent reading

the papers he'd brought from Buttle's, and attending to some minor household matters—accounts and so forth—that had arisen during his most recent absence.

He had also played a not-inconsiderable amount on his Érard, his aversion to which seemed to have been lifted by the deep familial calm engendered over Christmas. It continued to make him think of Paulette, but more happily, less wistfully, as if her teaching him to play were an ongoing beneficence that kept her present in their sitting room. Grey had invited Mrs. Hubble's family to remain for the holiday's duration, but Mr. Hubble firmly declined to impose himself, Angela, or his granddaughters any further on Grey's hospitality, and Grey did not press the matter.

In the afternoon of the last day of the year three, Grey posted back into London, thinking this the best ensurance of his being on time to Downing Street—particularly if New Year's was as snowy as New Year's Eve. As he rode to town, to Buttle's, he reminded himself that it was time either to become a member there or to find himself a boardinghouse. He could not decently continue much further on Pater's membership.

In the five steps from the coach to Buttle's entrance, Grey's tricorn accumulated a visible dusting of snow. As he stood a moment in the doorway, shaking the hat out onto the street, the porter Mathers appeared beside him. Mathers took the hat along with Grey's greatcoat, wondered if Grey would like a towel to dry off with, and welcomed him to the club, telling him that Mr. Pater could be found at the card table nearest the fire in the lounge. He called over one of the club's page boys to show Grey in.

"Are you busy for New Year's, Mathers?" said Grey, accepting the towel, which was warm, and using it to dry his face, which was bitterly cold.

"Not especially, Mr. Grey—besides the hunting, Christmastide sees the greatest departure of our members to their homes." Grey wasn't altogether surprised. The club had three types of member— the married, the unmarried, and the not-yet-married. The married members were with their wives, who, like all women, were forbidden anywhere in the club beyond the trailing edge of the foyer's carpet. The not-yet-married were with their parents, upon whom they depended, for the most part, for an income. Only the unmarried were at liberty on New Year's Eve. Pater, Grey's friend and man of business, was among this set. After having returned Mather his newspapers, Grey was shown to the spot Pater had selected for ringing in eighteen hundred and four: a green baize table by a roaring fire, where he was deep in a game of Short Brag.

Pater had just received the deal when, looking up to order another glass of toddy, he saw Grey and waved him over.

"Grey, my dear fellow, you're just in time to make a fourth."

"That we might switch to whist," said one of Pater's companions, who sounded as if he expected a new game to change his luck.

"I'm afraid Mr. Grey doesn't care for team games, ha ha, do you, Tom? Grey: Pond, Shepard." Grey shook the men's hands. He didn't particularly care for Brag either. Not because it was a game of chance—he enjoyed trying his luck—but because it was a game of chance masquerading as a game of skill. However, as Pater had spoken over the handshakes with the request, "Join us, won't you, Tom? Brag is a miserable game for just three," and because Grey didn't feel he could decently refuse the request, being Pater's guest, he sat down.

"Bring a hot toddy for Mr. Grey as well, would you, Parslow? A hot toddy, mind you: not a warm toddy or an indifferent one. Piping, sir, piping!" Parslow, who was approaching twelve years old, looked pleased at being addressed as "sir" and departed with a bow. At the same time, a cashier appeared, to change some of Grey's money into gambling markers.

The table was square and Grey's seat was the one furthest from the fire. Pater was to Grey's left, and Pond, backlit by the blaze, received the elder hand. In Brag, after the ante, each man is dealt three cards with the last turned up—the best of these denotes the elder, who brags first.

"I pass," said Pond.

"I brag," said Shepard, to Grey's right. "Half crown." He pushed five markers forward, each worth sixpence.

With the next eldermost card, Pater said, "Brag: make it a crown." He pushed forward ten markers—five shillings even.

Shepard looked at Grey, who shook his head. "Game for an angel?" said Shepard, raising his stake to six and eight.

"Half sovereign," said Pater, adding another five shillings.

"And I'll match you," said Shepard, making the pot even. "Gentlemen?"

"No," said Pond.

"Nor I," said Grey.

"Then I'll see your hand, Pater," said Shepard, laying down his own. Pater showed a sequence, and a strong one—knave, queen, king. But Shepard had a pair royal of three nines.

"I believe I have it," said Shepard, smiling.

"Damn their eyes," said Pater, sliding his court towards Pond and smiling at Grey. "You should have brought luck with you." Pater was a fine loser and a frequent winner, which, Grey believed, combined to make his relentless gaming seem less disreputable.

The deal had moved to Pond, and this time Grey had the elder hand. He opened with a brag of a shilling. Pater bragged next, doubling Grey's stake. Pond passed again, and Shepard made it a guinea, which made Grey toss in his hand. It continued in this spirit—of Pater and Shepard dueling; of Grey and Pond bragging on good cards and tossing on bad—for about an hour, which was, Grey felt, the amount of play time required of good manners. At the end of an hour, Grey was just slightly ahead of even—a shilling up—and was ready to call it a night. But there was something . . . He had noticed something about Shepard, who frequently raised the stakes when, to judge by the eventual outcome, he had rather poor cards. This, of course, was part of the game—the brag. But it appeared that whenever Shepard was counterfeiting to have a good hand, he would begin to examine his two faced-down cards with his left hand, reserving his right for the swishing of cognac. A sort of nervous gesture. And Grey's aversion to brag could not presume to withstand his love of cipher and pattern.

On the final deal of his night, Grey received a knave and a pair of fours—a middling hand at best. But seeing Shepard pick up his snifter, Grey decided to remain in the pot, bragging along with Shepard until first Pond and then Pater relented. Shepard's cognac became more agitated as the betting went on, until the pot was finally settled at fifteen guineas. Grey and Shepard both flipped their cards. Grey had his pair of fours, and Shepard, a high card of king. Grey took his money—or rather, his markers—and waved over Parslow.

"Mr. Parslow, please to take one of these for yourself, and use the rest to discount our expenses. Change what remains for a bottle of brandy, and serve it at midnight."

"Oh," said Shepard, shaking his head, "that's good of you, Grey, but I can't—"

"Do permit me, Shepard; gentlemen—my last chance of the year to earn some goodwill."

Shepard nodded in appreciation of the gesture, as did Pond and Pater. Grey stood.

"Thomas," said Pater, "you're never leaving us before the new year strikes."

"I'm afraid so. I have an early morning. But drink a good year for me, if you would. Have me inscribed in the book of life. Gentlemen—" Grey bowed to the three men and withdrew. A footman guided him to the overnight room into which Mathers had had Grey's effects unpacked.

At midnight, he was in bed, drifting off towards sleep. Below him he heard a dull roar as the disquantitied membership of Buttle's hailed eighteen hundred and four. Mathers's unexpectedly loud and commanding voice rose through Grey's floor to announce the toast:

"My lords and gentlemen, the toast is: the king, his country, absent friends, and the new year."

5

IT WAS DISTRACTINGLY cold and wet when Grey arrived by coach at 10 Downing Street. The sun hadn't come up yet. A red-coated soldier stood directly in front of Number 10's unremarkable black door, beneath a lantern that was somewhat brighter than the twilight.

"Bid you good morning, soldier. I'm Grey; I'm expected at eight."

"Yes, sir: please to go in, sir," said the soldier, who turned, knocked twice on the door, and stood aside for Grey to pass. The door opened, and Grey went through it.

A butler greeted Grey perfunctorily and led him down a long corridor, into a small anteroom. Around and above him, Grey could hear the sounds of men at work. He supposed wartime made early risers of His Majesty's government. The butler knocked on a door on the anteroom's rear wall—one of two side-by-side, separated by a large clock, which told Grey he was six minutes early. The butler stepped through the door, then came back out of it.

"You may go in, Mr. Grey," he said.

Within, Grey found he was at the end of a long room, which stretched out to his left and was mostly filled by a long rectangular table. At the near end of the table, a man sat with his back to Grey. A chair was pulled out to his left, and on a straight diagonal between the occupied chair and the empty one, was a chessboard. It looked like birch and ebony, with the pieces in their starting places.

"Sit down, Mr. Grey," said the man. "I'll be with you presently." After a moment looking at the two pair of Corinthian columns that stood directly before him, holding up what appeared to be a recently lengthened ceiling, Grey did as he was told. The man initialed the paper he was reading, took off his glasses, and looked at Grey. Grey recognized him, though they'd never been introduced.

"I'm sorry I couldn't accommodate you at a more civilized time on a more suitable day," said the prime minister's private secretary.

"Not at all, Sir Arnold."

"And we'll have to make this fast, I'm afraid. You have white, and it's your move."

Chess?

"I've not been told what this meeting is in aid of, Sir Arnold."

Arnold Woolworth, who was about sixty and very average in appearance, was cleaning his glasses' right lens.

"Well, I daresay Sir Edward will tell you at the appropriate juncture. The prime minister is meeting in the Green Room, so here we are instead. I will, however reluctantly, have to turn you out in a quarter hour, so do make your move."

Grey was tempted to push the point further, but feeling that Sir Arnold had exhausted his inclination towards explaining himself, he did, once again, as he was told. King's pawn, two squares.

Sir Arnold responded with his own king's pawn, two squares. Grey played king's knight to king's bishop's third. Sir Arnold, queen's knight to queen's bishop's sixth. King's bishop to queen's knight's fifth. King's bishop to queen's bishop's fifth. Queen's bishop's pawn, one square. King's knight to king's bishop's sixth. Bishop takes knight. Pawn takes bishop. Grey castles to the king's side. Bishop to king's knight's fourth. King's rook's pawn, one square. King's rook's pawn, two squares. Pawn takes bishop. Pawn takes pawn. Knight takes pawn at king's fifth. Sir Arnold advances his pawn to king's knight's third. Queen's pawn, two squares. Knight takes pawn at king's fourth. Queen to king's knight's fourth. Bishop takes pawn. Queen takes knight. Bishop takes king's bishop's pawn, and Sir Arnold has put Grey in check. Rook takes bishop. Queen to queen's first; check. Rook to king's bishop's first. Rook to king's rook's first; check. King takes rook. Sir Arnold's queen takes Grey's rook. Checkmate.

It happened very fast. Grey had been in a strong position . . . until he'd brought out his queen. Hadn't he? Sir Arnold had beaten him in fifteen moves. And their fifteen minutes were dwindling.

"Brilliant," said Grey, after a moment. The confusion at his circumstance, which had disappeared while his mind was in the game, was returning now with a new intensity. Why on earth should the prime minister's private secretary want to play a game of chess with him at eight in the morning of New Year's Day? It was absurd.

"Thank you," said Sir Arnold, who had taken a sheet of paper and was writing. "You play very well." Sir Arnold signed the paper, folded it in three, and handed it to Grey.

"Give this to Sir Edward, if you would. He'll be waiting for you at his office."

"At the Admiralty?"

"Yes, of course. And now," said Sir Arnold, checking a pocket watch he had open on the table, "I'm afraid I must ask for the room; Pettibone will show you out." Sir Arnold stood and shook Grey's hand. The butler—Pettibone, apparently—was waiting in the anteroom, and led Grey back up the corridor to Downing Street.

6

URNING LEFT at the end of Downing Street, it was a five-minute walk to Admiralty House. Grey let himself in a side door, and five minutes after that, he was in the outer office of the head of naval intelligence, waiting while the chief of staff showed Sir Edward Sir Arnold's letter.

"Go in, Tom," said Aaron Willys, returning to the outer office and suppressing a yawn.

"Late night?" said Grey.

"Yes," said Willys. "It's still going on. Maybe when we're done with you I can go home for a few hours to see if my children can recognize me."

"For my own part," said Grey, "I'm with child to learn what this is all about."

"You will, if only you'll move a little faster." Grey shook his head as he passed Willys at the threshold of the private office. "And Tom: If you ever again hazard comparably abysmal wordplay, I'll be compelled to ask you for a meeting." Grey smiled, then quickly adopted the appropriately taciturn expression for an appearance before his taciturn chief.

"Come in, Grey," said Sir Edward Banks. He was smoking a pipe, which he removed momentarily from his mouth, looking up at Grey with his cool, blue-gray eyes. As was his habit—adopted by virtually every man jack in his department—he wore no wig, and his short trimmed gray hair seemed just slightly disheveled. Willys must have been in earnest about their working all night. "Sit," said Banks, gesturing with the stem of his pipe. He had Sir Arnold's letter in front of him. "I imagine you're anxious to know what this is about."

"I am, Sir Edward," said Grey.

"What do you know of the Duchess of Bourbon? Bathilde d'Orléans."

"A *princesse du sang*, I believe. A friend of Benjamin Franklin's. Was one of the royals who supported the creation of a French republic."

"Just so," said Banks. "After the revolution, she made a gift of her fortune to the Republican government, only to be imprisoned by the Jacobins as a right-wing reactionary. Though several times a mother and in her middle forties, she—after eighteen months in a prison cell—was evidently still enough the famous beauty to seduce a constable twenty years her junior. He escorted her to exile in Spain, where, despite her treatment by the Assembly, she remained a dedicated Republican. She was an early supporter of Bonaparte, whom she believed would save democracy. When he assumed power, she was welcomed back to Paris, and into his inner circle—where she discovered she'd been very much mistaken in him. This prompted her, after a long period of estrangement, to secretly reconcile with her son. Louis Antoine, Duc d'Enghien."

Grey nodded. "I didn't realize she and Louis Antoine were mother and son."

"Are you and he acquainted?"

"We've never met, but I know him by reputation." The young Duke of Enghien—thirty or thirty-one, Grey believed—was the leader of the French resistance in the German states. In his early twenties he'd been one of the commanders of the French expatriate Armée de Condé that had tried to liberate France. The attempt failed, but it had won Louis Antoine a reputation for courage and tenacity. He always commanded his troops from the front.

"We have been working with Louis Antoine for some time, coordinating our efforts with the German émigrés. Two weeks ago his people delivered a message to us, from his mother—that Joseph Leclerc wishes to escape Napoleon's France and join the royalist court-in-exile, here in London. He hopes to be indebted to us for his rescue."

Grey leaned forward in his chair.

"Leclerc . . . one of Bonaparte's secretaries?"

"Precisely."

"That would be tremendous."

"It would."

"Why? And why now?"

"As to why: he has spent his life fighting for democracy in France; he expected the revolution to bring it, then Napoleon, and now the scales have fallen from his eyes. Like most of the émigrés, he has concluded that restoration and constitutional monarchy are the only practical way forward. As to why now—"

Banks tapped two fingers on Sir Arnold's letter.

"Let me turn to this. I asked Willys who the best chess player in the service was. He named you. I asked him to solicit a few further opinions. Most matched his own. To make certain, I asked the best chess player I know to have a look at you. Perhaps you have heard that in the seventies Sir Arnold beat the Mechanical Turk? That chess machine that had been touring Europe and beating princes at every stop." Grey shook his head. "He writes . . ."

Banks picked up the letter: " 'A fine player—needs refining—too eager to sacrifice pieces—could with training be a credible competitor.' "

"He beat me in fifteen moves," said Grey.

"He's a busy man," said Banks. "You were correct, regarding Madame Bathilde being friends with Benjamin Franklin. She was also his chess partner. She is, in fact, one of the strongest players in Europe.

"Since Philidor's death in '95, no player has emerged to claim his title of world's champion—as he was styled after beating Stamma in '47. Am I boring you, Grey?"

"No, sir," said Grey, who had failed in stifling a yawn. He sat up a little straighter to emphasize its involuntarity.

"The Free City of Frankfurt," Sir Edward continued, "is rather taken with mathematics and natural science. Emperor Joseph Second encouraged them, and the new one, Francis Second, does as well. As the Frankfurters host the coronation of the Holy Roman Emperor, they've decided to take it on themselves to crown a new champion of chess. In a tournament that will begin in two months. On February the twenty-ninth, of all days. I make no doubt it's a date of particular interest to economists and calculators.

"Invitations have gone to the courts of Europe and the New World inviting them to send their best players. The palace and the universities seem to have discussed nothing over the last month aside from the choice of whom to send. It is a matter of national pride, for us and for everyone else. The French will be sending their best players. Bathilde and Leclerc among them."

"You don't expect me to compete with them, sir?"

"No, of course not," said Sir Edward, striking a match, relighting his pipe. "The question I posed to Sir Arnold was not whether you could win, it was whether you could put up enough of a fight to lose without drawing attention to yourself. It is an elimination tournament, Grey—half the players will lose their first games and be done with. You need only be good enough to be a plausible contestant."

"And I am to use the tournament as covering for Leclerc's tracks towards England."

"You are. Napoleon's closest confidants—inasmuch as they are confidants—are kept under the constant watch of the Committee for State Security. It is unlikely the Maison Militaire would allow Leclerc out of the country, were it not for an opportunity to demonstrate the inherent superiority of the French."

"Is the tournament to have spectators?"

"It is."

"Then why bother competing?"

"As I say, Leclerc will have a bodyguard with him. All the contestants, however, are to stay at the Palais Thurn und Taxis, in whose ballroom the games will be played. Because of the large number of contestant guests, the courts have been advised that no servants will be accommodated; the palais's will attend to all. His bodyguards, who travel as his servants, will be out of the way."

"I see."

"Good."

"And Sir Arnold believes I'm good enough to lose."

"No. But he hopes you may be, with some training."

"Is he to train me?"

"The private secretary to a war cabinet, Grey? Willys has arranged for your instruction. At Cambridge."

"Oh, is that what they teach at Cambridge?" said Grey, and he and Banks shared a brief smile.

"George Atwood—I trust you know of him."

"The mathematician."

"Yes. And in his youth he was among the two or three best players in the world—I believe he may be the only man living to have beaten Philidor. They had an eight-game match at Parsloe's in '95. One game was drawn; Philidor took five and Atwood two. To hear Atwood tell it, he won those two only because Philidor was declining—he had been exiled from France—another 'counterrevolutionary'—and it was only a year before his death. Atwood is as old now, he says, as was Philidor when he died. That is why he declines to see Germany for England, but he has consented to teach you. You will meet him tonight at Trinity. Willys will tell you precisely where, and when."

7

IN A HALL ABOVE Neville's Court, Professor Atwood was demonstrating Newton's first law and the constant acceleration of gravity, using two equal weights connected to one another by a cord strung over a pulley. No matter where the two weights were in relation to one another—equally high above the ground, or with one nearly touching it while the other nearly touched the pulley—neither moved. They were in perfect equilibrium. To Grey, who had some small education in physical science and had spent innumerable hours with innumerable pulleys while a marine at sea, this still seemed counterintuitive. Having arrived early at Atwood's lecture, he had chosen to stand in the back of the hall to await its conclusion. He was surprised to find himself disappointed when the conclusion was reached and Atwood told his students that Newton's second law would have to wait for the succeeding lesson.

While Grey waited for the students to evacuate, he took a moment to consider that Newton himself had likely taught his first and second laws in this very hall, some hundred and fifty years earlier. Grey had not spent much time at Cambridge, but he supposed that, if one were being frank, he might find some small number of redeeming features to it.

"Professor Atwood," said Grey, approaching the bespectacled, berobed lecturer. "If you will allow me to introduce myself, sir, I am Thomas Grey."

"Yes, Mr. Grey. Your promptness is admirable. Come and walk out with me."

It was a clear evening, brisk but considerably less cold than the evening previous. "Have you taken a room somewhere?" said Atwood, as they passed through Neville's Gate.

"I have, sir. At the Bishop's Hostel."

"My man will arrange to have your things moved to my house."

"You're very kind, but I would hate to impose on you for the quantity of weeks I've undertaken to be here."

"Well, it's not a large house, but it sits on Coe Fen, so there's plenty of room for one of us to stretch his legs if you come on to irritate me. However, there is little enough spare time without having to wait for you to come and go from Bishop's."

The northern boundary of the Coe Fen, and Atwood's house, was a fifteen-minute walk from Trinity. Atwood, who had known in advance that whoever he would teach would first have played a game with Arnold Woolworth, asked Grey to go through it for him move by move.

"Good," said Atwood, as they arrived at his door. "Good. Sir Arnold is a very strong player, but you played intelligently. Come inside."

Atwood's house was cramped and dark—something like the inside of a man-o'-war, thought Grey—and seemed to date from the university's earliest days. Or, as the university was six hundred years old, at least to its earlier days.

"Go in there and set up the board. You will play white. I will be with you in a moment." Grey stepped into a small sitting room, and Sir Arnold had a word with his "man," who seemed to be— rather than a butler—a student, who, other than a pair of white gloves, was wearing academical dress. After carefully choosing the less comfortable of two chairs, Grey sat at Atwood's chessboard, which was laid-in to the center of a small wooden table. He began to extract chessmen from a scrimshaw box—under the watchful eye of a slowly ruminating sheep, who stood at a window on the room's south wall, part of a herd grazing on the fen.

The white was bone, and the "black," lapis lazuli. Grey was examining the black queen when Atwood sat down across from him. Grey stood and bowed, having failed to stand (or notice) when Atwood had entered the room. He replaced the queen on her color.

"It came from the Mogul," said Atwood. "Please begin."

Grey advanced his king's pawn two squares. Atwood brought out his own king's pawn, two squares. Grey's king's knight to king's bishop's third. Atwood's queen's knight to queen's bishop's sixth. King's bishop to queen's bishop's fourth. Queen's knight to queen's fourth. King's knight takes king's pawn. Queen to king's knight's fifth. Knight takes king's bishop's pawn, and Grey had Atwood's rook pinned. Queen takes king's knight's pawn. Grey's rook to king's bishop's first. Queen takes king's pawn. Check. Queen's bishop to king's second. Knight to king's bishop's third. Checkmate.

8

GREY AND ATWOOD's first game was the first of many that
ended quickly and in crushing defeat for Grey. After each
game, Atwood switched colors and replayed the game
from Grey's perspective, making the same moves Grey had, letting Grey attempt to play the same moves Atwood had, to come
to his own understanding of how Atwood attacked and defended,
and how he lured Grey into traps. Grey's principal weakness was his
aggression—his attacks were vigorous and featured the determined
exchange of pieces to clear the board. Atwood's principal lesson was
that an exchange or a sacrifice was acceptable only when accompanied by a concrete plan of what to do next. To throw your opponent
back on his heels briefly with unorthodox moves is well and good
when your opponent may be rattled into making a mistake. The players Grey would face in Frankfurt would not be rattled. These were
not the coin players at Parsloe's Coffee House, or Old Slaughter's,
gambling on their ability to bully rich dilettantes into costly errors.
These were men who kept the whole board in view.

On the tenth day, after perhaps a hundred and fifty games and a
hundred and fifty losses, Grey forced a draw. Atwood was, for the
first time since he and Grey had met, visibly happy. He had his man
open an old port and told Grey he was coming along very nicely,

and that he had earned a day off—in any case, Atwood had a lecture to give in the afternoon. Grey suggested he might come along, but Atwood told him it would be much better to clear his head somewhat than to add Newton to it. Why not take a turn around the fen, or the village. Grey decided he would take a turn with his rifle and come back with something fresh for dinner.

Grey's rifle was a rather unusual piece, an Austrian Girandoni repeater that fired lead balls from a 22-shot tubular magazine running along its barrel. It fired them using air stored in a conical iron reservoir that doubled as a buttstock. It fired a shot a second, fatal at a hundred yards and accurate to a hundred and fifty, and Grey would not have exchanged it for Excalibur. It hung diagonally across his back as he walked out of Cambridge, southeast, towards the Gog Magog Hills, where he heard he might take a few good rabbits of a foot or more. It took him an hour to get there, some short while longer to find a patch of flowering grass, and a few minutes beyond that to flush some coneys out. The best way to hunt rabbit, if you're a good shot, is to find some of their food and make noise. That sets them running and you take them on the wing, so to speak. As Grey walked as loudly as he could through the *Festuca* (as it had been identified in Kefauver's botany book), he couldn't help but think of the hunt in terms of moves and countermoves. He made his move into the grass—the rabbits made their move into hiding—he moved towards the thickest grass—they ran—he fired. It was a move that would typically call for a shotgun, but Grey felt confident of the Girandoni's accuracy, and its being a repeater saved him considerable time. In any case, he drew several exchanges but won six others, and went back to Coe Fen with a brace of rabbits each for himself, Atwood, and Atwood's servant.

WHILE ATWOOD's man prepared the rabbits, Atwood and Grey drank Armagnac, a rare bird in English wine cellars. Grey had not tasted it since before the revolution.

"Superb," he said, taking a small sip. "How on earth did you come by it?"

"I was in Paris last year to read a paper before the French Academy of Sciences, on orbital motion and the possibility of planets beyond George's Star. I brought a few bottles back with me."

Grey nodded. He was aware that Britain and France had a sub-rosa understanding that their natural scientists would continue to share work as if no war were going on—even to the extent of visits to the Royal Academy by Frenchmen and the No-Longer-Royal Academy by British and Irish men. It was slightly bizarre, but Grey had no objection to anything that tended to prove wrong Burke's allegation that, with the French revolution, the age of chivalry was gone, and that of sophists, economists, and calculators had succeeded.

Grey said this to Atwood—quoted Burke's famous remark. Atwood, who was reclined in his chair, leaned his head back and closed his eyes, and continued the quote: That chivalry—" 'that sensibility of principle, that chastity of honor, which felt a stain like a wound, which inspired courage whilst it mitigated ferocity—is all to be changed. All the pleasing illusions, which made power gentle and obedience liberal; all that decent drapery of life is to be rudely torn off; to be exploded as a ridiculous, absurd, and antiquated fashion. When lost, in an experiment to try how well a state may stand without these old fundamental principles, what sort of a thing must be a nation destitute of religion, honor, and manly pride, possessing nothing at present and hoping for nothing hereafter? All homage paid to women, as such, is to be regarded as romance and folly. The murder of a bishop or a father are only common homicide.

" 'Manners are required—sometimes as supplements, sometimes as correctives, always as aids—to law.' "

Grey shouldn't have been surprised that Atwood's memory was—evidently—perfect. Even so, the quoting of Burke as one might quote Shakespeare impressed him deeply. Atwood, who had reopened his eyes, noticed this.

"I don't memorize everything I read, you know. It's only that I knew Burke quite well. Interesting fellow. I can't say that I agree with everything he put forward. There is at least one ancient French tradition I do hope the revolution has stamped out. Do you know the ortolan?"

"The bunting? A small brown bird?" Grey's wife had been a naturalist.

"Yes. Some Frenchmen, practicing what they say is a legacy of Rome, force Armagnac down the birds' throats, then drown them in the stuff, roast them, pluck them, and eat them whole. Head, beak, bones, and all. They wear napkins over their head while they eat—to hide, they say, the shame of the act from God. And I wage my private war on barbarism by depriving them of their Armagnac, one bottle at a time.

"Which is not to say I dislike the French. I daresay the movement of art and science should be choked without them. Burke felt the same way. Called them the fountainhead of English civilization. But of course, he was Irish, you know. Those roast rabbits smell almost finished."

"May I ask you a question, Professor, that may sound somewhat silly and childish?"

"I'm a teacher, Grey. All I do is answer questions that are silly and childish. Please to proceed."

"What is it that makes chess, for some men, an obsession? It seems sometimes that its hold on devotees is less like a pass-time and more like a tincture of opium. When I play, I am captivated."

"Yes. That's hardly a childish question. I think everyone who plays on a nontrivial level asks himself that at one point or another. And I don't have an answer. What I think is that it has something to do with a man's drive to dominate nature. We build spires higher and higher; climb higher and higher mountains. Bulls are fought with nothing but a Spaniard's tablecloth. Men descend to the ocean floor in diving bells. Things that seem undoable are done, for the pride of victory—and victory over an opponent who is not a man; who is greater than a man. Perhaps we all have a deep-seated urge to wrestle with God as Jacob did, to prove our worth to him. Or to ourselves. Or very often, for men, to women." Atwood smiled.

"To dominate the game of chess requires an unnatural degree of forethought, in the same way climbing a mountain requires an unnatural degree of coolheadedness, or fighting a bull requires an unnatural degree of courage."

Grey nodded.

"On the first move of chess—the first half-move, actually; white's first move—there are twenty possible games. Since black has the same options open to him, that makes four hundred possible games by the end of the full first move. Now, the math is somewhat complicated after that point; you must allow for impossible positions—pawns in the first rank, that sort of thing—but an American has postulated the plausible number of possible chess games after just four moves as eighty-four million million. That is, eighty-four followed by twelve zeroes."

Grey pictured the number.

"To put that in some kind of meaningful scale, you could take every man—that is, every person: man, woman, and child—in Europe and assign to him one four-move chess game. To equal the total number of possible four-move games—and I should say, the shortest possible checkmate is on white's fourth move—you would need four hundred and twenty-five thousand Europes."

Grey pictured a gigantic stack of wall maps.

"Now, a serious chess game takes twenty moves, forty moves, a hundred moves—but how can a mortal being anticipate what his opponent will do just four moves ahead?"

No doubt having a perfect memory helps, thought Grey.

"Yet your Philidors can. To try to dominate the world of infinite possibility? That is truly, as Jacob did, to test yourself against God."

"And what would Burke say to that?"

Atwood shrugged. "To struggle with God is among our most ancient traditions. Burke's objection was to thinking that you've beaten him."

A ROUTINE had been established; it continued throughout January. Grey and Atwood would play, interminably; Grey would eventually manage a draw; Atwood would congratulate him and tell him to take an afternoon or an evening off. When they resumed, Atwood would play a faster and deeper game. It was a marginal blow to Grey's pride every time he discovered that Atwood had not been playing at full strength, but he understood the logic behind it: one must walk before he runs, and so forth. On days when Atwood taught at Trinity, Grey worked through chess problems Atwood wrote out for him in advance—trying to solve them in his head, and if that failed, on the board. At night, in a bed set against a chimney in Atwood's attic, Grey dreamed of chess. Sometimes of playing it, sometimes of being a piece in a great game.

By the end of January, Atwood claimed to be playing his true best, and Grey was drawing games at a rate of one or two a day. On January 28th and again on January 30th, Grey won, both times playing white. After the second victory, and two days before their February 1st deadline, Atwood pronounced Grey ready. He was still too aggressive in sacrifices, Atwood warned him, and ought to cease his occasional falling-back on the vulgar technique of moving wildly in hopes of knocking an opponent off-balance. But basically his play was sound, and good. Atwood was at all times blunt and straightforward, even as he and Grey became somewhat friendly, living cheek by jowl for a month. So when Atwood told Grey that he might, if facing a weak entrant in the first round, make it to the second, Grey took it as the high praise Atwood intended.

On their final day together, Atwood followed Grey out his back door onto Coe Fen, and Grey demonstrated the mechanics of the Girandoni, to Atwood's immense satisfaction. After squeezing off a few air-powered shots, they returned inside, shook hands, and Grey departed south in a chaise.

As he rode—feeling too stimulated to rest—he took the usual precaution, before he went abroad, of writing necessary letters. Power of attorney to Pater, along with a brief will. Also a letter to Mrs. Hubble to invite her father to avail himself of the piano anytime he wished; and to Canfield, suggesting that if the garden began to bloom before Grey returned, he might open it to the village.

Afterwards he leant back in the carriage and tried to let his mind wander, which it did, until—as the carriage approached Westminster—his eyes lighted on Old Slaughter's Coffee House. He opened the roof panel and asked the driver to stop, then climbed out and asked the driver to go on without him, to deliver his things to Buttle's. The carriage carried on, and Grey stepped into Slaughter's.

It was thick and hot and smoky inside; the smell of roasting beans wafted through the main room, competing with tobacco and sweat to dominate the ambience. Sock Spiller, Slaughter's head waiter (who'd been there since the fifties), was ambling back and forth, pouring punch and coffee for players and artists. While the artists discussed worldly trivia and tried to absorb some lingering airs of Pope, Dr. Johnson, and Glorious John Dryden, the players gambled on draughts, cards, and—principally—chess. Along the right side of the room ran a long bench, where regulars sat with their backs to the wall, accepting challenges, taking money off amateurs, and bilking drunks and naïfs. The artists' murmurs were mostly drowned out by the sound of chess pieces slamming down on checkered tabletops and of minute glasses being flipped, and of the regulars tongue-lashing their opponents. Grey had to walk deep into the room—about two-thirds of the way back from the street; to where the haze almost obscured any sight of the front windows—to find an empty spot. Grey sat down across from an unshaved man in a greasy brown coat who was eating cold chicken and playing with the coins he'd won off his last opponent.

The man looked Grey over, saw his clean and modestly expensive clothing, and said, "It's a shilling to play."

"A shilling stake?" said Grey.

"No, a shilling for my time," said the man.

Grey shook his head. "Not a chance."

"Then play with someone else," said the man.

Grey nodded and stood up.

"Oh, well, well then, if you're so sodding tight with a penny, sit down and we'll play for a stake."

Grey sat down. "Name it."

"Can you afford a pound, Sir Jew?"

"I think so," said Grey.

"Make it a guinea then," said the man, sneering, showing off coffee-stained teeth.

"Very well," said Grey, laying a pound and one down on the table. The man laid his own money down and scooped up a pawn of each color, one in each hand, and held them behind his back.

"Choose a hand," said the man.

"Right," said Grey.

"You're playing black," said the man, opening his hands. Conveniently, the black pieces were already set on Grey's side of the table. He suspected guests didn't guess white very often.

The Slaughter's regular—the coin player—made a conventional opening: king's pawn two squares. Grey responded with an equally conventional queen's pawn two squares. Pawn took pawn. Queen took pawn. The game was shallow, and Grey got the distinct sense that the regular was not playing to the fullest of his ability. He was subtle about it, but not nearly as subtle as Atwood had been . . . Grey saw himself being sharked. The man was playing a skillful, losing game, elegantly creating the impression that he was good, but not quite Grey's equal. Of course that was true (Grey hoped it was true, anyway), but the shark couldn't know it. The shark's game was deep, and it involved building up the wager before showing his actual strength.

Grey's instinctive response was to let the man think he was getting away with it. Grey won the first game, but just barely, after most of the board had been cleared. The regular proposed upping the bet, to two guineas, and let Grey win again. At the end of that game he was pretending anger. When Grey pocketed his winnings, the man ordered some gin, and soon began to pretend anger in drink. He lost a third game, for four guineas, and then—with the slightest hint of slurring his words—angrily challenged Grey to a game for twenty. Grey accepted. For a fourth time, the man (still playing white, the loser's prerogative) opened conventionally: king's pawn two squares. Grey responded with king's pawn, one square. The man advanced his queen's pawn two squares. So did Grey. Now the man brought out his queen's knight, to queen's bishop's third. Grey's queen's pawn took the shark's king's pawn. Knight took pawn. Knight to queen's seventh. The man brought out his second knight, to king's bishop's third. Grey brought out his second knight, to king's bishop's sixth. The moves were coming very fast now—the shark banging down each move, then flipping and banging down the minute glass. Grey moved just as fast and with equal vim. The man attacked with his king's knight, to its fifth. Grey responded with a defensive king's bishop to king's seventh. The shark attacked again with his knight, forking Grey's king's rook and his queen. The shark tasted victory and looked smug. King takes knight. Remaining knight puts Grey's king in check. Grey's king retreats to king's knight's eighth. The shark advances his knight to king's sixth, taking a pawn and threatening Grey's queen. Grey moves his queen to king's eighth—the only square where it isn't threatened—and the shark's smile expands with the pleasure of Grey falling into his trap. He advances the knight again, to queen's bishop's seventh, taking another pawn and again forking Grey's queen, this time with the queen's rook. Meaning Grey's next move could save either the rook or the queen, but not both. Losing either would cripple him for the remainder of the game.

But instead of moving either, Grey moved his king's bishop, to queen's knight's fourth—putting the shark's king in check, and at the same time opening a direct file from the shark's king to Grey's queen. Checkmate.

"My game, I think," said Grey, pocketing his winnings. The man threw his empty gin cup across the room, swept his arm over the board, knocking the pieces to the floor, and stormed away towards the front of the coffeehouse. Grey waved over Sock Spiller, who waved over a junior waiter to clean the mess. Grey apologized to Sock, paid the bill—adding something for both waiters—and then made his own way back towards the street. He was rather pleased; his chess pride had had a good evening.

Outside, he took a deep breath of cold air, lit a cheroot, and began the mile walk to Buttle's. Past Leicester Square, on Panton Street, he became conscious of men following him; footsteps coming closer at a fast walk. He turned. It was the chess shark, and a friend. The chess shark had a sap in his hand.

"We'll have your purse then," said the shark.

"No you won't," said Grey.

"I'll sap you down," said the shark.

"If you must," said Grey.

The shark stepped forward and swung the sandbag at Grey's head; Grey took the hit with his right forearm, and with his left hand, grabbed a handful of the man's right ear, hair and hat, and dashed his head hard into the masonry front of a house. Number 6, Panton Street. The shark's friend backed away a few steps.

"Cut along," barked Grey, and the man took off at a run. Grey stooped, picked up the dazed shark's sap, pocketed it, and continued on his way to Buttle's. He was greeted at the door by Mathers, who took his coat, hat, and sap. "Mathers," said Grey, "I feel I've trespassed too far on Mr. Pater's membership. You recall I'd folded my page in the signature book before leaving for India. Perhaps you could reopen it for me."

"Very good, sir," said Mathers.

9

A
T THE MAP TABLE in Sir Edward Banks's office, Willys toured
Grey through the final plans:
"You will travel under the name Thomas Caffery; these
are your credentials. Tomorrow you will meet the rest of the British
chess delegation in Harwich, here, at the dairy docks, and cross to
Holland. We have received assurance from the Dutch that they are
neutral in respect of the chess cartel—of course, they claim to be
neutral in everything—no one likes to admit he's a French puppet—
but in any case, we have a signed assurance of safe passage, so long
as your purpose is strictly gaming in nature. For that reason, on
the way out, you'll have to come through Denmark. But best not to
show our hand before we have to.

"You will land at Rotterdam and take the barge upstream on the
Rhine. The barges are privately owned, and mostly by Germans, but
now that the west bank of the Rhine is part of the French *patrie*, they
are forced to work within the French trading regime. The French,
of course, are party to the chess cartel, and they've always respected
the cartels in the past. Nevertheless, you will treat the barges as
hostile territory. If the frogs decide they don't like the cut of your
jib, there will be no relying on assistance from any German authority. Particularly because the French have made it clear that they will

cross the Rhine whenever they like, for whatever reason they like—in order to enforce their system for the continent, or to chase fugitives, or what have you. Who is there to stop them?

"Of course, it's the fugitive question that is relevant here: Louis Antoine informs us that Bonaparte's dragoons have taken to making people in the German states disappear in the night. Some reappear in Paris, very contrite about their crimes against the state. Others don't. We can be sure that they will want Leclerc back, though, once they realize he's gone, so obviously you will have to stay as far away from the Rhine and the border as you can. And to be, at all times, maximally discreet."

"Thank you, Aaron, for that advice," said Grey.

"In any case: a barge up the Rhine to the river Main, then up the Main to Frankfurt. Louis Antoine will contact you at the docks. You will wear a bottle-green jacket and no hat; he will ask you if you are the gentleman from Skye. Louis confides he will be able to remove you and Leclerc from the tournament, and from Frankfurt, without drawing notice. He will then escort you north through the Germans, across the Eider, into Sleswick. At Tönning, here at the Eider's mouth, you will signal one of our clippers standing off and on—long-short-long on the dark lantern—and she will take you off for a swift crossing back to England. The clipper will be there from the first of March, but won't expect you until the fourth or fifth. She will stay until you arrive."

Grey nodded.

"Is all of that clear?" said Willys.

"Abundantly. How many chess men am I meeting?"

Willys half smiled. "Very droll, Thomas. You are the eighth man in the detachment."

"The eighth? How many are playing in toto?"

"In excess of two hundred. Thurn und Taxis will evidently subsume the neighboring estates for the duration—they're blocked in the center of the city, so it will become one *grand palais*. Should be rather interesting."

"Yes." Grey was looking alternately at the principal map—a large map of northern Europe—and smaller illustrative maps. The Rhine Valley, the city of Frankfurt, northern Germany and Sleswick, and so on.

"Any questions, Grey?" said Sir Edward, who had remained seated at his desk through his chief of staff's discourse.

Grey shook his head. "No, Sir Edward."

10

GREY HAD WONDERED if any of the British chess men would be from the gambling set. In the event, they were mostly academics—two from Oxford, two from Cambridge, one each from St. Andrews and Glasgow. One was an elderly doctor from London named Mendoza, who spent most of his time discussing new techniques in surgery with the Glaswegian professor. Including Grey, the other six spent little time talking and considerable time playing each other in chess. During the crossing from Harwich to Rotterdam, Grey had a noticeable advantage, being the only one of their party, other than Mendoza, who was not struck with seasickness. Once they were on the Rhine (towed smoothly upstream by four giant Ardennais horses, who walked the towpath with casual, muscular authority, as if they were its sole proprietors), Grey's steadiness of stomach ceased to be an advantage. From that point on he won a few games, drew a few others, and lost several score, over five days that seemed to grow longer with Grey's irritation in defeat. At the confluence of the Rhine and the Main, the rotation of Ardennais was replaced with a Rhenish team noticeably less proud and somewhat smaller, but equally efficient. The barge arrived in the Free Imperial City of Frankfurt within an hour of its schedule, in the afternoon of Tuesday, February the 28th.

Grey was wearing the green jacket and not wearing the hat, but Louis Antoine, if he was there, had no chance to introduce himself. Rather unexpectedly, the six Englishmen and two Scots stepped off the somewhat dingy barge onto the somewhat dirty river dock, somewhat damp from an off-and-on rain shower, only to be greeted by footmen in white gloves and powdered wigs, who escorted them to a pair of gilded carriages. Clearly the Frankfurters were taking their chess coronation quite seriously. With the footmen standing on the boot boards, the coaches rolled west through the city, and in a quarter hour the *grand palais* of Thurn und Taxis hove into view, the largest and grandest house of a street of large, grand houses. Like much of Frankfurt's upper class, the family Thurn und Taxis had won their nobility through business, and with no legacy estate to maintain, they had preferred to stay at the center of things. The palais's exterior was neoclassical and ruddy-red; the carriages were waved to a stop by a marshaling servant outside the entrance arch, to allow a departing carriage right-of-way. A matching gilded carriage rolled outward, and the two coachloads of British subjects rolled in, under the arch and into a large courtyard, dotted with groups of freshly deposited chess players, whom servants were trying to usher inside.

A knot had formed around the only two women present—a lady's maid and her lady, whom Grey was at once certain was the Duchess of Bourbon, Bathilde d'Orléans. The reputation for beauty that preceded her throughout Europe had in no way been exaggerated, and even in her fifties, she was sufficiently captivating that otherwise shy and retiring academical types were vying for the privilege of escorting her indoors. Her overcoat—as the late February day was chilly, if not quite cold—was simple yet obviously of the highest fashion and most delicate couture. It was colored like a new merlot, with silver lace trimming. Her dense and elaborate wig was dark gray rather than white; the fur hat from which it protruded was white, as was the fan being discreetly used to keep her admirers at arm's length.

Grey approached Bathilde's circle; at the same time, a footman leaned through the admirers and whispered something in her ear.

"You will pardon me, gentlemen," she said, "I understand the English delegation has arrived, and I must greet my particular friend Mr. Caffery." She had picked out Grey, presumably by his jacket and hatlessness, and had locked eyes with him. Grey nodded, very slightly, and Bathilde approached him as if they'd known each other for years.

"Thomas my dear, how wonderful to see you."

"*Chère* Bathilde," said Grey, gently raising her outstretched hand to his lips, "you are—though it would seem impossible—more beautiful than ever." Bathilde let out a rich, tender laugh.

"Oh, my dear, you were always a terrible liar. But come, walk with me inside and tell me how you've been keeping yourself." To the other, disappointed chess players, she added, "By your leave," and with her right arm laced through Grey's left, they proceeded up the shallow steps to the palais's entry hall.

Once they were beyond the ears of Bathilde's followers—becoming part of the flow of players being urged towards the Thurn und Taxis's great hall, a giant, late Renaissance ballroom of brick and gilded plaster—Bathilde said to Grey in a quiet but conversational voice, "I understand our friend was unable to meet you at the docks. He was, I'm sure, very disappointed."

"It is all well, madame; I and the other British were expected and brought here directly. We should not have had a chance for a proper conversation."

"Just so," said Bathilde. "He will introduce himself this evening. And I am afraid there is a further complication for you to discuss." Grey nodded. "In the meantime, Mr. Caffery, allow me to introduce you to my fellow representative of the French school of chess: Mr. Joseph Leclerc." They had approached a solemn-looking man, whose eyes were pointed up, examining the hall's rib vaulting.

"Mr. Joseph Leclerc," she said, switching to French, "this is my especial friend, Mr. Thomas Caffery, of the chess players of the Court of St. James's."

Leclerc was dressed in the simple Republican clothes that were gradually falling out of fashion as Napoleonic France shrugged off austerity. He was shorter than Grey by two or three inches, and quite gaunt in appearance: sunken cheeks beneath prominent cheekbones. He extended a thin hand.

"Mr. Caffery."

Grey shook it. "Mr. Leclerc." With his third and fourth fingers, Leclerc slid a small, tightly folded piece of paper from his own palm to Grey's. "It's a pleasure, sir. And are these further members of the French delegation?" Two rather large and burly men had loomed up beside them.

"No," said Leclerc, with an unchanged frown. "They are my, eh, attendants."

"Honorine," said Bathilde, calling to her lady's maid, who—having followed her mistress and Grey inside—had remained by the entrance to the hall, standing invisibly against a wall. Honorine approached, and Bathilde said, with a gesture to the "attendants," "Perhaps you will show these gentlemen to a footman who can lead them to the servants' hostel. I'm afraid, gentlemen," she said, turning to Leclerc's bodyguard, "that our hosts are compelled to be most strict in accommodation, you see. If you are not quick, they may not even fit you in at the hostel—indeed, the lack of space has compelled poor Honorine to sleep on the floor in my own room."

The two men looked at Bathilde and then turned to a third man who was now stepping into the conversation, with a girl just over twenty on his arm. He nodded his assent to the two big men; one said, "Thank you, madame," to Bathilde, and both followed Honorine away. This third man turned to Leclerc and said, "Forgive me for interrupting—even when presented with the article herself, this Frankfurt petty-butler insists it is impossible to secure a room for your daughter. I have, however, been able to arrange a couch to be moved into your chamber and made up as a bed: I believe this is the only solution."

"Thank you, Théodore," said Leclerc, still frowning. "Most kind of you. Allow me to introduce you to a friend of Madame Bathilde's, one of the English players—Mr. Thomas Caffery. Mr. Caffery: one of our French entrants, Mr. Jean Théodore."

"Your humble servant, sir," said Grey.

"I am yours," said Théodore.

"And Mr. Caffery," said Leclerc, gesturing to the woman on Théodore's arm, "allow me to present my daughter, Geneviève."

"Mademoiselle Leclerc," said Grey, bowing shallowly, "it is a great pleasure."

"Thank you, sir," said Geneviève. Grey looked at her. She was a cold beauty; unsmiling, statuesque, and doubtless a rival for the Bathilde of her heyday. Palest blonde hair, greenest green eyes, and cheekbones that could have cut gemstones. If the Venus de Milo hadn't been disarmed . . .

"Come, Thomas," said Bathilde, "before the formalities begin, I must show you an exceptional portrait bust the Taxis have had from the Anatolian coast. It sits by the stairs. If you will excuse us——"

Grey followed Bathilde away, thinking of Geneviève Leclerc; thinking that he'd never seen a woman so entirely certain of her own beauty, and in consequence, so obviously disinclined to please. He had offered Bathilde his arm, and the warmth she evinced, nodding or smiling at everyone they passed, was as stark a difference from Miss Leclerc as could be imagined. Bathilde's beauty was a gift she was glad to bestow on others, as though it were twice blessed rain dropped from heaven. Grey wondered where the two women's paths had diverged.

"It's just ahead," said Bathilde.

"Are the Thurn und Taxis great collectors?" said Grey.

"Once, perhaps, but they have fallen on hard times with the collapse of their monopoly on the Kaiserliche Reichspost, now that Napoleon has his own ideas on postal organization. I have heard that nowadays they live mostly in Regensburg, and that this house is owned by the city burghers. Though I suppose I shouldn't gossip about it." She looked over her shoulder to see if they were out of Leclerc's and Théodore's earshot. "So you see what the new complication is."

"You mean the man Théodore, or the daughter?" said Grey.

"Théodore is a terrible man, part of the security committee; an

internal guard for Leclerc, I suppose, and quite a good chess player—
and yes, he is a complication—but no, I meant the daughter. Leclerc
concealed her from me entirely. She did not travel with us from
Paris, and I have only just been introduced to her this morning."

Grey nodded. They stood before an ancient marble bust of a
Roman patrician. "Leclerc passed me a note when we shook hands.
Perhaps it will explain."

"I imagine it will," said Bathilde. "Though I can guess what it
says. Who knows more about the foolish things parents do because
of their children."

Grey turned his head to Bathilde and smiled wryly. "As soon as I
can be alone, I will read it; I daren't do it here."

Bathilde nodded. "Do you expect you can accommodate her?"

"From the English view, yes, I think so—but it will depend more
on the arrangements our friend from the dock has made."

"Yes, quite," said Bathilde. "Though he sent word that he failed
to meet you, I have so far been unable to send word back about this
daughter." Grey nodded.

For a moment they stood in silence. Then Grey said, with a finger waved towards the marble bust, "This is rather fine, isn't it?" It
showed a slightly sneering, elderly bald man with a deeply creased
face and sagging jowls. It was near two thousand years old and so
remarkably lifelike that Grey felt almost as if he were looking into
the past.

"Yes," said Bathilde. "Very." They resumed their silence for a
moment. "Have you seen the great tablet from Rosetta?"

"I have," said Grey.

"Stolen from the French."

"'The spoils of war,' I believe you intended to say."

"Have they translated it yet?"

"Not yet, but the metropolis is consumed by the effort."

"Perhaps someday a peace treaty will send it to Paris."

"Doubtful, my lady," said Grey.

"Perhaps we can split it like Solomon's baby. Would you like the
Greek portion or the Egyptian?"

Grey chuckled. Behind them, a chime was struck. A finely dressed gentleman was standing on the second stair of the grand staircase, prepared to address the chess congregants.

"Lady Bathilde, and gentlemen—welcome." He said this in German, and then repeated the word "welcome" in French, English, Russian, Polish, Spanish, Italian, Turkish, Dutch, and after referring to a note card with a slightly embarrassed look, Swedish and Hungarian.

"I speak on behalf of our hosts," he said, resuming German, "His Grace Karl Anselm, Prince of Thurn and Taxis, and the burghers' council of the Free Imperial City of Frankfurt. As you well know, the men in this room represent the greatest chess players in the world. Perhaps among you there is a Philidor. We are gathered here to see. In the morning, at the hour of ten, the tournament will be opened by His Imperial Majesty Francis the Second. Do not be late. For those who require it, food has been laid in the antechamber there." He pointed. "Wine will now be served, and momentarily the footmen of the prince will begin to escort you to your rooms. Please to attend to the names I call from this place, and to cooperate with a prompt dispersal to your rooms, in order that you will have satisfactory rest before tomorrow's play. Thank you."

He ran again through the multitude of languages, saying "thank you" in each, before stepping down to speak with a clerk.

"What a charmer," said Bathilde, still standing beside Grey. The announcer—whatever his title was: director? steward?—climbed back to his place on the stairs. The chime was struck again, and when the room had quieted, he called, "Lady Bathilde. If you would approach."

"I am sent for," said Bathilde, offering her hand to Grey, who gave it another light kiss. "Let us hope that she who is first will not be last. Good evening, *mon ami*." She smiled at Grey and he smiled back. What a noble, captivating woman . . . he followed her for a moment with his eyes, before a touch on the elbow turned him around.

It was Mr. Jean Théodore.

"Mr. Caffery," said Théodore, in English, "we didn't have any chance to speak before, and, of course, because of the war, I rarely get an opportunity to speak to Englishmen."

"An unfortunate circumstance, Mr. Théodore."

"Depending on your point of view. Actually, the last Englishman I spoke to was Thomas Paine."

"Paine, sir—if I'm not mistaken—is very much an American."

"Well, so he said when he was arrested, and sentenced to death. Perhaps he was right, but we in Paris tend to err on the side of caution."

"You find execution cautious?"

"Oh yes. You know what they say, about having nothing to fear from a corpse. Of course, Paine was spared and became a great supporter of our first consul, Napoleon. But then caution in one can often lead to prudence in another. But I ramble. I wished to ask, how did you come to be acquainted with the Duchess of Bourbon?"

"I met her on my grand tour; I spent near a year studying in Spain. During her exile. Before she and prudence returned to Paris."

"Just so. Well, I must attempt to speak to the butler-general and learn if Mademoiselle Leclerc's couch has been installed. I shall see you again when play begins. Perhaps we shall have a meeting."

"One can only hope," said Grey.

II

THE THURN UND TAXIS footmen wore blue and gold livery; the gold lace reflected the torchlight illuminating the palace's upper hallways as Grey was led to his room. The hallways were something of a maze—wings had been added to grow the palais along with the family's postal fortune—but Grey and his modest luggage were soon delivered to a room on the top floor, with a sloped ceiling and a small rectangular window in the sloping outer wall. The footman handed Grey a lit candle in a pewter cup, asked if he needed anything else, and after accepting a groat, bid him good night and closed the door.

A moment after the door shut—as Grey was turning to examine his bed—a match was struck in the darkness. Grey turned to the sound. The match was being used to light a long, thin, clay pipe, and the flame illuminated the face above it. The face was smiling.

"Are you, by any chance, the gentleman from Skye?" He shook the match out, but the dim light of his pipe fire kept the wry smile visible. "If not, this will be terribly awkward."

"I am. His Grace le Duc d'Enghien?"

"Yes," said the duke, standing, "but do please call me Louis Antoine." He extended his hand and Grey shook it.

"Thomas Grey, traveling as Caffery. I remember reading of your exploits with the Condés in the nineties. Doing, they said, in the figure of a lamb the feats of a lion."

Louis chuckled and shook his head. "It was much ado about nothing." Grey smiled and Louis went on, "But it's kind of you to say. I must apologize for failing to see you at the docks; there was rather more going on than I had anticipated."

"All's well that ends well, Your Grace. Please sit. I'm afraid that a complication has arisen."

Louis resumed his seat. "Théodore, you mean."

"No," said Grey, sitting on the bed, leaning back on the headboard, lighting a small cigar. "Mr. Leclerc has brought his daughter."

Louis frowned; Grey was unfolding the note Leclerc had pressed into his palm. He scanned it quickly and then read it aloud:

" 'Sir: I hope you will forgive my deceptive omission regarding my daughter's accompanying me. I will not leave her behind, and I would not take the chance that you would have been advised to refuse to include her in your plans.' " Grey looked up from the letter. "Why would I have been advised to refuse to include her in my plans?"

"Mademoiselle Leclerc," said Louis Antoine, "is known to be an ardent Bonapartist. She has published poems in praise of him and the new France, led subscription drives for soldiers wounded in his service, that sort of thing."

"I see," said Grey, and continued: " 'I freely confess to this attempt to force your hand by waiting so late to reveal a fly in the ointment. I have waited with her as well: for the sake of discretion, she knows nothing of our plans, nor will she, before the final moment. I hope you will believe my expressions of deepest shame at this shabbiness, and that you will be able to accommodate us both, because I say again, I will not go without her. Yours, etc., LeC.' "

Louis nodded. Grey held the letter to the candle. As it burned, Louis scratched his chin and nodded again. Grey looked at him. He was thirty-one and handsome in the way some might deride as pretty. Certainly there was nothing in him that bespoke a man of action. He looked like wealth and leisure. Or perhaps just leisure, as Grey noted, for the first time in the dim light, that Louis Antoine was wearing the livery of a Taxis footman.

"Yes," said Louis, following Grey's look, "I was able to come to an arrangement with the underbutler. A very discreet arrangement— you needn't worry—but he was kind enough to outfit me in a way that I might come and go without attracting any attention. And his help will, later on, be important to executing my plan of escape."

Grey knocked some cigar ash into his candle's drip tray and nodded for Louis to continue.

"The plan is this: As you know, Frankfurt is a great market town, the center of local commerce. Roads radiating out in every direction, and—most importantly—there is a great farmers' market held on the first of every month. Which, happily, is the second day of the tournament—the day after tomorrow. March first.

"At the end of play on the second day, there is to be a sort of celebratory ball—in celebration of the tournament, and in anticipation of the champion, as all but the final two players will have been eliminated by then, with the grand finale to happen the following noon, under the eyes of various rich and mighty burghers and courtiers. In any case, during that ball, Leclerc will excuse himself from his bodyguard, complaining of digestive trouble and seeking the privy closet. There you will be waiting, to help him through the high window and out onto my waiting carriage, which will whisk us away into the night.

"Meanwhile, at the ball, my underbutler friend will wait as long as he can, until a Frenchman breaks away from the party to check the privy, and then loudly announce that Mr. Leclerc's vermiform appendix has burst, and that he has been rushed by some Thurn und Taxis servants to the nearby home of a doctor who specializes in, uh . . . appendices."

Grey grunted a chuckle.

"I have arranged for this doctor not to be at home. If—or, as I should say, when—the two guards and Théodore go there to find him, the doctor's servants will inform them that the doctor had been called away by another emergency, south to Darmstadt, and that the coach carrying Leclerc has taken off in pursuit of him. This will, I believe, send the French guardians off on a long chase in the wrong direction. At a minimum, they will lose an hour; if we are lucky, much more. By the time they realize what has happened, we will have disappeared north into the Rhenish hinterlands, well on our way to the Danish coast."

Grey was nodding thoughtfully.

"What do you think?" said Louis, tapping out his long pipe and beginning to refill it.

"Very neat," said Grey. "Very good. I'm certain I could not improve on it, for Leclerc—but what allowance can you make for his daughter?"

Louis was lighting and inhaling. "Yes, she is, as Leclerc wrote, a fly in the ointment. Hmm." He drew a few times on the pipe. "Well, it seems to me that the only difficulty is getting her to the carriage. It should be no difficulty, nor at all implausible, to say that when her father became suddenly ill, she insisted on accompanying him to the doctor. I will simply add this to the explanation our underbutler shall give. But how to extract her without drawing any attention? Hmm."

Grey gestured out the small room's small window. "The garden out there, is there a gate at the far end?"

Louis shook his head.

"How high is the wall?"

"Seven or eight feet."

Grey nodded. "Instead of my helping Leclerc through the privy's window from the inside, could you help him from without?"

"I believe so," said Louis, with a slight grin as he anticipated Grey's solution.

"Well, if we can match our watches, I need only persuade Mamselle Leclerc to exit to the garden . . . I might say that Lady Bathilde wonders if she might wait on her for a moment, a problem that requires a woman's ear . . . Or pass her a note written in her father's hand. And then once she's out there, we—me on the inside, you on the other with the carriage—might get her over the wall without too much difficulty."

"Willingly or unwillingly?"

"Well, I assume—once she understands her father's plans—willingly."

"I wouldn't be so sure. French girls do what they want. The English think that makes them easy." Louis laughed. "In fact, it makes them very difficult."

"Well, either way, I don't anticipate much problem. She can't weigh more than six or seven stone. I'll toss her over if I have to. Her father can mollify her afterwards."

Louis nodded. "Very well: we shall plan on it."

"Very good. Now, if you would, tell me about Théodore."

Louis's pleasant expression dropped into a sneer of contempt. Perhaps even of hatred. "He is as odious a man as God has ever made. One of Robespierre's principal terrorizers—a man with no conscience at all. No, nothing even resembling a conscience. And therefore very adept at shifting with the political winds. When Robespierre's star abruptly fell, Théodore was already on the reactors' side. This secured him a place on the security committee—as a chief bloodletter—until Napoleon's return from Egypt. He joined with the Corsican quickly after the Assembly was supplanted, which let him keep his post. Though I doubt even as hard a man as Bonaparte could have any feeling for him other than contempt. I won't tell you in any detail what he has done to enemies . . . to his friend's enemies . . . to anyone whose suffering would advantage him. What he's done to their skin. Well, in any case, let us say simply that he is a man to be wary of."

Grey nodded, and for several long moments he and Louis smoked in silence.

"What about his chess game?" said Grey.

"What?" said Louis.

"How strong is Théodore's chess game?"

"Who cares?" said Louis.

12

A FTER THEY'D MADE PLANS to meet the following day for luncheon, to discuss any problems that might have arisen, Louis had slipped out of Grey's room, concealed by his Taxis uniform, and Grey had gone quickly to sleep. Now it was the morning of the tournament's first day—February 29th of the year four— and Grey was standing, well rested, washed, and shaved, among the throng in the grand hall who awaited the emperor's entrance.

The steward, or director (or what you will), stood on a low platform set in the center of the great marble-floored, high-ceilinged, gaudily mirrored hall, looking towards the main entrance for a signal to announce the emperor's arrival. Grey was pleased to be getting a look at Francis II—he hoped that seeing the man in the flesh might help resolve some of the evident contradictions in what Grey had heard of his personality. Francis had been a child spoiled in the Florentine court of his father Leopold, before being sent in his middle teenage years to Vienna, to prepare for his eventual accession to the throne of his childless uncle Emperor Joseph II. The spoilage of Tuscany had been replaced, in Austria, by strictest discipline: Joseph had tried to make a man of a "mother's boy." Reports that Grey had read in London called Francis self-centered and self-interested, yet said when his uncle sent him to the Austrian army, he was a good and capable soldier, both in taking orders and leading troops. Joseph had reportedly said that, for all his other shortcomings—which Joseph did not hesitate to list—Francis had an inherent and unswerving sense of fairness and justice. And yet, when Danton had offered to negotiate the release of Francis's aunt, Marie Antoinette, Francis had refused to make even trivial concessions to the Jacobins, which would have saved Marie from the guillotine. Francis hated Napoleon, but to end the War of the Second Coalition, he'd given Napoleon all of his empire west of the Rhine, along with a tacit veto over the Germans' affairs. Was this compromise or cowardice? Joseph had called his nephew unimaginative, but as his uncle had sponsored the greatest artists of the eighteenth century, Francis was perhaps the world's most important royal patron of the sciences. Machines animated by heat and steam were coming to life on the Danube. Yet Francis loathed democracy.

Francis was about Grey's age, but had been emperor for almost fifteen years, since his early twenties. At an age when Grey had responsibility for half a ship's marine company, Francis had responsibility for tens of millions of men, women, and children. It was a difficult strain to imagine.

"Honored burghers of Frankfurt; lords, ladies, and gentlemen," said the director, loudly. "His Imperial and Royal Apostolic Majesty Francis II, by the grace of God, Holy Roman Emperor." Grey's German was not good enough to hear accents, but he believed the director was speaking with considerably more precision than he had the day before.

Francis walked into the room quickly, with a vague frown on his long, thin face. For an emperor, he was dressed simply—no cape or train, or satin and sashes. Instead he wore a stiff-collared black coat over a silver waistcoat and black breeches, a well-powdered wig, but none of the customary medals on the breast. He stepped onto the stage, waved away the director, and addressed the hushed room.

"My subjects and guests, it is my pleasure to welcome you today. As you know, I was crowned in Frankfurt; it is most suitable, therefore, that the new Caesar—or should I say, the new Philidor—of chess be crowned here as well. Though not, perhaps, at the cathedral." He smiled, very slightly. "I wish you all the best of luck, and let play commence." He stepped down from the stage and walked quickly out of the room, to considerable applause.

After a mannerly interval, the director stepped back onto his platform. "If the esteemed noncompetitors would kindly withdraw to that end of the room"—he gestured to an area by the entrance, where footmen stood ready to separate the players from the spectators with a long velvet rope—"we may shortly begin." There was considerable shuffling about, but soon the audience had been concentrated where they wouldn't get in the way. At the same time, eight long tables, with chessboards set on them, were carried in from the room's rear. The director resumed:

"Lady Bathilde; gentlemen: there are one hundred and fourteen chessboards laid out for play. The rules are simple: white and black have been assigned by lottery, as has each man's opponent. The winner of each game will proceed to the second round, while the loser will be eliminated from further play. In the event of a draw, the man playing black will be deemed the winner. Coming to Frankfurt from across Europe and the world, there is a total of two hundred and forty-two competitors. Therefore, fourteen have been selected— again, by lottery—to pass by the first round, and enter competition in the second. They are as follows . . ."

The director began to read off a list of names; Grey's was the second spoken. He felt an immediate, crushing disappointment—for two months he had awaited this moment of action, and having been honest with himself, he had felt that his only realistic chance of winning a game would be in the first round, where the weakest players would still be playing. He had a bitter taste in his mouth.

"If these fourteen gentlemen will withdraw to the spectators' area, I will begin to read out the place assignments, beginning with white at the head of the first table."

Grey had been standing with his countrymen. He bid them all good luck, shaking the hand of each, and then made his way towards the enroped audience. Along the way, Bathilde caught his eye. She winked at him and he felt somewhat better about his bad luck.

He and the other thirteen pass-bys took their place among the spectators, and the two hundred and twenty-eight players, in a slow succession, took their seats. Grey was annoyed (further annoyed, this time with patriotic displeasure) that two of the Englishmen had drawn each other as opponents, considerably worsening their national odds.

"Is everyone in his place?" asked the director. He paused a moment, and when no one answered, he said, "Then, please to begin."

This not being Slaughter's or a gamblers' den, there were no minute glasses forcing fast moves; still, everyone playing white had had more than time enough to settle on an opening. In the few seconds after the director's instruction to begin, the room was filled with the soft mallet sounds of stone and wooden chess pieces hitting stone and wooden boards (the sets were not uniform; Grey wondered where they had all come from—lent by the burghers perhaps). Otherwise, the room was silent.

The spectators numbered about fifty when play began, but quite quickly dwindled to two dozen or so, as half realized they couldn't really see much, and would prefer to await the results in the foyer or courtyard, where they could talk and be waited on. From the spectators' position, Grey could only see the moves of the game being played at the head of the nearest table. Grey wasn't sure who the players were—between the waiting for his room assignment and the waiting for Francis II, he had been introduced to, oh, a hundred-odd chess players: fewer than half the total. He hadn't met either of these . . . though a few games back, he could see one of the Americans he'd been introduced to, one Castor Baucom, whose accent Grey had found nearly impenetrable, and who—in the midst of three hundred men in formal dress: mostly breeches, or boots over trousers—had chosen to wear heavy cotton work pants, a collarless shirt, and what Grey assumed were West Indian moccasins. Admittedly, he did look comfortable. After his, the most noticeable deviation from the standard European fashion of the moment was among the Ottoman and Russian contingent, some of whom favored robes or long jackets over loose-fitting pants. A Georgian player Grey had met was wearing a long, close-fitting, flat-fronted white jacket that came to his knees and was tightened at his waist by a broad leather belt. An Ottoman Jew from Jerusalem wore a long jacket over a collarless shirt and trousers; he was one of the few players with a beard, and the only one, other than the London doctor Mendoza, with his head covered.

The two men at the table-head nearest Grey were dressed as he was: dark jacket, dark waistcoat, white shirt, light brown trousers, leather boots. They were both playing well, playing conservatively, moving slowly, driving Grey to the brink of madness as they lingered over even the obvious moves. Grey's attention wandered to the people standing around him—the fellow first-game pass-bys he had exchanged a few words with; assorted Germans, Slavs, and Scandinavians; the upper-class Frankfurters enjoying the spectacle, such as it was (and it was not Ascot). And then there was Geneviève Leclerc, standing with Bathilde's lady's maid Honorine, who looked to have appointed herself as her attractive young countrywoman's chaperone. Grey moved gradually towards her, as if adjusting his view of one of the less easily watched games. When he was directly beside her, after a polite nod to Honorine, he spent several minutes watching the play before saying anything to Geneviève, whose single-minded squint was directed at her father, somewhere in the middle of the second table.

"I'm sorry I can't offer you a pair of opera glasses," said Grey, finally.

Geneviève turned to him and smiled slightly, the way a girl of breeding does to show she is well mannered without inviting a conversation.

"They would be helpful, sure. But I make do. He seems to be playing with a conventional French defense. He always handles that well."

"One associates the French more with offense, these days."

Geneviève smiled again, in the same not-especially-amused way, and said nothing. After a moment, Grey continued. "Do you play yourself?"

"I do. Sometimes as my father's sparring partner. But my game is shallow; he uses me only to stay in practice when there is no stronger player around."

"I gather he plays with my dear Bathilde."

"Yes," said Geneviève. "They have lately become quite inseparable, as they have both prepared for this tournament. But of course everyone wishes to play against Madame Bathilde, to get a degree closer to the famous Mr. Franklin."

"Ah yes. Did you ever meet him?"

"My father says he complimented me in the cradle—that my 'voice was ever soft, gentle, and low. An excellent thing in infants.' " Grey laughed, and Geneviève smiled again, for the first time with a little actual warmth. Though not too much.

"I gather your father works in government. You haven't by any chance met the famous Mr. Bonaparte."

"I have had that honor, yes. Though I fear it would be indiscreet to discuss our first consul with—if you will pardon me—the enemy."

"Am I your enemy? There's no war in Frankfurt."

"I bear you no ill will, sir, but you are English, are you not?"

"I am."

"And I am afraid that this is base and ground enough to make you France's enemy. Though we are gathered here as neutrals. Frankfurt's docks on the main are full of trade and bustle while France's lie empty, blockaded by your ships." She cocked her head towards Grey. "Though of course I don't mean to suggest that I hold you personally responsible." Her face suggested she did.

"Perish the thought."

"Indeed. However, if you will excuse me now, I should hate to miss my father's play."

"Of course, mademoiselle. Your servant."

She nodded, and Grey retreated slightly. He turned back to the slow game he had attempted watching at the start, and when he could stand no more, decamped to the courtyard for some fresh air and a cigar.

Over the next two and a fraction hours, the group in the courtyard—some talking, some pacing, some accepting coffee or chocolate from the footmen—awaited news of the first round's conclusion. It was brisk outside, but not uncomfortable. Not uncomfortable enough, anyway, to incline Grey to retrieve (or send a footman for) his greatcoat. Grey exchanged a few polite words with a few of the other passed-by players who had, over time, wandered outside. None of them felt like talking; each was playing games in his head. The game Grey was playing was somewhat, not altogether, different: the moves that would get Geneviève Leclerc quickly and quietly to her father's escape coach.

Periodically he checked his watch, or stopped to listen as one of the other players inquired about the progress inside. After two hours, two-thirds of the games were over, with the vanquished filing occasionally out into the yard. Some were cavalier in defeat, putting on a brave face—others sought each other's company to talk through their games and examine their mistakes. A few said nothing outside of curt orders to footmen to retrieve their luggage and servants and summon transportation. A few victors came out too, though mostly they seemed to be staying inside, perhaps basking in their triumph, or using the silence of the main hall to avoid losing their concentration before the second round.

The second round was supposed to begin in the early afternoon, before a break for luncheon. However, after the footmen's explanation that the first round had "not yet ended" became monotonous, and one o'clock came and went, Grey went inside to investigate the situation for himself. A handful of his fellow awaiters followed.

Back in the great hall, Grey discovered that only a single game was now being played; the spectators were visibly annoyed that the first-game winners had ringed this final contest, obscuring their view. Figuring his status as a contestant permitted his approach, Grey joined the viewing circle, to see two players he'd very briefly met earlier in the day—a Pole and a Russian—engaged in a vicious endgame: a king, a rook, and a knight against a king, a rook, and a bishop. No pawns remained; it was a slow chase and counterchase, around the board, each man looking for an angle in which to entrap his opponent. There were murmurs of a stalemate, but it would mean a de jure defeat for the Russian, who was playing white—and neither the Russian nor the Pole seemed to want the game to end that way.

From the time Grey appeared, the game continued another quarter hour, until the Russian allowed his bishop to be pinned behind his king in check, so in moving the king, the bishop was forfeit. With this move, the Russian resigned, and said something to the Pole in a mutually intelligible Slavic language, of whose precise origin Grey was unsure. The Pole bowed his head in appreciation of the Russian's remark; the two men shook hands, and the Russian departed. Another Polish first-round winner stepped out of the ring to shake his countryman vigorously, clapping him on the back and jostling his shoulders as they both smiled; there was general congratulation and murmuring over the game and its conclusion. There was a chime for silence, and from the stage the director announced that, due to the delay, the second round of games would begin after luncheon rather than before, and that the players should be back in the great hall by four in the afternoon.

Louis Antoine had suggested he and Grey meet at a small and out-of-the-way restaurant named the Kleine Fleischhaus. Grey found the name singularly unappetizing, but Louis Antoine promised a meal Grey would not regret, and Grey had been prepared to take his word for it. He walked up increasingly narrow, brownish streets, and when he realized he'd taken a wrong turn, retraced his steps to the correct hole in the correct wall by following his nose. The heavy smell of smoke and spice that wafted out the little flesh-house's open door was like a signal cannon in the fog.

Grey stepped inside, out of the chilled afternoon and into a beautifully warm brick room, where a half dozen tables competed for space with a jungle of dangling sausage strings, links, chains, and giant stand-alone sausages whose tremendous size forced Grey to wonder if they'd been cased in the guts of an elephant.

"*Mein lieber* Thomas," said Louis Antoine, who was seated against a wall, beside a meat hook on which he'd hung his coat, jacket, and wig. He stood up, shook Grey's hand, and they both sat. "Did you win this morning?"

"I didn't play this morning; I received a pass to the second round."

"And you're not pleased?"

"I hate a delayed action."

Louis nodded. "Indeed. Did *Mutter* win?"

"She did. So did Leclerc and Théodore, for what that's worth to your sense of . . . *Vaterlandliebe.* If that's the right word."

"The only action of Théodore's that could make me proud would be his sudden and—would it be horribly un-Christian to say painful?—death. But I am, of course, glad to hear the French contingent may distinguish itself. But let us lay that, for the moment, to one side. Let us discuss meat."

"Meat?"

"Yes. Here is the best meat restaurant in the known world."

"Ground meat."

"Even the most perfect cut of the most aristocratic cow ranks below this greasy little place."

"Have you ordered already?"

"You don't order here. You sit and they bring you your meal."

"Which will be . . . ?"

"A variety of sausages, hot and cold, on dry bread. Day-old bread."

"No mustard."

"Correct. Nor sauerkraut."

"Beer?"

"Apfelwein."

"Very well. Your reputation is staked on this."

"Without reservation."

Moments later, a man in a red-stained apron brought over two large wooden trenchers with a dozen ovular slices of hard white bread on them, and a dozen diagonal slices of sausage on those, in a variety of colors and textures. A pitcher of cider and two Geripptes glasses followed. Every time a trencher was exhausted, it was replaced, and with a new variety of sausages. Louis Antoine and Grey talked a little of their past adventures, a little of the progress of the fight against their mutual enemies in Paris, but mostly they discussed the competing attributes of various grease-dripping bits of meat-stuffed intestines. The meal was overwhelmingly delicious. On his way back to the Thurn und Taxis, Grey stopped at a public fountain and splashed some near-freezing water in his face, just to wake himself up again; to stave off the nap his body now felt entitled to.

He was back with fifteen minutes to spare—time he used to imbibe several pints of coffee and, in a moment when he felt no one was looking, to slap himself hard in the face. Then he exchanged pleasantries with a few of his fellows and waited for the director to reappear, ring his chime, and read out the list of pairs and colors.

Grey was to play white, against a smiling, determinedly sociable Pomeranian—who, like Grey, had indulged at his luncheon perhaps more than was prudent. And not in sausage, but in beer. Or so Grey deduced from his breath and manner.

"Is everyone in his place?" said the director again. When no one answered, he repeated the instruction, "Then, please to begin."

"Good luck, sir," said the Pomeranian, in German so heavily northern (Grey presumed) in accent that it took Grey a moment to grasp its meaning.

"And to you, sir," answered Grey. "Shall I?"

"Please do," said the Pomeranian, and Grey made his opening. As he did, he felt his nostrils flair slightly, and some of the hair on his arms and neck stand up. Finally the game was afoot.

Grey's opening advanced his king's pawn two squares. The Pomeranian answered with his queen's pawn, one square. Grey brought out his king's bishop, to queen's bishop's fourth. Queen's knight to queen's seventh. King's knight to king's bishop's third. King's knight's pawn, one square. King's knight to king's knight's fifth. King's knight to king's rook's sixth. Grey's king's bishop to king's bishop's seventh—checkmate. In five moves.

The Pomeranian stared for a moment at the board. Grey looked at him, feeling, for some reason, guilty.

"An improbable stroke of luck, sir," said Grey. The Pomeranian nodded, then fainted and fell backward, exciting considerable attention from the rest of the room.

13

REY WAS THE first winner of the second round. Once the Pomeranian was collected and helped up the stairs, towards his room, Grey was offered admittance to a waiting room, where a fire burned opposite a table of reborative drinks and fruit. Grey ate a dried pear and tried not to let his focus drift too far from chess—there was still one round to go, the late-afternoon-turned-evening session. A few minutes later, another winner arrived, and after him, a strengthening succession followed. Happily, one of the early arrivals was Leclerc, who joined Grey in the ostensible admiration of a small cuneiform tablet.

"Mr. Grey," said Leclerc.

"Sir," said Grey.

"What do you think of this," said Leclerc.

"Personally," said Grey, "I can take cuneiform or leave it alone. How was your game?"

"I beat an Albanian. Shall we discuss other matters? These moments of seclusion from my friends will not last long."

"Just so, Mr. Leclerc. The younger of our mutual acquaintances has arranged something quite elegant. Tomorrow evening, at the reception, at a signal, your digestion will be troubled." Grey ran quickly, quietly, through the plan while Leclerc listened and said nothing. At the conclusion, Leclerc simply nodded. Grey asked, "Has your daughter been enlightened?"

"Not yet," said Leclerc. The director's chime rang, and the second-round winners began to reassemble in the great hall. From two hundred and forty-two to one hundred and twenty-eight, to sixty-four; the assembly was dwindling. Conversely, the pool of spectators was growing, as a large number of defeated entrants—those not too badly embarrassed by their losing efforts—chose to stay to see the results. After all, remaining meant a congenial atmosphere and free accommodation, whereas going home meant announcing failure. Grey wondered how many of those announcements would be slightly fictionalized . . . losing later and among thirty-two or sixteen instead of one or two hundred.

The director was visibly annoyed at the time it took the contestants to quiet down—there were fewer of them, but buoyed by victory and having become reasonably well acquainted with one another, they had grown chatty. Bathilde, who had won her second game as well as her first, remained a focus of attention. Encouraged chess-victors worked their way towards her in hopes of exchanging views on some opening or other, and recounting to her their brilliant endgames.

"Quiet, I must insist on quiet!" said the director, finally raising his voice. Bathilde put up her fan to warn her adherents to stop speaking to her, and this finally began a wave of silence spreading through the remaining sixty-four.

"Thank you," said the director, with blank-faced Teutonic contempt. "I will now, if I am able, read the pairings for the final round of the day, beginning again with white at the head of the first table."

The odds of a meeting shortened with every round, so perhaps he should not have been surprised, but he was, and equally pleased: for the third round, Grey was playing black, against Jean Théodore.

The two men sat opposite each other and said nothing. Théodore seemed determined to intimidate Grey before they started. Grey felt quite certain Théodore didn't know who he was—perhaps he had been slightly suspicious of his association with the former exile

Bathilde, but Grey's impression was that Théodore disliked him either as a matter of instinct or of habit. Théodore's stare of cheerful malice was very refined, and Grey could easily imagine it striking fear into his enemies. Grey's look of impassive indifference was equally refined, however, and after thirty-odd seconds, Théodore made his opening move. King's pawn, two squares.

Thirty moves later, it seemed the two men were very well matched. Thirty moves after that, it was clear that Théodore had the advantage. By the ninetieth move, Théodore had Grey in full retreat—on a mostly clear board, he had two rooks to Grey's one rook and a pawn. Grey's pieces were lined up in the king's rook's file: his king on the third, his pawn on the fourth, and his rook on the eighth. Théodore's rooks were side by side on the fourth lateral: the king's rook at king's bishop's fourth; the other at king's fourth. His king was at king's seventh. He was using his rook advantage to slowly drive Grey towards a corner and checkmate.

He made his mistake eight moves later, when he moved his king to the king's knight's place, in line with his rook at its fourth. It was a move calculated to end the long chase, locking Grey's king in the corner. Mate in two, he thought. This was the last game being played, and had attracted a crowd. Grey's only move to stave off the inevitable was to sacrifice his rook, which he did, moving to king's knight's eighth. Théodore took it and then realized, with a look of undisguised shock, what he had done. With the rook gone, Grey had no move. It was a stalemate. A draw. A draw at ninety-eight moves.

And because Grey was playing black, this meant he won by default.

At first Grey thought Théodore would snarl at him—he had a certain curl in his lip that seemed ready to issue a challenge. But Théodore mastered it, stood, and extended his hand.

"I congratulate you, sir. Brilliantly played."

Grey stood and shook.

"Thank you, sir."

Théodore looked around at the spectators. "*C'est la vie*," he said, smiling genially. "I must join the other losers, as we lick our wounds." There was a murmur of laughter. "Gentlemen——" He bowed shallowly and withdrew, as the crowd began to issue Grey its own congratulations, which were cut short by the director ringing his chime and dismissing everyone for the evening. Grey returned to his room with a deep sense of satisfaction. Certainly, some luck had been involved. But does a man make his own luck? In any case: he had made it to the final thirty-two.

14

T HE NEXT MORNING, after a splendid night's sleep, Grey was
eager for the day's events to unfold. In the morning he would
do his damnedest to win another game or two; he had woken
up feeling unbeatable. In the evening, the game action would be
replaced by real action, and the escape to freedom of Joseph Leclerc
would commence. Louis had told Grey to check the garden wall
for a sign that everything was proceeding according to plan: Atop
the wall, in a spot visible from Grey's window, Louis would place a
brick. Parallel to the wall's face if everything was to plan; perpen-
dicular if a meeting were required. The brick had been in its spot,
parallel, and everything was going swimmingly.

Some in deep thought, some in lively conversation, some in their
cups of coffee or tea, the thirty-two remaining players stood in the great
hall, awaiting the director's chime. Grey felt a touch on the elbow, and
turned to see it had come from the tip of Lady Bathilde's fan.

"My dear Thomas," she said, "how are you on this gray, exciting
morning?"

"Very well, my lady," said Grey. "And yourself?"

"Equally well," said Bathilde. "I am a competitive woman,
Thomas. It is a flaw, to be sure, but not a mortal one, and I daresay
that this has all been very good for my spirit."

Grey smiled. "A more spirited woman I've rarely seen, my lady."

"Rarely? If modesty didn't forbid, I would say I'd be damned if you'd met a woman whose spirit exceeds my own."

Grey laughed.

"Here, sir, is where I would open my fan and hide my face coquettishly—my coquette is good as it ever was—but I'm afraid it's somewhat cold to open the fan. So you will have to take my word."

"Might I get you a cup of tea?"

"Thank you, no; I've had several already, and it would never do to have my hands trembling." The word "trembling" was accompanied by the director's chime.

"Silence, if you please," he was saying.

Bathilde took Grey's hand in her own and squeezed it tightly. "The very best luck, my dear."

"And to you, my lady."

Once Bathilde was a fair dozen steps away from him, Grey lit a cheroot and waited to hear his name called. It didn't take long. He was playing white, against one of the Americans. Not the peculiarly dressed fellow; one of the others. This one was dressed quite normally, like an Englishman, but with the somewhat simpler look favored by the Americans' puritanical streak. Altogether he was sufficiently nondescript that Grey, to whom he had been briefly introduced on the preceding day, might not have recognized him were it not for his large mustache, an embellishment few Englishmen favored.

"Good morning, sir," said the mustachioed American, shaking Grey's hand over the table as the two found their places.

"And to you, sir," said Grey. "I confess I'm glad to be playing you—one saves considerable energy speaking in his own language."

"I couldn't agree more, sir."

"Your accent, sir—if I don't mistake—makes you a New Englander?"

"Correct, sir; from Boston."

Grey smiled. "Yes, I thought it had a familiar timbre. If you will forgive me intruding personal matters—my mother was a Bostonian."

"Indeed?" said the American, in a friendly tone. "So we are half brothers. Though I must say, one does not generally hear of immigration west to east. The Tories and Loyalists who chose to leave after '76 generally settled in Canada, I had thought."

"My father was in Boston before the war. In fact, I entered the world on a king's ship in Boston Harbor."

The American laughed—"Why then, sir, you are an American yourself! That's our common law, you know—oh very good—you know that gives our United States three of these final thirty-two? Near-as-makes-no-difference to ten percent. Very good indeed, ha ha."

Grey chuckled. "Well, the subject of my Americanness was one very often debated by my parents—that is, was I born 'in the harbor' or was I born 'on the ship.' Of course at the time, it made no difference."

The American went on smiling as if looking at a long-lost relative. "Though from the British point of view, it seems still to make no difference."

"You refer to the pressing of seamen, sir?"

"I do, Mr. Caffery. But I apologize; I should not have brought in politics."

"An apology is quite unnecessary, sir—in fact, it is I who must apologize, because, I confess, I have forgotten your name."

"Parker. Philo Parker. And I believe we have a mutual acquaintance. Though he doesn't know it, I just . . . happen to have seen you two in company. I mention it only inasmuch as, though America won't side with those impressing our seamen, we still prefer to see Europe moving towards British democracy—such as it is—than towards Napoleonic dictatorship. I thought you might find that worth knowing, in a pinch." Parker was speaking in a low, though not secretive, voice. The words caught Grey off his guard.

"Who is the mutual friend?"

"A cove by the name of Louis. But let us begin. You have white, sir."

Grey nodded and made his opening move. Interesting. The Americans seemed to have come a long way quickly not only in chess, but in more useful forms of intelligence. Of course, what could be a more perfect occasion than this tournament for a young intelligence service to make connections with imaginative men from all over the world?

Grey opened with his king's pawn, two squares. Parker answered with his own king's pawn, two squares. King's bishop's pawn, two squares. King's bishop to queen's bishop's fifth. Knight to king's second. Queen to king's bishop's sixth. Queen's bishop's pawn, one square. Queen's knight to queen's bishop's sixth. King's knight's pawn, one square. King's knight to king's rook's sixth. King's bishop to king's knight's second. King's knight to king's knight's fourth. Grey moved his king's rook to the king's bishop's place, but didn't castle. Parker's king's knight to king's rook's second. King's bishop's pawn takes pawn. Grey now had Parker's queen threatened. Without seeming to give it much thought—Parker sacrificed his queen, taking Grey's rook. Grey was taken aback. Was Parker playing Grey's game of disquietingly aggressive moves? It couldn't be a mistake. But, having lost the rook, Grey couldn't afford not to accept the exchange. Even if he could, Parker's queen put him in check. Bishop takes queen. King's knight to king's bishop's third . . . and that was checkmate. Grey had lost. Inwardly hurling oaths at himself, he stood and offered his hand.

"A damned fine move, Mr. Parker." They shook.

"You're too kind, sir," said Parker. "I hope at some future date we may meet again—perhaps someday you will favor me with a visit to Boston."

"Perhaps, Mr. Parker, and I appreciate it."

Parker nodded; Grey nodded back, and the men went their separate ways—to join the winners and losers, respectively. Grey took himself out to the courtyard for a little brisk air and to further harangue himself for losing. He was the first out of the round of thirty-two. After a few of his small, narrow cigars, he forced himself to shift his thoughts from chess to Leclerc. He told himself he'd gotten much further than he'd expected, or had any right to expect. This was no help at all. What helped was reminding himself of his genuine, abiding hatred for the French regime. Which was not difficult. The time for play maneuvering was over; it was time now to prepare for the real thing.

Returning inside, Grey met Bathilde, who was discussing with Honorine the process of packing her bags; what to leave out for the evening's reception. Bathilde had lost as well, and also to an American, the strange-dressed fellow in the moccasins.

"Castor Baucom: strange man," said Bathilde. "He speaks the most curious dialect of French—calls it 'trapper French'; he's a fur trapper, and says much of the American northwest frontier is French-speaking; many of the Indians on the Canadian River picked it up from dealing with our *habitants*. But there seem to be so many other languages mixed in that I could follow no more than two-thirds of what he said. I asked him to switch to English. But I couldn't really follow that either. He's a mumbler. Shy, I think. You have never seen bluer eyes, though. I think he used them to distract me, ha ha."

"Was it a decisive win?"

"I'm afraid so," said Bathilde. "Even if I am only the seventeenth-best player in the world, I shall bear it bravely. How did you fare?"

"I was demolished." He was bearing it bravely too. "Perhaps I will get a rematch in the next leap year. Leclerc?"

"He won. Soon he will play among the final sixteen."

"I hadn't realized his play was so strong."

"Yes. He is considered one of the finest tacticians in Paris; I believe it is what earned him a place on Bonaparte's staff. I'm not sure what our first consul would do without him."

Grey nodded. "An estimable man."

"Just so," said Bathilde. "Thomas dear, did you happen to see a stray brick on the wall this morning? I had been meaning to tell the gardener about it. Wouldn't do to let it become an eyesore."

"I did, my lady. I'm sure it will be taken care of by tomorrow."

"I'm glad of it, sweet. Now—shall we watch the survivors play? I believe I heard the chime."

It took just a few moments to divide the sixteen remaining players into eight games. Leclerc played Philo Parker and beat him; the trapper Baucom beat an Italian; a different Italian won, along with two of the Englishmen, and three Germans of various nationality. The eight resisted the director's motion to break for lunch, but he insisted. After a short retirement during which few spectators and no players left the premises, play resumed, with the great hall having been rearranged—the eight long tables, which had each supported one of the final eight games, had been replaced by four desk-sized tables, arrayed in a square of about five yards to a side, ringed with a velvet rope, for more intimate viewing for the audience. Grey was glad not to have played in such intimate circumstances. The four games of the final eight were played amidst a heavy, intrusive silence. The two Englishmen, Joseph Wilson and Jacob Sarratt, both lost; Grey made sure to shake the hand of each and to offer some commiseration—he had idly hoped that the two men might face one another in the final game the following morning. The Italian, Feste Verdoni, won; so did two of the Germans, Messrs. Johann Baptist Allgaier and Aaron Alexander. So did Leclerc. It was late in the afternoon now, and there was a pause of just fifteen minutes before the two games of these final four were played. Leclerc paced about the circle and said nothing. Allgaier left to splash some water in his face and came back looking refreshed. Verdoni and Alexander chatted happily with each other while the audience pretended not to eavesdrop.

In the event, Verdoni played Allgaier, and lost, and Alexander played Leclerc, and lost. Grey was irritated that Leclerc would now be more at the center of attention, but—as there was nothing he could do about it—decided to hope it would lend credence to the story of his urgent leaving to seek a doctor. After all, what man on the precipice of being crowned the world's chess champion would leave voluntarily?

This proved to be a maddeningly prescient surmise.

THE FINAL game was set as Leclerc against Allgaier. This game would be played on a grander scale, with a grander audience. The last vestiges of the mass play were dispensed with, and the foundations laid for the last-evening ball. It was to be a chance for the players who hadn't quit Frankfurt in disgust to socialize with one another, and a chance for aristocrats and great men of the Holy Roman Empire to meet them and discuss their own dilettante interest in the game. Perhaps fully half of the discussions revolved around attempts by aristocrats to solicit secrets of the Mechanical Turk, but if any of the tournament players knew how it worked, they kept it to themselves. Most of all, it was a chance for the burghers of Frankfurt to establish acquaintances with powerful men from all over the world. They saw that, with Napoleon pushing the Germans towards unification, the great power among them would either be Prussia or Austria, and one or the other would have power to dictate to the free cities unless they could build commercial empires of their own first, the way Amsterdam had two hundred years earlier.

Grey, as did the greatest part of the chess players, left the great hall to change into formal evening wear. Before he changed, he indulged himself in a two-hour nap, which he expected to be the last sleep he would have for the next day or two. After waking and dressing, he packed his luggage—what there was of it—and left it for Louis Antoine's underbutler to retrieve. He returned to the great hall to find the ball already in motion, with a string quartet playing the latest tunes from Vienna and Salzburg and swirls of chess men vying for the attention of the rich and mighty, the rich and mighty vying for the attention of the preeminent chess men, and everyone vying for the attention of Bathilde. Grey was content to hang around the edges, waiting to see Leclerc make his move to the room's rear entrance and towards the privy closet. He waited for nearly an hour, before Leclerc was able to break away from the adulation and walk not towards the privy, but towards Grey.

"Mr. Caffery, a word?" said Leclerc, in a low voice.

"Mr. Leclerc," said Grey. "Certainly. Are you quite well?"

"Yes," said Leclerc. "Quite well. I had thought before I might have some pangs of discomfort in the abdomen, but they have subsided."

Grey looked discreetly around them. They were near one of the French doors to the garden, where the cold night made the hall chilly; the crowd was denser in the warmer, further-in reaches of the room. Satisfied that no one would overhear, Grey kept a conversational expression on his face and said, "Explain yourself."

"I can't leave before the final game. It would attract too much attention."

"That's nonsense," said Grey, evenly. "Unless you think there will be less attention after the final game. When you are either crowned champion or ushered back to Paris."

"There will be a natural break between the tournament and the packing and so forth. That is when I can best slip away. Do you think your forethought in this matter exceeds my own?" Leclerc took a sip from the punch glass he carried.

"I think your forethought is clouded by the prospect of glory on an imaginary battlefield, fighting fictional, wooden wars of no consequence. That is, by vanity."

"It is my neck on the guillotine's block, sir—"

Grey spoke over him—"The plan is for *tonight*. The arrangements are for *tonight*. Your bodyguard will descend on you again the very moment—"

"It is my affair, sir; my life is concerned."

"Not yours only," said Grey, affably miming a move on an imaginary board. "You pigheaded son of a bitch."

Leclerc smiled: his contribution to the appearance of a friendly chat. "Tell Louis Antoine to re-lay his plan for tomorrow after the game. I have nothing else to say on the matter." He offered his hand.

Grey shook it and said, "Think of your daughter, sir."

Leclerc stared daggers back at him and said nothing. He turned and walked away, and was quickly interdicted by Emperor Alexander of Russia, who, as grandson of Princess Marie Auguste of Thurn and Taxis, was leading an entourage around the party as if he were its host.

For a moment Grey watched the twenty-six-year-old czar. He was in his third year on the throne, following his father's assassination. In some ways, he was an even greater enigma than Kaiser Francis. There was no question that he was a man of the Enlightenment—he had moved quickly to relinquish the near-absolute authority of his predecessors in favor of constitutional monarchy. At the same time, he was thought to be changeable, almost whimsical, in his swings from liberalism to monarchism. At times he was the greatest champion of the new age of reason. At others, he wished to be the last great champion of the old system, wherein Europe was controlled by an intermarried family of rulers who answered to no one but each other. He seemed to see empowering the Third Estate as both desirable and dangerous. He aggressively laid the groundwork for reforms that never seemed to grow to seed.

Grey moved on, past the czar et al., the varied groups of the cloyed and cloying, towards the grand staircase, around it, and out into the hallways beyond. It was a short if somewhat confusing walk to the privy at the palais's absolute rear, where the night soil could be conveniently removed from outside the building. The privy was empty; Grey closed the door, closed the seat of ease, stood on it, opened the high window, and leaned out.

He was almost face-to-face with Louis Antoine d'Enghien, who was sitting on the high-up driver's seat of a large coach, smoking his long white pipe. He was back in Thurn und Taxis livery.

"Thomas," he said, looking unperturbed, "I was not expecting you."

"No," said Grey. "Are we alone?"

"There's just my driver Helmuth, at the corner. He can't hear us. And I wouldn't worry if he could. I trust him implicitly."

"Good," said Grey. "Unfortunately, our man won all his games today."

"So?"

Grey raised his eyebrows.

"Ah," said Louis. "He doesn't want to leave without his crown."

"Just so," said Grey.

"Sacred blue," said Louis, under his breath, exhaling smoke. "Vain, damnable—vain, damnable fool. It would be just service to leave him behind."

"Yes," said Grey. "For the moment he is being admired by the Czar of All Russia."

"Oh, is Alexander here?" said Louis.

"He is. You know him?"

"We are cousins. After some remove. After the revolution, he hosted me for a time in his court. A good fellow, I think. A little indecisive, but no more, I'm sure, than the average emperor."

Grey nodded. "Is there any European ruler to whom you're not a cousin?"

"None but Boney," said Louis. "So what does our idiot genius Leclerc propose as an alternative to a very carefully laid plan?"

"He wants to disappear after the game concludes tomorrow, at the moment of greatest confusion between the chess and the return to humdrum."

"Humdrum?" said Louis.

"To normal life," said Grey. "Can it be done? You will have to rearrange the doctor and his coterie."

Louis tapped the pipestem on his chin and was for a moment silent.

"It can be done," said Louis. "I'm not certain how exactly—not yet—but it can be done. Tomorrow, when the game is over . . . around noon?"

Grey nodded.

Louis continued, "Win or loss, get yourself as close to Leclerc as you can, and look out for me. And when things start to happen, follow the current."

Grey nodded again. "Very well; until tomorrow," he said, and began to close the privy closet window.

"Stop," said Louis, smiling.

"Yes?" said Grey.

"I've already seen your damned trunk collected. And I won't have time to get it again tomorrow; it will have to stay here in the coach. Would you like a change of clothes?"

Grey chuckled, then started to laugh. Louis was swept up and laughed with him. At the corner, just outside the light of a streetlamp, Louis's driver turned around to see what the fuss was about.

15

OVERNIGHT, THE GREAT HALL went through a lepidopteran transformation. When Grey descended from his room in the morning, he found a circular stage set for Leclerc and Allgaier, and around it, at a ten-or-so-foot radius from the stage, a ring of high-backed chairs. The one closest to the entrance was gilded with special extravagance. Evidently a throne. In fact, several looked like thrones of more or less majesty. This was not altogether surprising, Grey supposed, when one considered that there were two emperors in attendance. How many prince-and-princesses and duke-and-duchesses would likewise be in the fleet? There were about two dozen chairs in the circle. And there would be a duke somewhere in the laymen's crowd as well. Louis Antoine—disguised as a footman? Perhaps just in unobtrusive street clothes.

The drawing room where the winners had congregated had a light German breakfast laid out. Grey had a slice of tasteless cheese on black bread, and wondered if he would have the opportunity of saying a few words to Lady Bathilde before the game began. He was certain there would be no goodbyes afterwards. In the event, she didn't come down until near the last moment before the entrance of the great guests. Instead, Grey had some inconsequential conversation with some of the other defeated players who'd remained to watch the finale—and a surprisingly interesting conversation with the trapper Castor Baucom, on the methods and ethics of beaver trapping. Beavers, it seemed, were deeply industrious animals, more than Grey had suspected. Baucom claimed to have seen a beaver dam more than a hundred yards across. And a beaver, said Baucom, cannot abide the sound of rushing water—whenever a leak is sprung, he rushes out of his lodge in the mind of a ship's carpenter searching for a shot hole beneath the water line. Baucom said that whereas American and English trappers laid bait for beavers, the French and Indians simply smashed holes in their dams, and when they came out to do repairs, knocked them over the head. Baucom said the general consensus among Americans was that this wasn't very sporting, and that the consensus among the Indians was that a dead beaver doesn't much care how he came to be dead. Grey could see both sides of the argument, but before they could settle the point one way or the other, a fanfare announced the arrival of the czar of the Russian Empire. Grey and Baucom and everyone else filed out of the breakfast room and saw that the rest of the aristocrat chairs had been filled, by various and doubtless distinguished guests. Grey recognized a handful, but most were unknown to him—he assumed they were either courtiers or wealthy self-mades. Following the fanfare, the czar waited to make his entrance until stillness prevailed. Then he came in, dressed more or less simply as a Russian officer, with his German czarina Elizabeth, née Louise of Baden, beside him. Once they were in their places and a discreet interval had passed, another, longer fanfare was played, and Emperor Francis entered. His empress, Maria Theresa of Naples and Sicily, was not with him. The czar was to his right, and some anonymous bigwig to his left. Indeed, the man might have had the good sense to take his wig down, lest it tip over onto the Holy Roman Emperor. In any case, Francis sat down, waved everyone else to be seated, and waved to the tournament director, who was standing opposite the emperor, where there was a small gap in the chair ring.

The director bowed to the emperor and tolled his chime. Joseph Leclerc and Johann Baptist Allgaier descended the grand stair together, side by side. Grey, standing among the audience that was slowly encircling the circle of chairs, found these theatrics silly, but kept his expression austere—austerity seemed to be the theme. The final two walked abreast through the chair gap and onto the stage. The director followed them up, holding his palm open in front of him.

"I am holding," he said, "a twenty-kreuzer silver piece. The obverse shows the laureled profile of the emperor. The reverse, his arms. It has been agreed that if the obverse lands up, Mr. Allgaier will play white." He flipped the coin and caught it with his right hand, and held it covered on the back of his left.

"Are the two gentlemen satisfied by the toss?" Leclerc and Allgaier nodded in turn.

"Very well," said the director. He uncovered the coin and showed it first to Leclerc, then to Allgaier. "It is the head of the emperor," said the director. "Mr. Allgaier will now be seated at the white pieces, and Mr. Leclerc at the black."

As the men took their seats, the director waved a pair of footmen over, carrying a large mirror, which they placed on the stage behind the chessboard, tilted forward, so the game could be seen top-down in its reflection. Of course, reflected Grey, it only showed the game to Kaiser Francis and perhaps three or four guests on either side, and those standing directly behind him. For those opposite, it made seeing the game more difficult. But Grey liked it. A cute solution.

"Gentlemen, begin," said Francis.

Allgaier made his first move, and the director announced it: "Mr. Allgaier: queen's bishop's pawn advances two squares."

Among the defeated players—Grey included—and among the chess-savvy others, there was a bit of murmuring. It was an unusual opening. Leclerc waited more than a minute to make his first move.

"Mr. Leclerc: king's pawn, one square."

"Mr. Allgaier: king's knight to king's bishop's third."

"Mr. Leclerc: queen's pawn, two squares."

"Mr. Allgaier: queen's pawn, two squares."

"Mr. Leclerc: king's knight to king's bishop's sixth."

"Mr. Allgaier: queen's knight to queen's bishop's third."
"Mr. Leclerc: king's bishop to king's seventh."
"Mr. Allgaier: queen's bishop to king's knight's fifth."
"Mr. Leclerc castles to the king's side."
"Mr. Allgaier: king's pawn, one square."
"Mr. Leclerc: king's rook's pawn, one square."
"Mr. Allgaier: queen's bishop to king's rook's fourth."
"Mr. Leclerc: queen's knight's pawn, one square."
"Mr. Allgaier: pawn takes pawn, to queen's fifth."
"Mr. Leclerc: knight takes pawn, at queen's fifth."
"Mr. Allgaier: queen's bishop takes king's bishop."
"Mr. Leclerc: queen takes bishop."
"Mr. Allgaier: knight takes knight."
"Mr. Leclerc: pawn takes knight."
"Mr. Allgaier: rook to the queen's bishop's place."
"Mr. Leclerc: bishop to king's sixth."
"Mr. Allgaier: queen to queen's rook's fourth."
"Mr. Leclerc: queen's bishop's pawn, two squares."
"Mr. Allgaier: retreats queen one square, to queen's rook's third."
"Mr. Leclerc: rook to queen's bishop's eighth."
"Mr. Allgaier: king's bishop to queen's knight's fifth."
"Mr. Leclerc: queen's rook's pawn, one square."

Grey found that he was holding his breath, and let it out quietly. No one had ever seen a game develop like this.

"Mr. Allgaier: pawn takes pawn, to queen's bishop's fifth."
"Mr. Leclerc: pawn takes pawn."
"Mr. Allgaier castles to the king's side."
"Mr. Leclerc: queen's rook to queen's rook's seventh."
"Mr. Allgaier: bishop to king's second."
"Mr. Leclerc: knight to king's seventh."
"Mr. Allgaier: knight to queen's fourth."
"Mr. Leclerc: queen to king's bishop's eighth."
"Mr. Allgaier: knight takes bishop."

Emperor Francis slapped the arm of his chair, prompting those who didn't follow the game to turn and look at him.

"Mr. Leclerc: pawn takes knight."

"Mr. Allgaier: pawn to king's fourth."

"Mr. Leclerc: pawn to queen's fourth."

"Mr. Allgaier: king's bishop's pawn, two squares."

"Mr. Leclerc: queen to king's seventh."

"Mr. Allgaier: pawn to king's fifth."

"Mr. Leclerc: king's rook to queen's knight's eighth."

"Mr. Allgaier: bishop to queen's bishop's fourth."

"Mr. Leclerc: king to king's rook's eighth."

Allgaier had pushed Leclerc's king to the furthest corner of the board . . . but it was well defended there.

"Mr. Allgaier: queen to king's rook's third."

"Mr. Leclerc: knight to king's bishop's eighth."

"Mr. Allgaier: queen's knight's pawn, one square."

"Mr. Leclerc: pawn to queen's rook's fifth."

"Mr. Allgaier: pawn to king's bishop's fifth."

"Mr. Leclerc: pawn takes pawn, at king's bishop's fifth."

"Mr. Allgaier: rook takes pawn, at king's bishop's fifth."

"Mr. Leclerc: knight to king's rook's seventh."

"Mr. Allgaier: queen's rook to king's bishop's first."

"Mr. Leclerc: queen to queen's eighth."

Leclerc had nothing to do but shuffle his pieces defensively, waiting for Allgaier to attack. He had, in essence, not yet made a single offensive move. Though, so far as Grey could tell, he hadn't yet made a wrong move either. But Allgaier was relentless.

"Mr. Allgaier: queen to king's knight's third."

"Mr. Leclerc: queen's rook to king's seventh."

"Mr. Allgaier: king's rook's pawn, two squares."

"Mr. Leclerc: king's rook to queen's knight's seventh."

"Mr. Allgaier: pawn to king's sixth."

"Mr. Leclerc: king's rook to queen's bishop's seventh."

"Mr. Allgaier: queen to king's fifth."

"Mr. Leclerc: queen to king's eighth."

"Mr. Allgaier: pawn to queen's rook's fourth."

"Mr. Leclerc: queen to queen's eighth."

"Mr. Allgaier: queen's rook to king's bishop's second."

"Mr. Leclerc: queen to king's eighth."

Leclerc was vamping, moving his queen back and forth, waiting for Allgaier to give him an opening. Or was he playing for a stalemate?

"Mr. Allgaier: queen's rook to king's bishop's third."

Surely Allgaier wasn't playing for a stalemate . . . which would mean he would draw the game but lose the championship.

Leclerc moved his queen back again:

"Mr. Leclerc: queen to queen's eighth."

"Mr. Allgaier: bishop to queen's third."

And again. But what else could he do? Allgaier was closing in like a shark swimming in a tightening spiral.

"Mr. Leclerc: queen to king's eighth."

"Mr. Allgaier: queen to king's fourth."

Then Leclerc took the initiative—shaking Allgaier's position by putting his queen under threat.

"Mr. Leclerc: knight to king's bishop's sixth."

But instead of sacrificing the initiative, Allgaier sacrificed his rook for a knight:

"Mr. Allgaier: rook takes knight."

The exchange drew a gasp from Lady Bathilde, who was standing almost directly behind Czar Alexander, with her lady's maid Honorine at her elbow.

"Mr. Leclerc: pawn takes rook."

"Mr. Allgaier: rook takes pawn."

"Mr. Leclerc: king to king's knight's eighth."

"Mr. Allgaier: bishop to queen's bishop's fourth."

Leclerc was cornered now; had no move but to return his king to the absolute corner.

"Mr. Leclerc: king to king's rook's eighth."

"Mr. Allgaier: queen to king's bishop's fourth."

Leclerc surveyed the board for about twenty seconds. Then he nodded his head and gently laid his king on its side. He stood and extended his hand. Allgaier stood and shook it.

"Mr. Leclerc resigns. Mr. Allgaier wins."

Francis got to his feet and began to applaud. When the Holy Roman Emperor stands, everyone stands—so everyone got to his feet and began to applaud—those who did not understand the genius of what they'd just seen, and those who did. Leclerc, who knew he had played brilliantly, but had been beaten by a perfect game, joined the applause. Allgaier nodded to him in appreciation and respect. Leclerc stepped down from the stage, and as he received shakes of the hand and half-admiring, half-obligatory nods, he moved away through a crowd now eager to congratulate Allgaier. The kaiser and czar each shook Leclerc's hand, as did the czarina and kaiserette, who had entered as the game concluded. And Grey looked around for some sign of Louis Antoine.

While he looked, a hand touched him softly on the elbow and withdrew. Grey caught a glimpse of the face it belonged to, moving past him; saw it was Louis, in an Ottoman costume and glasses. Grey followed him through the crowd, towards Leclerc, who was looking for his daughter.

Louis slowed and let Grey pass him, saying quietly into Grey's ear, "Watch me and then grab the girl." Grey nodded and continued on, towards Leclerc's daughter.

An instant later, there was a scream—or rather, a shriek:

"*How DARE you, sir!*" shouted a woman's voice, in French. Grey watched the action out of the corner of his eye, while he kept on his course for Geneviève Leclerc. The voice belonged to Honorine, Bathilde's lady's maid. She was facing . . . Grey turned slightly to see . . . she was facing the French security man Théodore. Just as Grey turned, Honorine drew back her hand and slapped Théodore as hard as she could, across the face.

The slap was now the center of the room's attention; Grey turned back towards the Leclercs, and saw Louis Antoine put his arm on Joseph Leclerc's arm and begin to lead him towards the foyer. Louis had a strong grip and was clearly not waiting to see if Leclerc was ready to leave—but Leclerc followed along with him, waving subtly to his daughter to follow. His daughter's face showed intense confusion, turning back and forth from the scene with Théodore—where Honorine was now shouting something about being pinched—to the inexplicable sight of a Turk leading her father away by the elbow. Her father waved again for her to follow; she didn't move, and Grey arrived beside her a half moment later.

"Mademoiselle, I'm here at your father's request, please to come with me at once." He grabbed her left elbow with his right hand and began to lead her along after Louis and her father.

"Now see here, sir!" she began to say; but before the sentence had emerged from her mouth, Grey had switched his right hand from Geneviève's elbow to her mouth and clapped it tight, so that he was wrapped around her the way one might be if giving instruction in swinging a cricket bat. Now he took her left arm with his left hand and ushered her forward.

"Go along, mademoiselle, or I'll be forced to carry you."

Geneviève tried to stand fast, and bit Grey's hand. Keeping his right hand over her mouth, Grey locked his left arm like a vise around her waist and lifted Geneviève's feet a foot off the ground, carrying her along like an uncooperative, oblong sack of oats.

All this happened in a matter of seconds. Over his right shoulder, Grey could see the crowd that continued to be fascinated by Honorine's vocal defense of the Honor of French Womanhood—and on the far side, he could see the two large bodyguards, who had been watching the turmoil around Théodore, but were now looking for their charge, Leclerc. As Louis ushered Leclerc out of the great hall and into the foyer, the two guards began to walk quickly in that direction; quickly noticed Grey with Geneviève and forced themselves not to break into a run. Grey was working out how he could fight them off with an angry, fettered girl in tow, when providence— or rather, an American cousin—intervened. As the two bodyguards wended their way through the crowd, the Bostonian Philo Parker put his foot on one of the now-vacant spectators' chairs and slid it across the slick marble floor into the path of the further bodyguard, at the same time grabbing the collar of the nearer man and yanking him backward, off his feet.

Clearly, thought Grey, with intense relief, he'd been right about Parker being an American intelligence man. For an instant he and Parker locked eyes; Grey mouthed "thank you," and Parker nodded slightly, then began to help the two Frenchmen up, apologizing profusely for his clumsiness.

Before they were on their feet, Grey was into the foyer.

Louis was out the front door and walking down the steps into the courtyard. Grey followed, five yards behind. Louis ushered Leclerc into a waiting coach, then turned to help Grey lift the tumultuous, kicking Geneviève inside.

Grey followed her in, his hand still on her mouth, and pushed her into the seat beside her father.

"GO," shouted Louis to the driver, who snapped his six-in-hand reins and had the coach tearing out the courtyard's entry arch while Louis was still standing on the running board. Grey grabbed him by the shirtfront to help him keep his balance as he climbed inside; over Louis's shoulder, Grey could see Théodore emerge from the Palais Thurn und Taxis at a full run. Théodore's eyes locked onto the coach—and a split second later he was out of sight; the coach had rounded the corner out of the palais's entry drive and was racing through Frankfurt's midday traffic.

Louis closed the coach door behind him and sat down beside Grey, who had one hand pressed into Geneviève's stomach to keep her in place.

"Kindly remove your hand from my daughter, sir," said Leclerc.

Grey did, and the moment he did, Geneviève grabbed for the door handle. Louis grabbed her, and she dug her nails into his cheek, leaving four streaks of blood.

"*Geneviève!*" commanded her father, his hand on her shoulder. "*Be still!*"

"Your help!" she yelled through the closed carriage window at some passersby. If they heard her, they made no indication of it.

"I'm sorry," said Grey, pulling a handkerchief out of a waistcoat pocket. "I give you my word that this is immaculately clean. Louis?" he added, nodding to Geneviève. He grabbed the lady by her shoulders, and Grey gagged her with the cloth. "Your turban?" said Grey, again to Louis, pointing with his chin at Louis's disguise-topping headpiece.

"Help yourself," said Louis.

"Stop fighting," said Grey to Geneviève, "or I'll bind your hands and feet."

Geneviève kicked Grey as hard as she could, in the thigh, missing her target.

"Very well," said Grey, pulling Louis's turban off his head. It unraveled in his hands, and Grey began to seize the lady's legs together.

"That won't be necessary," said Leclerc.

"Are you blind?" said Louis, with a hint of laughter in his voice.

"Desist, sir!" said Leclerc.

"If it weren't necessary, sir," said Grey, "I wouldn't be doing it." He had moved on to binding Geneviève's hands.

"Damn you, remove your hands—"

"I'd advise you to be quiet, sir, or by God I'll seize you up next. God's *truth*!" said Grey, leaning back in his seat and taking a breath. "Perhaps, Mr. Leclerc, instead of wittering at me, you should tell your daughter that this is all at your own request—and a damned large favor it is, too."

"Now, now, gentlemen, your tempers," said Louis. "Recall that there is a lady present." Geneviève Leclerc attempted to tell Louis, through her gag, what he could do with his chivalry.

Leclerc scowled at Grey for a moment before putting his hand on his daughter's elbow.

"What the Englishman says is true, my dear. I did request this. Or something in its nature. It is vital for us to travel to England, and these two men made the necessary arrangements. Now please do not scream; I will remove the gag."

"Perhaps you'd better explain a little more completely first," said Grey.

"I'm afraid, my dear," said Leclerc, ignoring Grey and feeling for the gag knot at the base of his daughter's skull, "that our government has gone astray. It is not what I believed it would be. It is not what you believe it is."

The gag fell free. With her tied-together hands, Geneviève pulled it away, and then felt the corners of her mouth, where it had been tightest.

"What are you saying, Father?" she said, balling up the gag handkerchief in her hand, making eye contact with no one.

"What I am saying is that so long as Napoleon Bonaparte wields all-but-absolute authority over the people's government, the dream of the Enlightenment is dead in France."

Geneviève—cautiously, so as not to provoke Grey's or Louis Antoine's ire—opened the window a crack. She took a breath of fresh air and then tossed Grey's handkerchief out through it. Louis laughed. Grey looked at him.

"That was a Christmas gift from my housekeeper, you know." That didn't stop Louis from enjoying its ejection, however. Geneviève ignored them both.

"I am afraid, Father, that I am forced to disagree. It is only through the strength of the first consul that the Enlightenment can be saved from the tyranny of the Jacobins. The damage done by the 'people's' government—which we both know it never was—must first be reversed, before freedom and democracy are possible. We must have a General Washington before we have a President Washington."

"I had believed that to be the case, dearest, but it is not. The first consul is not Washington, he is Octavian. And I believe that if he is not stopped, soon he will be Augustus."

Again Geneviève was silent. After a moment, her father began to undo the binding on her wrists.

Louis gestured for him to wait. "If you would indulge me, sir, let us have some resolution first. What has your daughter to say?"

"You said," said Geneviève, "that you believed if First Consul Bonaparte is not stopped, he will become a new Augustus?"

"I did," said Leclerc. "And I do."

"And you mean to help the English stop him?"

"If I can," said Leclerc.

Again Geneviève was silent. She looked out at the passing buildings. They were close now to the outskirts of Frankfurt. The breeze that blew into the carriage through Geneviève's open window was surprisingly warm. Or at least, surprisingly not-cold. Perhaps spring had arrived a few days early. Grey, of course, did not believe in "signs" . . . but surely this was a good sign.

"If that is your belief," said Geneviève to her father, "and that is your intention, then you are a traitor to France."

Her father looked deeply wounded. This was the first time Grey had seen his crest fall. He looked at the coach's floor.

Moving from French to English, Louis shook his head and said, "How sharper than a servant's tooth."

Grey looked at Louis out of the corner of his eye, but didn't correct him.

"I'm very sorry you feel that way, my dear," said Leclerc to his daughter, "but I'm afraid your convictions on the matter make no practical difference. I have sown the wind, and you are caught up in the whirlwind. Willingly or unwillingly, it carries you to England."

"Out of respect for you, sir," said Geneviève to her father, "I will remain in this company till you are safely away. But I will not go with you."

"Yes," said Leclerc, "you will."

"Do you intend to have me watched every moment, from now until my death? Because at the first opportunity, I return to France."

"It will not be safe for you there."

"I do not believe that."

"You know nothing of the world, my dear. I have sheltered you all your life."

"And in deference to that, I will go along with you until you are safely away. But not one step further. Now please untie me. My hands are growing numb."

"Can we trust you?" said Grey.

"My father can," said Geneviève. "That is enough."

Grey looked at Leclerc. Leclerc nodded.

"Very well," said Grey, and sliding a small knife out of his cigar case, cut Geneviève's bonds. She rubbed her wrists. No thanks were offered.

The coach was rolling through farmland now, towards the Oberwald, the thick forest north of Frankfurt. Green seemed to be budding everywhere, and crocuses dotted the sides of the road.

"Is the start of spring always so abrupt here?"

"Abrupt?" said Leclerc, not deigning to look at Grey. "No. But it is always like this."

"Yes," said Louis. "Lovely, isn't it?"

16

LOUIS TOLD EVERYONE he had arranged for a farm at which to change horses, but that they had a long way to go first, six or seven hours at least, and they might as well try to get some sleep. Grey was still unconvinced of Geneviève Leclerc's intention to remain aboard—but the fact was, he cared very little whether she came with them or not. That was her father's affair. In any case, the coach was driving too fast for her to jump. So he followed Louis's lead and slept, not giving a fig whether the Leclercs joined them.

When he next woke, it was dark, with only some thin moonlight illuminating the coach's interior. Louis Antoine and Leclerc were asleep. Geneviève had her head back and was gazing out the window, looking deeply sad. A bit of the moonlight bounced off her cheeks, which were damp. Grey watched her for several minutes before she realized it. Then she turned and looked at him, expressionless.

"I'm sorry to have been so rough with you earlier," said Grey.

She said nothing, but after a moment nodded and turned back to the window.

"You should really try to get some rest," said Grey. "We shall be on the go constantly for several days."

"Rest?" She made a sound something like a snort of contempt.

"How can I rest? Torn from my home, my friends, my country. Given the choice of losing my father or losing myself."

"You can still keep very much yourself in England, Mademoiselle Leclerc. A great many of your countrymen have settled there, while they wait out the storm."

"Traitors," said Geneviève. "And to think of my own father as one of them." She blinked against tears.

"Since being introduced to your father," said Grey, "I confess that I have found him rude, officious, and unpleasant."

"To hell with you," said Geneviève.

"But I knew him long before we were introduced—by reputation. In '81, he was an officer with the French expeditionary force at Rhode Island in the United States. After a year of standing on the shore watching the French fleet trapped in Narragansett Bay by our British blockade, your father persuaded the Comte de Rochambeau to march west and join with George Washington's army. Perhaps when you speak of Washington you should remember that your father knew the man. And that without Rochambeau's reinforcing him, he might not have been able to, uh . . . eke out his victory against us at Yorktown. It was an enormous risk, marching five and a half thousand men hundreds of miles with no naval support. Had it failed, your father might have hanged for it. But he believed that the only hope for a free France was a free America. With the armies combined, he marched with Washington and Lafayette to Yorktown, where he volunteered to lead one of the assaults on the British redoubts. These assaults had to be made not only under cover of darkness, but with muskets unloaded, to prevent an accidental discharge alerting our men before the final charge. He led a detachment of French regulars under the Marquis de Deux-Ponts to capture the Ninth British redoubt—one of our defensive forts—while Alexander Hamilton attacked the Tenth. Armed only with his saber, he led a bayonet charge against a fortified position, vaulted the barricades, and beat our useless German mercenaries into submission.

"Eight years later, he was at the Tennis Court and took the Oath. Remember that opposing the monarchy then meant a good deal more than it means now—his signature, among five hundred and seventy-six others, was the first blow against absolute monarchy in Europe. Five years after that, he and a force of fewer than four thousand Republicans defended the fortress of Metz against an Austrian army of twenty thousand. You can ask the Duc d'Enghien about it—" Grey nodded to the sleeping Louis Antoine. "He was there, on the other side, and not much older than you are now. Leading French royalists in the Austrian coalition. And just about the only Frenchman there, on the royalist side, who did himself any credit.

"But I digress. Of course you must have heard—perhaps from Napoleon himself—about your father's service at Mantua and Hohenlinden. But, of course, as he is your father, you must know him far better than I do. So if you say he is a traitor to France, a traitor he must be."

Grey had laid his head back on the leather bolster, and was being lulled towards sleep by the repetitive sway of the coach.

"In your place I might have wished to consider his particular reasons for doing what he's doing. Knowing that he has seen what he has seen. Sees what he sees. But you're about twenty, aren't you? Yes, I'm sure you know best."

Geneviève Leclerc held his eyes for another moment but said nothing. She turned back to the window, and Grey went back to sleep.

17

"THOMAS, AWAKE," SAID Louis Antoine, jostling Grey with his elbow. Grey yawned and looked outside. Dawn was close enough to see a morning mist hanging over a plowed field; the sky had brightened from pure black to inky blue. Louis was tightening his bootstraps. At some point during the night he had shed his Turkish robes, and was dressed in a shirt and trousers.

"We've reached the farm," he said. "I'm going to see the horses changed, keep an eye on our guests, would you?" Across from the two of them, the Leclercs were sound asleep.

"Surely," said Grey, following Louis out of the coach. Louis began to walk towards a farmhouse, and Grey took his bearings. They were pulled up by a stable not far off the road. Grey began to pace, stretching his legs, did a slow circle of the coach, and spoke to Louis's driver Helmuth, who was sipping from a canteen.

"Good morning, sir," said Grey, in German.

"And to you, Mr. Caffery," said the driver. "Care for a nip, sir?"

"Yes, thank you," said Grey, and caught the canteen that the driver tossed down. He drank from it. It was water. Grey must have translated "nip" incorrectly. Anyway, he wetted his throat and tossed the canteen back up.

"Much obliged," said Grey. "I take it we're not changing drivers along with the horses."

"No, sir."

"Would you like me to take a spell at the reins?"

"Thank you sir, but I am not weary."

"Very good." Grey pulled his shoulder blades together and stretched his chest and back. "I'm going to have a look up the road; can you whistle for me if the passengers stir?"

"Certainly, sir."

Grey nodded thanks and walked down the wagon path to the road. He had to confess surprise at the quality of these Frankfurt highways. Smooth and well packed. He wondered if the Thurn und Taxis mailmen had something to do with their maintenance. He yawned again and looked north up the road, and south down it.

As silent as a church. Perhaps even the farmers were still asleep. He turned to walk back to the coach—

And stopped. He looked south down the road again. Had he seen something move in the mist? Was it his imagination—or had he seen a shape, the tall, thin silhouette of a man on horseback?

He squinted at the spot at which he thought he'd seen it. There was nothing—just twilight and some morning fog. He held his breath and listened for the sound of hooves. But there was nothing.

Still, he'd been doing this sort of work for too many years to take chances.

He walked quickly back to the coach, where two two-horse teams had been changed. Now the leaders were being put in harness by a heavyset German farmer and his son, while Louis stood on a step halfway up to the driver's seat, talking to Helmuth about routes or weather or some such.

"Louis," said Grey, when he was close enough not to have to raise his voice, "there may be someone following us. A rider."

Louis nodded, made some last remark to Helmuth, and jumped down. "We had better get moving then."

"Just so. Can the farmer direct us to a detour—I think we had better get off this road."

Louis shook his head. "These roads are too little used for it to make any difference—if we are being followed and we turn off, there won't be enough traffic to cover our tracks. No, we must increase our pace, stay ahead of whomever a scout might be scouting for. If they had the men here to try something, they would have tried it already." He shook his head again. "The only alternative would be to leave the coach and go on foot for a while, but that would leave us awfully exposed."

"Yes," said Grey, "it would. Then let's make haste; there's not a minute to lose."

"Quite," said Louis. "Check the horses." Grey made sure the bridles were all fast, and Louis gave some money to the farmer and shook his hand. Grey climbed back into the coach, Louis behind him, saying "Go" quietly but emphatically to Helmuth as he did. Helmuth took up the reins and pulled the coach in a tight circle, and then back onto the road.

Joseph Leclerc and his daughter slept on through most of this, until the driver had whipped some life into the six fresh horses and the coach returned to its full speed, amplifying the small bumps of the wide, flat, plumb straight road. The road was straight enough that Grey, even though he and Louis were seated facing backward, had to keep watch behind by opening the window and leaning his head out.

After an hour or so, with his hair thoroughly tousled—the coach was driving hard through the countryside at better than half a mile a minute—Grey was starting to think he had, in fact, imagined the predawn rider. He was almost prepared to ask Louis to take a spell on watch, to stave off a permanent crick in the neck, when he caught a flash of light in the distance—somewhere in the dim morning haze.

At first he thought it was the powder flash of a rifle. But that first point of light was joined by another, and then by a dozen more, and then Grey knew what it had been. The glint of sunlight off the brass helmet of a French dragoon.

They broke out from the fog then, as Grey reached over to tap Louis on the shoulder. Red-fronted bottle-green jackets—white crossbelts—black jackboots—the plumed brass helmets of Napoleon's myrmidons.

"Right," said Louis Antoine, after sticking his head out the window on his side of the coach. He bent over and pulled a case from beneath the seat.

"What is it?" said Leclerc.

"*Le deuxième dragons*," said Louis. Leclerc set his jaw. Geneviève's face showed a difficult mix of relief and anxiety. Louis opened his case. Inside were two pair of dueling pistols. He checked the flints and held one out to Grey.

Grey shook his head and said, "Give it to Leclerc. I've a rifle in my trunk." Louis nodded and offered the pistol to Leclerc, who accepted it and rechecked the flint and powder tray.

"Can she load?" asked Louis, nodding to Geneviève.

"I can," said Geneviève, with the stress on "can" to make it clear she was not certain she would. Grey did not wait to find out. He took off his jacket and opened the door on his side of the coach, firmly gripped the handrail at the door's latch, and swung himself out into the brisk German morning.

The force of air that runs outside a coach being pulled by six strong Rhenish horses at full gallop is considerable; Grey's shirt and hair were whipped about like sails tacking through a strong headwind. Grey reached up and grabbed the rail of the luggage rack, put one foot on the sill of the window he'd leant out, and heaved himself onto the coach's roof.

To another man this ascent might have been daunting, but with his years spent in the rigging of ships as a royal marine, Grey was used to having his shirt and hair blown and buffeted. He slid a foot through a luggage rail to brace himself, and yanked his trunk free of its tie rope.

Behind the coach, the dragoons were gaining; as fast as six Rhenish horses might pull, a single cavalryman is inevitably faster. Soon they would be close enough to open fire. Reloading a muzzle-loaded piece was impossible at a gallop, so every dragoon carried, along with his carbine, two pistols at least; often more. The dragoons being Napoleon's pride and joy—the spear tip of his army—they were begrudged no expense.

Grey opened his trunk and dug through his clothes (a few blew away; a dragoon deftly ducked a pair of Grey's trousers) to find *his* pride and joy—his Girandoni repeater. With its buttstock air reservoir detached, it fit nicely in Grey's traveling bag, where he kept the magazine loaded and the reservoir charged. There was a carbine shot from the dragoons—testing the distance for the dozen of them, as they rode tight-packed in six rows of two. The shot sang past Grey's left ear as he screwed the reservoir into the Girandoni's trigger-and-barrel assembly. He loaded the first ball and took aim at the dragoons, now less than thirty yards away. They were beginning to spread out from their tight phalanx, into a broken line that was wide instead of long, most leaving the hard-packed road for the farm fields around it, without breaking their gallop.

A minute had passed since the dragoons appeared in the mist—now another ranging shot was fired at the coach by one of the closest. Before Grey could answer, a shot cracked out from beneath him, from the coach's left window; it was followed an instant later by a shot from the right. Louis and Leclerc had got their pistols loaded, and taken their aim well: two dragoons were thrown from their saddles. If the shots hadn't killed them, the tumbles certainly had; Grey imagined he had heard the sound of limbs and necks shattering.

But now the line of dragoons had come close enough for shots fired at full gallop to be aimed with a degree of accuracy, and the two shots from the coach were quickly answered by a rolling carbine volley. It thundered from one end of the line to the other, like the broadside of a man-o'-war, and ten lead bullets smashed into the coach and the trunks atop it. Through a cloud of cork and cloth—the debris of shredded luggage—Grey drew a bead on a dragoon sergeant and pulled the Girandoni's trigger. A gush of air and the sergeant was thrown backward off his saddle, as if his torso had run into the limb of an invisible tree.

A pistol bullet passed through one of the cases and tore a strip of flesh off Grey's thigh. He ignored it and took aim again. Before he pulled the trigger, another pair of shots were fired by the men below him in the coach. This time only one dragoon fell. Grey shot, and got another dragoon for himself—but only in the arm, which was badly shattered by the impact, along with the man's pistol. With remarkable composure, the man dropped the reins from his left hand, drew another pistol from a saddle holster, and was taking aim at Grey when Grey shot him again. This time he went down.

Grey swung his gunsights away from the dismounted dragoon's riderless, galloping horse, searching for his next target. He noticed now that along with the twelve blazing-brass-helmeted dragoons, there was a thirteenth rider, hanging slightly back—not dressed in dragoon green and red, but in the dark blue of a French regular.

But not a full uniform, either—an officer's jacket worn over the shirt and trousers that the man had been wearing the day before. It was Théodore. Major Théodore, apparently. Both of his hands were on the reins of his galloping horse, and that meant he was not an immediate threat, so Grey moved his gunsights again, to another dragoon, and fired. Another gout of air; another .46-caliber bullet tearing through a French cavalryman. This one was dragged for a moment by a stirrup before falling away.

The concentration of the dragoon's first carbine volley had given way to a less organized barrage from reserve carbines and pistols, fired at will. Already six dragoons were dead, but the remaining six were closing fast with the coach. Grey brought his rifle to bear again, and pulled the trigger. He and either Louis or Leclerc had chosen the same target, and a gaping hole was torn in the dragoon's chest. At the same time, on the other side of the coach, two dragoons had ridden to within feet of the coach's sideboards, and—their finite supply of powder weapons evidently exhausted—seemed determined to put the coach's occupants inside the length of a cavalry sword. One grabbed onto the luggage rail with his left hand, let his horse ride out from under him, and with his right hand stabbed a saber in through one of the windows. There was a scream—from Leclerc—and a shouted oath from Louis—as he kicked open the door and sent the dragoon flying off the coach. Now the dragoon screamed, till he was silenced by a loud thud. The second closed-in dragoon was scampering up the coach's tailgate. Grey fired the Girandoni into the man's face at a range of less than a yard.

But now Grey had to drop the Girandoni, there being no time to swing the long barrel around to a third dragoon, who had succeeded in mounting the coach's top. In a half-crouch, the man was swinging his saber down at Grey's shoulder; Grey grabbed the man's arm and stopped the swing, and the two struggled, wrestled, crouched on the flying, bouncing coach-top, each trying to trip the other and throw him overboard.

The dragoon got a leg in; Grey lost his footing and fell, sliding over the top of a trunk, grabbing blindly about for a handhold—expecting at the instant to plunge off into the abyss—finding a grip, but seeing it was too late. The dragoon was looming over him with his sword raised for a killing blow. Before the blow could fall, the man's face twisted in pain as Helmuth turned in his seat and lashed the dragoon across the back with his driving whip. The distraction was enough for Grey to grab the dragoon by his belt and hurl him into the airstream.

At the same time, a still-mounted dragoon, drawn even with the coach's front, drew a pistol and fired it into Helmuth's stomach. Grey grabbed what was left of one of the trunks and hurled it into the path of the rider, knocking him off—killing him, Grey hoped. Grey scrambled forward to Helmuth, who was already deathly pale. He still had hold of the reins with one hand, and tried to reach them back to Grey. That, with his last breath. As he turned, he slumped backward and fell from the coach, dragging the reins with him. Grey made a grab for them, but was too late.

Feeling the release of the reins' tension, the horses knew instantly that something had changed, something was wrong; and they began to fall out of step with one another. Grey got his footing at the driver's seat and leapt forward, onto the back of the right-rearmost horse. He nearly slipped off—grabbed the horse's mane to steady himself—and then, swinging his right leg over, stepped onto the central harness bar that ran from the rearmost team of the six-in-hand rig to just behind the leaders.

Grey inched forward, with his only handholds the handfuls of hair on the backs and manes of the galloping horses. He needed to get to the front team, to one of the leaders, and rein it in. Or else, at the first turn in the road, the driverless coach was certain to turn over. And just as certain, everyone it carried would be killed.

Close behind Grey there was a shot—out of the corner of his eye, he could see one of the two remaining dragoons veering from his steeplechase path beside the road, towards Grey and the coach horses. But the shot hadn't come from him. Grey's head twitched instinctively back towards the coach just in time to see Louis throw out the inanimate body of the other remaining dragoon (such as he had been).

Another shot. This time it *was* the dragoon veering towards Grey. The bullet whistled inches over Grey's head; close enough that he imagined he could feel it blow through his hair. And another shot from the coach as Louis, leaning out the door, fired again, and delivered a bullet through the cheek of the dragoon.

Louis shouted something that Grey couldn't hear, but—still clutching the manes of the two middle horses—Grey could see Louis waving for him to look in the other direction. Grey swiveled his chin from his right shoulder to his left—

Just in time to see Théodore with his pistol drawn, and aimed—not at Grey—but at the head of the left-hand leader. Théodore fired, almost point-blank, into the coach horse's head. The horse collapsed in a tangle of its own dead limbs. The other five horses were yanked off-balance, and suddenly everything was turning, spinning, screaming, as the horses and their coach began to roll and tumble. The harness bar on which Grey stood dug into the road, and he was thrown forward. He had to protect his head. That was his last thought before unconsciousness.

HE WASN'T out long, though—he was dragged awake by the sound of screaming. Not of men, but the screaming of horses. A truly terrible sound. Grey's first instinct was to feel around his body for his rifle—for a pistol—for anything with which to end the animals' suffering. He was facedown on the ground, with his legs splayed awkwardly around him. (Like a camel—the thought popped unbidden into his head.) He rolled onto his back. His left arm wasn't working. He lifted his head and tried to blink his vision clear.

Before him was a dead horse, and its five broken companions bellowing their agony. Behind them was the coach, on its side, a mess of splintered trim and bent metal. From behind the coach came Théodore. He was reloading his pistol.

Thank God, said Grey to himself. He's going to put down the horses. Even with everything Grey had worked for, for months, lying around him in shambles, he felt a moment's relief. Even a moment's regard for Théodore. But as Grey watched, Théodore walked among the screaming horses without seeming to notice them. He slid the ramrod out of his pistol, having seated the ball and wad. He opened a powder horn and filled the lock. He ignored the horses and walked towards Grey.

He took his aim at Grey's face. Grey felt fury well up inside him—strangely, less at his impending death than at Théodore's inhumanity to the suffering horses. Grey looked from the gun to the animals, his heart breaking, his blood boiling, and through the ringing in his ears, he heard Théodore say, "Can you hear me?"

And from beyond the horses, Grey saw a pale, shaken, but seemingly unhurt Geneviève Leclerc climb from what remained of the coach.

"Yes," said Grey, looking away from Geneviève, to Théodore, "I can hear you."

"Usually," said Théodore, "I like to leave theatrics to the Austrians and Italians. But I thought it would be cruel to deny myself the pleasure of ensuring your knowledge of our game having ended, ultimately, in a rather dramatic victory for me. And a crushing, and very final, defeat for you."

"Yes," said Grey. "So it appears." From the corner of his eye, he could see that Geneviève was carrying a pistol. But for whom?

he wondered. "But how many men did you lose in the process?" said Grey.

"The Second Dragoons? There are more than enough of them left somewhere. These few may have looked like knights, but they were—believe me—no more than pawns. A few pawns to recapture a rook is a small price."

"Well, I'm flattered, of course, but I'm no rook."

"No, of course not," said Théodore. "I was, of course, speaking of the traitor Leclerc. And, of course, the bishop 'Duke of Enghien' is a nice addition." Speaking in French as they were, Leclerc used the French name for the piece: the "jester" Duke of Enghien. "But you, Caffery, are just a pawn scarified by the other side. A piece of no significance."

Théodore cocked his pistol. "If you're offended, you needn't worry about satisfaction," he continued. "I will receive enough for the both of us."

"A final word?" said Grey. Geneviève used two thumbs to cock her own pistol. The sound was drowned out by the horses.

"Very well," said Théodore. "Speak your piece." He waited. Grey tried to think of something clever to say about the weakness of Théodore's endgame, but his head was too thick.

"Nothing?" said Théodore. Why hadn't Geneviève fired? Grey's eyes darted to her; betrayed her. Théodore spun around. He looked at her, pistol held before her with both hands. Both hands shaking. Her lip quivering. He started to laugh.

"Will you shoot me, child? Put that silly thing on the ground before you hurt yourself."

Geneviève fired into Théodore's chest. He fell. Grey lowered his head and drifted back into unconsciousness.

18

GREY WAS SNAPPED AWAKE by Louis Antoine—foot on Grey's shoulder—yanking Grey's dislocated left arm and popping it back into its socket.

Grey swore, and Louis said, "Yes, I thought that might wake you up." He smiled. His face was badly scraped, and much of his right ear appeared to have been torn off.

"Sit down," came the commanding voice of Geneviève Leclerc. "I told you not to move while I cut the bandage."

"Pardon me, mamselle," said Louis. "Just thought I'd get it over with."

"Sit," repeated Geneviève. Grey was lying flat; he watched Louis lower himself onto a rough-hewn wooden chair, and Geneviève begin to dab away some fresh blood beneath his disfigured ear before placing a folded pad of cotton over it and beginning to wrap Louis's head in a sackcloth.

Grey looked around. They were in a small wooden cabin. Grey was lying on a blanket on the floor. Off to his right, past Louis and Geneviève, Joseph Leclerc was lying on a bed, either asleep or unconscious, with a damp rag on his forehead.

"How does Leclerc?" said Grey.

"Very ill, thanks to you," said Geneviève quietly, and with real anger in her voice.

"And how do you?" said Grey.

"Very ill too," she said.

"Though of the lot of us," said Louis, "she's clearly the strongest. Only one who made it standing out of the crash. Fetched a farmer to help destroy the horses and get us off the road before any more Bonapartists came along." Geneviève scowled. "Present company excepted," said Louis.

"And what else are you missing?" said Grey to Louis. Louis laughed.

"Less than you are."

Grey felt to see if his ears were still there. He checked his nose. Both his eyes seemed to be working, and both legs. He searched his midsection.

"We had to cut away your clothes," said Geneviève, continuing to bandage Louis's head.

Grey hadn't noticed—it hadn't occurred to him—that he was *dénudé*. He sighed his relief. Louis laughed again.

"Geneviève and the good farmer were able to recover some of our clothes from the wreck," he said, gesturing to a messy pile of things in the corner. "Along with this—" He reached to a table beside him.

"If you move again," said Geneviève, who was trimming Louis's bandage, "I shall cut off your other ear. And not by mistake." Louis held up Grey's Girandoni repeater.

"What a remarkable thing," said Louis. "I've heard of these but never actually seen one. How on earth did you come by it?"

"Is the air canister intact?" said Grey, with a hint of anxiety in his voice.

"It is," said Louis. "I wish I could say the same for my pistols. Not one survived with its lock. I've had them since before the revolution." He said this with a hint of flippancy. And then with real sorrow. "I hadn't had Helmuth as long," he said. "But one can get very attached to a comrade-in-arms . . . let alone his driver. A hell of a good man. I shall miss him."

"He saved my life," said Grey, and after a moment's reflection, added to Geneviève, "As did you, Mademoiselle Leclerc. I am deeply in your debt."

"Yes, you certainly are, Englishman," she said, spitting out the words and not looking at him. "How do you suppose I shall ever be able to return home now? Having killed a French officer in cold blood."

"There wasn't a drop of cold blood for a mile around you, mamselle," said Louis.

"It is the end," said Geneviève, mostly to herself. No one else said anything for a while. Geneviève moved to stand over her father, removed the compress, and felt his brow.

"He's feverish," she said.

A man walked into the cabin—the farmer, Grey presumed, to whom it belonged. He carried a pitcher of water, which he handed to Louis.

"A thousand thanks," said Louis, who offered the pitcher to Geneviève. She ignored him, so he took a deep drink and handed the pitcher down to Grey, who was sitting up, leaned back against the wall. Grey—who had now noticed his own intense thirst—drank deeply and handed the pitcher back. Louis offered the pitcher again to Geneviève, who took it absently, dipped her fingers into it, and sprinkled some of the cool water onto her father's face. He groaned softly.

"How is he?" said the German farmer.

"No better, I'm afraid," said Louis. To Grey, he added, "He got a saber across the chest, and his right leg is mangled. I'm not sure how badly," and then, speaking again to the farmer, "This one at least"—he pointed his thumb to Grey—"is awake."

The farmer nodded. "My wife is gathering some food for you. You mustn't stay long. It will not be hard to follow a trail from your accident to my stead."

"Yes," said Louis. "As soon as we can."

"No," said Geneviève. "My father cannot be moved. Not until the fever passes."

The farmer shook his head.

"He's right," said Louis. "We can't stay here. A squadron of dragoons cannot disappear without drawing a great deal of attention. We have to get back on the road."

"Bumping and heaving along in a cart? It will kill him."

"If he stays," said the farmer, "it will kill us all. You must go."

"Let me look at him," said Grey, climbing uneasily to his feet. Dizziness struck and he fell back against the wall. He pushed forward, and Louis held his shoulder until he had his balance.

"What good will that do?" said Geneviève. Still there was venom in her voice.

"I was at sea for many years," said Grey. "I've seen more broken legs than you've had hot dinners." Geneviève scowled, but stood aside for Grey to examine her father.

Gently, Grey felt along the length of Leclerc's leg. There was a break, but only in the narrow outer bone of the lower leg.

"It's broken, but not too badly. Just here, where the color is. But she's right," he said, turning to Louis. "If he bounces along these roads, the break will widen and threaten gangrene. He would lose the leg, and with the chest wound"—Geneviève had cleaned and bandaged it already, but Grey could judge its extent by the blood that showed through the white cloth—"it would probably kill him. Poisoned blood."

"You cannot stay here," said the farmer.

"No," said Grey. "We can't. Have you a handcart?"

"Yes," said the farmer. "It is how we got you here."

Grey nodded. "Will you sell it to us?"

"I will," said the farmer.

"We will take him to the Rhine," said Grey. "And take a barge to the sea. How far is the nearest river dock?"

"Near fifteen miles by the road—but I can show you a forest path where you can go more slowly and carefully, and arrive in perhaps twenty miles or a little more."

"Very good," said Grey. "Please fetch us the food and the cart, and we will begin immediately. Louis, would you be a good fellow and produce some of my clothes? And if it survived, my purse? Now," to Geneviève, "let us splint this leg."

19

THE PATH THROUGH THE FOREST was old and rutted—a pre-Roman road, probably, following a rivulet to the Rhine. Its value lay in being miles and miles from anything like a real road. With the farmer having helped cover their track to it, they were able to take time and care not to jostle Leclerc too severely. He lay, somewhere between delirium and unconsciousness, on a bed of straw, on the farmer's handcart.

They followed the path for the rest of the day and the following night, slowing frequently but never stopping except to clean and cool the party's various bandages in the water of the stream they traveled along. They arrived at the banks of the Rhine at dawn of the next day, the morning of March 4th. The new river dock, the farmer had told them, was less than a mile downstream of some old stone pilings of a dock long disused that stood where the forest path ended. Where the path emerged from the forest, at the confluence of their stream and the river Rhine, Geneviève gave her father a sponge bath while Grey and Louis bathed themselves; then she bathed herself while Grey and Louis discussed how much bandaging they dared have on in public. Between the two, they were able to assemble from the recovered bits of luggage gentlemen's clothing for three; they dressed Leclerc as well. And ultimately, Louis commandeered Mr. Leclerc's wig, which, though slightly too large for him, covered his ruined ear.

While Geneviève dried and dressed, they laid out their new plan of escape in detail they hadn't wished to discuss in the farmer's presence, and hadn't had the energy to discuss before the icy cold bath had brought them somewhat back to life. They would flag down the first northward-bound barge willing to pick up passengers from an unscheduled port of call (the dock they would be using belonged to the hamlet of Linz am Rhein). They would insist on private rooms, if necessary waiting for a barge that could offer them, and then shut themselves up until they reached Rotterdam. Once there, they had only to avoid discovery over the few hundred yards between the river docks and the sea docks, and to buy passage on a merchant ship for England, to be safely out of Paris's reach.

That agreed, they took a moment to discuss the icy demeanor Geneviève had adopted—treating them more or less as strangers who happened to be going her way, and speaking very little. They agreed she could not be blamed, under the circumstances: her father's indisposition coupled with her first time killing a man. The only point of contention was as to whether she could be trusted. Grey felt sure she could—how could he feel otherwise, he said, after she had killed Théodore to save him? Louis, however, preached caution. If Georges Danton had spoken of *mise en garde* instead of *l'audace*, said Louis Antoine de Bourbon, Duc d'Enghien, Danton's head would still be attached to his shoulders. Grey dared say no one could accuse Louis of a lack of audacity, but further conversation on the subject was preempted by the completion of Geneviève's ensemble.

With Geneviève following silently behind—resting her hand on the shoulder of her still-feverish but finally sleeping father—Grey and Louis resumed pulling the cart, now along the riverbank towards Linz. The town appeared gradually between the water and the forest, and they passed little traffic between its outskirts and its docks. Grey bought a loaf of bread and half a cheese wheel for them to share while they waited. Once Louis had raised the dock's signal flag to let the riverboats know they were interested in coming off, there was nothing to do but wait and eat. And look at the far bank, at what was now France. There was little conversation.

Though the long, narrow riverboats passed almost constantly— there was little merchandise in west Germany or eastern France that hadn't traveled on the Rhine—it took the best part of an hour for the appearance of a travelers' barge with an inclination to take on passengers. Even so—once a shouted negotiation with the still-moving barge had secured them two rooms to Rotterdam—it was touch and go, with the barge never coming to a full stop, and Grey having to step onto the moving boat with Leclerc in his arms while Geneviève and Louis did their best to support his broken leg.

An idler steward showed them to their rooms, on the boat's western side; the gangway between the cabins and the gunwales was so narrow that Grey was forced to carry Leclerc onto the cabins' roof, where the polemen stood (as if on a giant gondola), and then to lower Leclerc down to Louis, with the help of the idler and a passenger who'd been on the roof taking sun. Geneviève explained her father's injuries as the result of a bad fall from a horse.

The barge was no royal yacht. In fact, it was different from the Rhine's freight barges only inasmuch as the freight it ferried was men. Even so, the cabins were perfectly tolerable—each had a cot, and a hammock to sling above it, a table and a chair, and—to accommodate large Rhenish families—each pair had communicating doors, which meant a river breeze was not out of the question.

Once they had Leclerc settled, and once Mademoiselle Leclerc had persuaded Grey and Louis that she would on no account agree to sleep in the other cabin's cot, but would sling the hammock in her father's cabin, Grey and Louis retired to what was now their cabin. They agreed that the man who stood the first watch would stand a dogwatch and get the cot for the duration, and then shot Morra for it. Grey had evens and won, and elected to sleep first. He'd never minded hammocks.

Four hours later—with the time kept mostly by the clocks of passing church steeples; the ferry barge rang no bells, and neither Grey's nor any of the Frenchmen's watches had survived the coach crash—

Louis woke Grey up, with nothing to report other than that they had passed Bonn, letting off and taking on half a dozen passengers. A crew steward had been unable to provide a list of names, as no passenger list was kept, but he was able to tell Louis that none were officers, and that no one on the docks had inquired as to whom the barge might be carrying. Louis added that this particular steward was not suspicious of the questions because Louis had told him that they were a family escaping from bad debts that the wayward son—Grey—had accumulated with his drinking and gambling. Grey affected a mirthless laugh and left a tired but optimistic Louis to his rest.

Grey's watch lasted past nightfall and the barge's arrival in Cologne. He roused Louis then, to take over for ten minutes while Grey disembarked to buy them all some food from the dock vendors. He came back with a string of pretzels and two pocketfuls of small apples. There was water to be had from the barge's scuttlebutt, but he'd bought also some bottles of beer, as a precaution. And (most importantly) after an irritable day and night, he had finally been able to replenish his tobacco supply. Louis took a pretzel and a beer and went back to his cot, mumbling that he would try to reassemble his shattered pipe in the morning. Grey knocked softly on the door of the Leclercs' cabin, and after a moment Geneviève opened it, stepped outside, and said her father was finally sleeping peacefully and what did Grey want?

Grey offered her a pretzel and an apple. She took the pretzel and began eating it slowly, tearing off small pieces with her hands and nibbling on them. Tired of trying to talk to her, Grey said nothing, instead working his way through a couple of apples and a bottle of beer while watching the French *patrie* roll past. The Cologne docks where they'd touched had been on the French side—it was the first time Grey had been in France since he'd come off a Norman beach in a smuggling skull. It had been an exhausting few months since, just the thing to keep his mind off his private life. He wondered if his garden and piano were getting any use.

"I suppose," said Geneviève, "I should thank you for the care you've taken of my father."

"I'm happy to do it," said Grey, taking a final bite of an apple and throwing the core into the Rhine. Geneviève resumed her silence, and Grey used the cutting knife from his empty cigar case to cut the stem out of a new apple and bore a hole in its top, and to cut two orthogonal holes in its torso. He tapped in some of his new tobacco and lit it using the stem as a match and one of the ship's running lights for fire.

He puffed away, lost less in his thoughts now, and more in contemplation of the curious but pleasant taste that baked apple and tobacco have in combination.

"You killed the best part of a dozen men yesterday," said Geneviève.

"No," said Grey, "I don't think I can rightfully claim more than half of them. Louis Antoine and your father handled the rest."

"How does it make you feel?" said Geneviève.

"How?" said Grey, surprised. He shrugged. "I don't see killing as anything to be ashamed of, if you do it for the right reasons. It's murder that's a sin."

"And that was not murder?"

"Well, I can say that, for my part, if I hadn't killed those men, they would have killed me. The rules of the world say that if a man tries to kill you, you're perfectly entitled to kill him back."

"The man I killed, though, would not have killed me."

"He would have killed me, though. If you like, I will assume responsibility for his death. It won't keep me up nights."

"I'm afraid it doesn't work that way." She sounded very solemn. They fell into another brief silence.

"He would have killed you," said Geneviève, "because you were his enemy. He was a soldier."

"Not exactly," said Grey. When she didn't go on but seemed to wish him to, he added, "What was your reason for shooting him? At the time. It wasn't to save me, I gather."

"I was afraid for my father."

"And with good reason," said Grey. "Théodore's sort of soldier does cruel things to his enemies."

"And yours does not?"

"Mine?"

"A spy? A poacher? A thief in His Majesty's service?"

Grey shrugged. "What you will. But I am sorry to disappoint you—no, my sort does not."

Geneviève Leclerc let out a very short, contemptuous laugh. "And what is it you claim that a French officer would do beneath your own level?"

"It is not a question, at all, of being French. I daresay you've noticed that Louis is French. It's a question of . . . oh, I don't know—attitude. France has been guided by a new philosophy that says that the ends justify the means. We—that is to say, those who are on the other side of this fight—do not."

"And how many Americans and Irishmen have you killed in your efforts to persuade them that ends do not justify means?"

"That is a perfectly fair point," said Grey, puffing on his apple. "But I would point out that there is a distinction between weighing good and bad, on the one hand, and on the other, declaring that the desire to do good makes bad into good. During the American war, the American side was taken up vociferously by many Englishmen, including many members of Parliament. Likewise, Parliament is invariably full of defenders of Irish rights. The American president—or maybe the previous one, they run together a bit in my mind—but he, before their revolution, served as attorney to the British soldiers accused of the so-called Boston Massacre. An ardent revolutionary, mind you, and he's said to say that defending those soldiers was the proudest moment in his life, because every man deserves equal protection of his rights. I'm rambling, I suppose. These pretzels, I'm afraid, have gone to my head." He tossed an empty beer bottle into the river. "But if you knew what your precious National Assembly and the directorates and the first consul had got up to . . . your stomach would turn."

"So you say."

"So I do. I can hardly believe it's been almost a year since my arms were nearly pulled off by a professional torturer in the dungeon of the Conciergerie."

"You should have visited before the revolution," said Louis Antoine, behind them. "It appeared to better advantage when it was a parliament instead of a prison." Louis was standing in the open door of their cabin; he stepped out onto the narrow gangway and leaned onto the gunwale railing. "Where are we?"

"A little north of Cologne."

"Very good. I relieve you. And will take custody of the beer."

"Much obliged, Louis," said Grey. "Good night, Mademoiselle Leclerc."

"Good night, Mr. Caffery."

Louis and Grey both laughed. Grey stepped into the cabin, leaving Louis to explain, if he chose to. Grey was asleep almost before his hammock was slung.

20

G REY SLEPT MOST OF THE NIGHT, and when Louis woke him in the morning, having checked with his steward friend that no officers had boarded the barge or asked about its passengers, he and Grey agreed that the immediate danger of their having been tracked from the scene of the coach crash had passed. The prudential course for the rest of the trip would be simply to keep their heads down. With a minimal outlay of cash, they were able to secure, through Louis's steward, the pilfering of cards and a peg-board from the barge's small communal room near the bow. They spent most of the day—after a short nap by Louis and several games of solitaire by Grey—in a desperate, cutthroat match of cribbage. The gentlemen forgot themselves to the point of Geneviève being forced to pass in through the communicating door and scold them for the incessant bellowing of "Muggins."

Louis invited her to join them, and after some initial reluctance, and being persuaded that the best guarantor of quiet would be her being able to berate them at will (this was Grey's suggestion), Geneviève acquiesced, and was dealt in for the next match.

She was a good hand at cribbage and took several games, but proved unable to get her blood to the fever pitch of competition that sustained the lives of Grey and Louis. Before long she declared that she would take some air on the roof deck, and leave the men to their histrionics. If she came back to find her father disturbed, she added, ears would be forfeit.

A half hour later, she returned. Her face was white. "One of the Dutch players is on board," she said urgently, as soon as the door was closed behind her.

All thought of cribbage was instantly banished. "One of the chess players?" said Louis. "Did he recognize you?" said Grey. She nodded yes to Louis and said to Grey, "Yes. He asked about my father's abrupt departure."

"Did he give his name?" said Louis.

"Yes," said Geneviève. "Dekker."

"Describe him," said Grey.

"Shorter than you are," she said to Grey, "and still somewhat too thin for his height. Small nose, slightly feminine. Thin lips. Red hair and freckles."

"The *barbarossa*," said Louis, "yes, I remember him."

"Yes," said Geneviève, "he has a beard, of sorts. A Dutch beard."

Grey nodded. He remembered the man. Won his first match and lost his second. "Did either of you speak to him in Frankfurt?" he asked.

Louis shook his head.

"Yes," said Geneviève. "He is an ardent supporter of the Batavian Republic."

"You mean he's a Bonapartist."

Geneviève hesitated a moment, and then nodded.

There was a short pause while each of the three chewed the situation over. Louis restarted the conversation by throwing down his cribbage hand and saying:

"This is rather unfortunate."

"Mm," said Grey, nodding his agreement, and then, thinking aloud: "When we touch, he could raise the alarm—but there are only German cities between here and Rotterdam. So that would not likely do him much good. But . . . he could pass a note to any

Frenchman who happens to be at a dock on the east bank. And there would be a dragoon regiment at the next dock to arrest us."

Louis nodded. Geneviève was looking down, glancing occasionally at the door that led to her father's cabin.

"But——" said Grey.

"There are only two more stops before Rotterdam," said Louis, finishing Grey's thought. "We have only to keep an eye on him at each—a very close eye—and then, at Rotterdam, ensure that we get off before he does. And that shouldn't be much problem."

"Just so," said Grey. "We should probably, though, keep an eye on him, beginning now."

"Yes," said Louis. "Do you know which cabin is his?"

It took Geneviève a moment to realize Louis was talking to her.

"No," she said.

"Never mind," said Louis. "I can find out easily enough from our friend the barge steward. I'll be back," he said, standing, edging past Geneviève, and exiting onto the deck.

Geneviève cursed quietly in French, and said she would go check on her father.

21

THE DUTCH CHESS MAN had taken a cabin on the barge's eastern side, quite far forward. As Louis was less likely to be recognized than Grey—having been at the tournament as a faceless footman rather than a competitor—he insisted on taking the first watch. Grey argued that he'd been awake all the preceding night, but Louis was determined, and Grey agreed instead to take over as soon as the sun had set enough for Grey's features to be somewhat obscured. Until then, Louis would stand in the bows with his back to the wind, watching the Dutchman's door, pretending to be out for a leisurely smoke. With grim resignation, Grey parted with the newly purchased tobacco and wished Louis luck with the repairs to his formerly long-stemmed clay pipe.

After Louis had located the Dutchman's cabin, before his departing to his watch post, Geneviève reemerged from her and her father's room and suggested perhaps she should share in the surveilling duty. Louis dismissed the idea, said looking to her father's health was more important, and left. Geneviève looked irritated at not being given a chance at rebuttal, and sat down on Louis's cot.

"My father is still asleep, and his fever seems to have broken," she said. "He's stopped sweating."

"Has he had enough water?" asked Grey. Geneviève nodded. "Good. I'm glad to hear it."

"What were you saying before about the Conciergerie? I asked Louis Antoine but he told me it was not his business to discuss."

"I was a guest there last year. A guest of First Consul Bonaparte's."

"What had you done?"

Grey held her gaze and said nothing.

"You were tortured?" said Geneviève.

For another moment Grey said nothing; then relented. "I was."

Geneviève looked away from Grey, waited a moment, and asked: "What was it like?"

"Being tortured?"

"Yes."

Grey looked at Geneviève Leclerc curiously. No one had ever asked him that before.

"It was, uh . . . very painful."

"What did they do to you?"

"I was racked. You know, tied at hands and feet and stretched."

"And that was very painful?"

"It was something like being tied between two plow horses who are driven in opposite directions . . . You're a bold thing, aren't you?"

"Children of the revolution have no need of the artifice of the past."

"Is that so?"

"Yes, it is."

"If only the gentleman who had me tortured was so open-minded . . . He was, among other things, terribly put out that I'd f——d his sister."

Geneviève blushed deeply, stood, and left the room, returning to the cabin where her father slept.

Grey chuckled quietly to himself—no need of the artifice of the past, ey?—and began to deal a hand of solitaire.

Then he started to feel ashamed, and decided to take a nap instead.

.   .   .

THE NAP and solitaire killed the remaining hours till dusk, and then Grey took over from Louis; assumed his spot in the bows, casually taking the evening air and hoping the relative darkness would keep the Dutchman, if he emerged from his cabin, from recognizing him. When he relieved Louis's watch, Louis told him that the steward had confirmed earlier that the man was in his cabin, and that since then, no one had come in or out of it. Grey pointed out the communicating doors between cabins, but Louis saw nothing for the Dutchman to gain by subterfuge . . . in any case, Louis had been able to see everyone who entered or exited the dozen starboard cabins, and none had been the Dutchman.

Not long after taking over the watch, the barge arrived at Düsseldorf, and the Dutchman stuck his head out of his cabin and called one of the boat stewards. The steward followed the man into his cabin, and a moment later stepped out of it again. As Grey watched, he walked aft, said something to a bargeman at the dock's edge, and then stepped ashore. Grey followed in his footsteps.

To the same bargeman, Grey said, "I'm stepping off for some dinner . . . How long till we set off again?"

"Ten minutes, and don't be late."

Grey nodded and walked over the docks and into the city, keeping the steward just ahead of him. As soon as they were out of sight of the boat, Grey closed ranks with the steward, grabbed him by the shirt at the small of his back, and pushed him into an alley.

"I'm sorry to trouble you," said Grey, "but I wonder if you could tell me what the red-bearded Dutch fellow asked you."

"He didn't ask me anything," said the steward.

Grey reached into his pocket and pulled out four shillings.

"If you'll tell me what he said, I will keep it to myself, and you can keep my payment as well as his."

The man looked as if he expected Grey to go on and add a threat: a stick to counterbalance the carrot. In fact, Grey had contemplated threatening the man, but decided it would be unnecessary. He was right. After a moment, the man shrugged and held his hand out for the money. Grey dropped one shilling onto his palm.

"What did he want?"

"He wanted me to deliver a note."

"To whom?"

"To a French officer."

"To what French officer?"

"To any French officer. That is all. My money, sir?"

"Let's have the note."

The steward took a moment to consider if the note should command an additional fee, but figured he oughtn't to push his luck. He reached into his pocket and pulled out a small folded paper under a wax seal. Grey dropped the remaining three shillings into the man's hand, and he handed Grey the note.

"Don't go straight back," said Grey. "Wander around a bit; take as much time as it would have taken you to deliver this. Does he expect you to report back to him afterwards?"

"Yes," said the bargeman.

"Good. As I say, tell him everything went to plan and keep both payments. And tell me, which of these greasy-looking dock carts sells the best food?" The servant pointed to a sausage man and took his leave. Before he went, Grey added, "If I find you've told the Hollander about this meeting of ours, I'll break your right arm." The man just nodded, and Grey broke the seal on the note and read it.

It was brief and to the point: the man identified himself and said he believed some enemies of the Republics, French and Batavian, were traveling on barge so-and-so, and briefly described the disappearance from the Thurn und Taxis. Grey pocketed the note, bought some links from the sausage man and some tobacco from a chemist, and returned to the barge.

In fact, this had all been rather fortunate. The Dutchman would believe he'd discharged his duty. He might be surprised when no one was waiting at Duisburg to arrest his denouncees, but Duisburg was the last stop before Rotterdam, so there wouldn't be much he could do about it. For once, things seemed to have taken a fortunate turn. Grey hoped this signaled a sea change. There was this night, another day and night, and then they should all be safely on a butter boat across the English Channel.

Louis agreed with Grey's conclusions, but felt they should keep up the watch on the Dutchman's cabin. Grey agreed with that, and resumed his place in the bows.

THE REST of the night was quiet. Grey saw the servant deliver his report to the Dutchman. He moved down the gangway close enough to catch a few words, and was satisfied that the servant hadn't sold them out. Besides that, Grey stood on deck, enjoyed the brisk river air and the glide of water down the barge's sides, looked occasionally at the stars and picked out some of his favorites (one doesn't spend as many years as Grey had at sea without developing attachments to certain signposts of celestial navigations). He paced a while and smoked most of his new tobacco. By the inky early morning, he was down to his last apple; he should, he reflected, have had the foresight to buy a pipe or some paper. Then, in a stroke of genius, it occurred to him to roll up the Dutchman's note and smoke that. He had smoked it almost down to the signature when Louis came again to relieve him. Dawn was approaching. Grey couldn't see any point to keeping himself hidden now—the Dutchman had clearly deduced their presence. But Louis pointed out that, if for no other reason than his being up all night, it made no sense for Grey to continue on, so he returned to their cabin.

He was slinging a hammock when the door to the Leclerc cabin opened. Geneviève stepped in and closed the door behind her.

"How's your father?" said Grey, when the door was latched.

"Better, thank you. He woke a few hours ago and asked for some water, and then fell back asleep."

"Good," said Grey. "I'm glad to hear it."

"I've come to apologize."

Grey went on hanging the hammock. "I'm the one who should

apologize," he said. "I'm sorry to have embarrassed you like that; it was inexcusably rude."

"I provoked it," said Geneviève. "I behaved abominably, prying into your personal life. I wished, of course, to find some excuse for my countrymen. But if our places were reversed, I'm sure I would not have escaped a blow."

"Well, let us call it even, for the moment." Grey finished with the hammock and looked at Geneviève, who was still standing, silently, with her back to the closed communicating door.

"Can I offer you something? I've got some various greasy German foods wrapped up on the cot. And there's some beer left."

Geneviève started to cry. Grey, who felt like rolling his eyes but didn't, took the girl by the elbow and sat her down on the cabin's chair, and then sat himself opposite on the cot. He put on his most avuncular expression and was going to attempt consolation when she spoke.

"What am I going to do?"

"You'll come with us to England, live in great comfort with your father—who, I can tell you, will be a *most* honored guest—and then, in a few years, when the war is over, return home to France."

Geneviève shook her head. "I can never go home to France."

"Why not?"

"I killed that man. Théodore. I shot him in the heart."

"You were defending yourself and your father. In any case, when the war is over, no one will give a da— . . . no one will give a second thought to who killed whom. People are too relieved to be at peace again, and the successor regime—whoever takes over the losing country from the losing leader—will place all the blame for all the deaths on his predecessor, so that everyone else can move forward with a blank slate.

"When that happens, you will be free to go where you like, see who you like, do what you like . . . everything will be the way it was before."

She had stopped crying and now, more than anything else, looked tired. She leaned back against the cabin wall—the bulkhead separating Grey's room from the cabin where her father lay sleeping—and sighed.

"That's easy to say when you haven't lost what I've lost. Home, friends, country. All my possessions save a few trinkets and the clothes on my back. Maybe for you things will be as they were when the war ends. But not for me."

The sympathy that had been growing in Grey for this rather sincere young lady shriveled. He didn't care to discuss the death of his wife with her. He'd already been far too personal with her. In fact, she was older than his wife had been when they'd married, but Paulette had had a preternatural tact and understanding . . . wisdom beyond her years. This callow, pretty little slip of a girl had no idea what the world was like, and Grey had no inclination to unfold it to her.

"Mm," said Grey. "Well, time will tell. And in the meantime, the best thing will be to distract yourself. A nap, perhaps."

She shook her head and slumped slightly further back against the wall. Poor hurt fowl. Grey was growing tired of this. If only he'd left Geneviève and grabbed Bathilde instead.

"Is something funny?" said Geneviève.

Grey was smiling. He straightened his face.

"No, excuse me. I was just . . . thinking about the end of the war. How joyous, et cetera. And your father, and you, will play a large role in bringing that about."

Geneviève was frowning at Grey, and said nothing.

"Would you, uh . . . care for a game of cards? Cribbage?"

Geneviève nodded. "Do you know Brag?" she asked.

Grey rolled his eyes.

22

AFTER PERHAPS three-quarters of an hour of Brag, Grey pointed out that he'd stood watch all night, begged off, and went to sleep. Geneviève asked if he minded if she stayed in the room and played solitaire, as she didn't wish to disturb her father. Grey said certainly, climbed into his hammock, and was, inside of two minutes, asleep.

"Wake up," said Louis, shaking him. "We have trouble."

Grey snapped awake. "What is it?" He was already grabbing a ceiling beam and lifting himself out of the hammock.

"We've just gotten into Duisburg, and a French officer has boarded—I saw him come on and sent our steward to investigate. He's been attached to the French embassy to The Hague. Our Dutchman hasn't seen him yet, but if he does . . ." Louis gestured a decapitation slice across his neck.

Grey nodded. At the same time, Geneviève—who had fallen asleep on the cot—was stirring. "What's going on?" she said, lifting herself up on one arm.

"A complication, mamselle," said Louis. "We must go have a word with our Dutch friend."

"Do you want me to go along with you?" said Geneviève, sitting upright, ready for action.

"No," said Louis. Among the miscellany recovered from the coach crash was a pistol—not one of Louis's, but one of the dragoons'—and several knives. Grey offered the pistol to Louis, who shook his head. It wasn't loaded, anyway, so it would only serve for dramatic effect. Grey slipped it into the waist of his trousers, against the small of his back. Into a similar spot in his own waist, Louis slid a long cavalry dagger, then slipped a smaller one—a steel and wood switchblade—into a pocket. Grey checked that the cutter knife was still in his cigar case. He nodded to Louis; Louis nodded back, and opened the door.

"Stay here," said Louis.

"And we're soon to return," added Grey. The men exited the cabin and followed the gangway forward, towards the barge's bow. They passed through the common room, where Grey was able to get a sidelong glance at this French officer. Grey guessed he was waiting on a room being cleaned for him. In whatever case, he was looking out the propped-open shutter windows that gave a view of the barge's bow, and didn't notice Grey or Louis passing by. There were another three or four in the room, talking and eating, so there was no reason for them to draw his attention. On the starboard side of the boat now, Grey and Louis made their way aft to the Dutchman's cabin. Long, thin shadows were cast on the starboard gangway by the bargemen's poles as they pushed the barge away from the river's edge and out into the current. Grey looked over his shoulder to make sure no one was watching them, and Louis knocked on the Dutchman's door.

Grey tapped Louis's shoulder, asking him to give way. He did, and Grey slipped the pistol out from under his jacket just as the door opened. The Dutchman's eyes went wide as the pistol jabbed into his navel. His hands went up, and Grey pushed him into the room and down onto his cot. Louis followed and shut the door behind them.

"I hate to have to intrude on you like this, my dear fellow," said Grey, in Dutch. Such a strange-sounding language, to the English ear, but so close to English that Grey didn't bother affecting an accent.

"But for reasons that I'm sure you've deduced—being the smart fellow that you are—we can no longer let you enjoy the liberty of the barge." Louis was stuffing a kerchief into the man's mouth. "The officers you are waiting for will not be arriving. Your note wasn't delivered. But it won't be held against you. We will simply ask you to remain here in your cabin until we've docked at Rotterdam and the rest of the ferried passengers have disembarked. No harm will come to you if you cooperate.

"Louis," he said without turning to face his partner, "what's the most unusual language you speak?"

"Hungarian?"

Grey chuckled and shook his head.

"Romanche perhaps?"

Grey looked over his shoulder at Louis. "Be serious."

"Russian?" said Louis.

"All right," said Grey. To the Dutchman: "Do you speak Russian?"

The Dutchman shook his head.

"Your mother's a c——," said Grey, in Russian. The Dutchman had no reaction.

"Good," said Grey.

Louis was stripping a cord out of the room's hammock. "Turn around," he said, in Dutch. "I'm going to bind your hands."

"F—— you," said the Dutchman.

Louis shook his head tiredly, pulled the switchblade out of his pocket, and flicked it open. He stuck it into the tabletop and repeated the instruction, "Turn around."

The Dutchman complied.

"I'll stay with him till we're in Rotterdam," said Grey, in Russian, "and you are safely away with the Leclercs, to a butter ship bound for Harwich."

"Don't be absurd," said Louis. "You have to get back to England, and I've no intention of going to Harwich. I'll stay with him."

"It will draw too much attention to you, Louis. The Duke of Enghien will be a pleasant prize for the Batavians, and Napoleon will want someone in exchange for losing Leclerc. But I—they won't have any idea who I am; I'll get dumped in a Dutch gaol for a few days; it won't trouble me."

"The Leclercs will need you on the other side—a troika of Frenchmen showing up in Harwich would cause more of a stir than any of us would like. In any case, as I said, I've no intention of leaving the continent. I have work to do here."

From his tone, it was clear that the discussion was over. There was no need for Grey to make a show of insistence. "Very well, Louis Antoine. I want to give you my Girandoni. If you—with great reluctance—have to kill this one, or anyone, it is quite quiet."

"Thank you, no," said Louis. "Much as I covet your rifle, it will be too much of an encumbrance. I do plan on slipping away afterwards, you know." Louis had tested, to his satisfaction, the bindings on the Dutchman's hands. He spun the man around and sat him down on his cot. "No," said Louis, "I will use the switch and the stiletto, if it comes to it. But I doubt it will. Once we dock at Rotterdam, we should have at least ten or twenty minutes before they turn out the rooms. I'll barricade myself in here, pretend the door has been jammed by accident. I can promise you, I believe, one hour. No more."

"That will be more than enough," said Grey. "It's only a few minutes' walk to the other side"—meaning the North Sea—"and it won't be hard finding a ship to take us across."

"Yes, there's a constant stream of them in and out, but let me advise you: Don't bother looking for one that seems not to care for the French. They carry supercargo all the time, and a generous handful of silver will carry the day further than politics."

Grey nodded. He stuck out his hand.

"This is goodbye then. I am deeply in your debt, Louis. I hope we'll meet again so I can settle the score."

"Nonsense, Thomas. But if we don't meet again in the field, come and find me in Paris when this is all over. I think I can promise you victory settlements of the first order." He smiled his wide, careless smile, and the men shook hands. The parting wasn't drawn out any further than that. Grey opened the door to the deck, stepped through it, and closed it behind him. He walked forward, to cross back to the port side of the barge, again through the common room.

The French officer was still there, sitting on a bench, trying to light a pipe. His match went out as Grey passed by.

"Pardon, sir," he said to Grey. "Would you mind handing me the candle out of that thing?" He pointed up to a lantern by Grey's head. Grey flipped the lantern's door open and slipped the candle out of its holder, held it for the Frenchman while he lit his pipe, and then put it back.

"I am much obliged," said the French officer, after a few puffs. He stood and extended his hand. "DeJordy, sir."

"Schmidt," said Grey, extending his hand. They were speaking in German.

"Could I interest you in a game of cards, sir? Or chess?"

"You are kind, sir, but I'm afraid I must get on."

"Yes of course; I don't mean to detain you. Though I imagine you will be able to find me here later if you change your mind."

"Were you unable to secure a cabin, sir?"

"I'm afraid not—they are all full. I didn't care to wait for the next barge, and a night in the lounge won't put me out."

"*Bonne chance*," said Grey.

"*Danke*," said DeJordy, with a pleasant smile. Grey passed through to the port side and went aft to the cabin he'd been sharing with Louis. Geneviève was there, and despite the close quarters, was pacing.

"You're back!" she said. "Tell me, what happened?"

"We've had to confine the Hollander to his cabin," said Grey. "A French officer's come aboard and we can't risk the two meeting. Louis will stay with him tonight. In the morning, we will be in Rotterdam."

"I've been imagining such terrible things," said Geneviève. "That we'd been found out. That you and Louis were caught and killed. What would I do with my father if we were left alone? I don't know the details of what you have planned. Where would we go? What would we do? We would be caught like rats in a trap."

"Everything is fine, Mademoiselle Leclerc—"

"Oh, for the dear's sake, stop calling me that! My name is Geneviève."

"Then Geneviève: Everything is well in hand for the moment. However, were you in fact left to shift for yourself, you would disguise your father's face and then hire a dockhand to take you to the sea side of the port. Do you have money?"

"Yes."

"Have the dockhand take you to any boat or ship bound for England—delivering butter, or Edam, or something—and pay him to take you along. Pay everyone liberally and there should be no problem. Once you're in England, look for any man in a uniform and tell him that you must get to the Admiralty in London at once. Tell him you and your father are carrying dispatches; that will get the point across."

Geneviève nodded.

"In any case, once you're on the water you'll be safe. Both the French side and the English are agreed on letting the Dutch continue to sail back and forth. The French have accepted that the Dutch and their farmers need the money, and the English, for some unknowable reason, *cannot live* without Dutch butter."

It was a weak effort at lightening the mood, but Geneviève, whose brow had been deeply furrowed, laughed at it. The tension that had built up in her popped like a soufflé. As is often the case when imagined fears are supplanted by a little information. "You don't care for butter?" she asked.

"I do," said Grey. "What I mean is that, as I am told, England does in fact accommodate and employ a large number of cows. They must be terribly work-shy."

Geneviève, who looked as though she'd just completed a herculean trial, plopped down on the cot. She said, not in a superior tone, "Butter from all the Netherlands has more fat in it than English butter."

Grey, who had never really thought about it before, raised an eyebrow. "Really?"

"Mm-hmm," said Geneviève, nodding.

"Huh," said Grey. "It's funny, in all these years I'd never actually considered what the difference was. It's like Scotch whiskey. One doesn't think much about why it's better than English. It just is. Do you mind if I take off my jacket?" The cabin's air was hot and inanimate.

Geneviève shook her head. Grey took it off and took a seat.

"I'm afraid whiskey is outside my sphere," said Geneviève. "But I do know my butter."

"Because you're French?"

"The Leclercs have been dairy farmers from time immemorial. Not my branch of the family, anymore. But my country cousins. After my mother died, they looked after me. While my father was away with the army."

"You're a farm girl?"

"Are you surprised?"

"I am," said Grey. "I don't know why exactly. But I am."

"Leclerc is not an aristocrat's name," said Geneviève.

"And yet you are at the heart of Paris society."

"Indeed. Because it is a post-revolution society where nobility comes not from one's blood, but from the blood one spills."

"Is it preferred that the spilt blood be your own, or someone else's?"

"Very droll," said Geneviève, without smiling.

"I'm sorry—in fact, I do admire a system that prefers achievement to birth. I only worry about empowering a dictator to decide what constitutes achievement."

"And who do you think should decide?"

Grey shrugged. "No one. Or God. Or if you prefer, common sense."

"Why are you British so obsessed with God?"

"You mean, why haven't we replaced worship of God with worship of the fatherland? I thought after you de-capped Robespierre, you all agreed that that hadn't been a good idea."

"Not worship of the state—devotion to the common good. As

opposed to devotion towards words written thousands of years ago by some Jews in the desert."

"I suppose the question is, who's to say what is and is not for the common good? That's why we have a parliament. To let the commoners decide for ourselves. And to make sure the parliament doesn't execute everyone who disagrees with it—the way yours did—we have a king beholden to the old, desert Jews' ideas. I think it strikes rather a good balance. It's the test of time, you know."

"Are you very religious?" said Geneviève.

"No."

"And that doesn't make you a hypocrite?"

"I don't think so," said Grey. "I think of the church as something like the Royal Navy. Even when I don't participate, I'm glad to know it's there."

Geneviève smiled. "Yes, I too think of the church as being like the Royal Navy. Blockades our ports, stops our intercourse, and keeps us from doing the things we like."

Grey snorted. "So you are a liberated woman? Freed from those shackles?"

"I am."

"And here I was feeling ashamed for having shocked you before. With my coarse remark about . . . that fellow's sister."

"I wasn't shocked, per se. I was indignant. It was as if the enemy had . . . made a coarse remark about all France."

"I see," said Grey. "Well, as I hope to have made clear, it is only the government of France to which I am an enemy. I have nothing but affection for the people."

Geneviève shrugged. "Perhaps you will have convinced me of that by the time we reach Rotterdam."

23

THROUGHOUT THE river journey north, Mr. Leclerc had remained in his cabin—first delirious, and after his fever broke, in nearly round-the-clock sleep. In the final day, he had been able to sit up, with Geneviève's help, and had even managed to keep down some bread mashed up in a cup of water. (More impressive when Grey considered it unlikely he'd have been able to keep it down himself.) Leclerc was still very weak, and had said almost nothing—nothing more than the occasional inquiry as to where they were—but there was no time left for him to recover. It would be a short crossing through the yards from the Rhine to the North Sea, but Leclerc had to be conscious and upright. Anything else would require Grey hiring help, as he couldn't carry a stretcher by himself. If at all possible, Grey wanted to avoid involving anyone else. They were now in the homestretch, but there was still the chance of being tripped up by an inquisitive Republican stevedore, wondering why he was being asked to carry a litter to a ship bound for England.

So as the barge approached Rotterdam, Grey left Geneviève to sleep and went looking for Louis's steward, who was able—with the craftsmanship customary of men who work on boats—to assemble a shoulder crutch. He also, after a brief search, furnished Grey with a long, scratchy scarf and some sailcloth, the latter of which Grey would use to make a bundle of the disassembled Girandoni. Grey paid handsomely for all, and the steward wished him better fortune in drinking and gambling.

When he returned to the cabin, Grey set about bundling his rifle. He was rolling the sailcloth tightly around the detached barrel and air reservoir when Geneviève awoke. She smiled at him; he smiled back, and said, "We'll be at Rotterdam in less than an hour. We must get your father ready."

Geneviève nodded and slipped through the communicating door. Grey filled his pockets with the various bits and pieces of his possessions that had survived the coach crash and checked to make sure he'd left nothing behind. The empty pistol he slipped back into his waistband; the rifle bundle was tucked under his arm. Then he picked up the crutch and let himself into the Leclercs' cabin.

Occasional airings had kept it from becoming too fetid, and Miss Leclerc had worked hard at keeping her father clean. Grey wondered where she'd learned to shave a man's face. The shave didn't matter, really, because Grey intended to wrap the bottom half of Leclerc's face in a scarf—but no doubt it made him feel a little trimmer. That was the effect it had had on Grey. During the night, while Geneviève slept, he'd shaved out on the gangway, in the brisk river air, occasionally able to catch a glimpse of his progress in the passing water, where it was lit up by the barge's sidelights. He rubbed his face.

"Mr. Caffery," said Leclerc, wanly, "good morning." Geneviève was helping him sit up.

"Good morning, sir," said Grey. "If you'll pardon me—" As he had regularly since the crash, Grey smelt Leclerc's broken leg. No gangrene.

"How is it with you, sir?" said Leclerc.

"Well," said Grey. "And your leg seems to be too."

"Hardly," said Leclerc.

"I mean, sir, there is no putrification. I would say you'll more than likely keep it."

Leclerc nodded. "If we make it to Harwich."

"We will," said Geneviève. Leclerc looked at her with mild surprise.

"Has Mr. Caffery brought you around to my way of thinking?"

"No," said Geneviève. "I remain convinced that he is a fool, and that you are another. So clearly I can't leave you to fend for yourselves. When you are settled in England and out of danger, then I will decide what to do with myself."

Leclerc nodded, trying, failing, to conceal his intense relief. She was a capricious girl, this Geneviève. Flighty, even. And Grey had half expected she would dig her heels immovably into Rotterdam: to say, once her father was aboard, that she was going back to Paris to face the guillotine for killing Théodore, and that she was sorry only that she had but one head to give for her country. But this was a good sign.

"Where is the duke?" said Leclerc.

"Covering our withdrawal," said Grey.

Leclerc nodded. "Very well," he said. The barge had slowed, and now started to turn as it was poled out of the current and towards a dock berth. "Let us begin."

"Cover your face with this," said Grey, handing the scarf to Leclerc. Leclerc took it and began to wrap it round his chin. Geneviève helped, then stepped back. Everything below the nose was covered, and the long scarf's ends tucked into Leclerc's shirt.

Grey nodded. "Good. Try to look ill, won't you?" Leclerc emitted a single snort of laughter.

Geneviève stepped forward again to help her father to his feet. Grey touched her arm. "Allow me," he said. "And, if you would, carry this"—he handed her the wrapped rifle—"and hold this"—he gave her the crutch. He leaned over and put his hands under Leclerc's arms. "Ready?" he asked.

Leclerc nodded, and Grey lifted him to his feet. Leclerc gritted his teeth and suppressed a groan. "Give me that," said Grey, and Geneviève handed him the crutch. Grey pushed it under Leclerc's shoulder, the shoulder opposite the broken leg, and then put a firm arm around Leclerc's waist. Leclerc took hold of the crutch's shaft, checked that it could take his weight (it was nothing fancy: a very long-shafted capital T), and then slung the other arm over Grey's shoulder.

"I'm told the barge turns before it docks, so we'll be able to disembark this side," said Grey. "As soon as we touch, we're off. Are you both ready?"

"Yes," said Leclerc.

"And me," said Geneviève. She was carrying Grey's parcel, as well as a small bundle of her and her fathers' own pickings-up from the coach crash.

"Good," said Grey. They all felt their balance shift slightly as the barge touched the pier. "Let us go."

Geneviève opened the door, and Grey helped Leclerc through it. It was a gray, chilly, early morning. And it was an awkward sideways shuffle along the gangway, to the gunwale port opened for departing passengers to step up onto the pier. "Up" because it had been a dry season on the continent, and the barge lay lower than it would usually. This was an irritating complication. Grey first helped Geneviève up, and handed her the crutch. He was preparing—trying to figure how best—to lift Leclerc off the barge, thinking perhaps he would pick him up at the waist, as he had Leclerc's daughter— then thinking better of it, looking for a steward to assist—seeing they were all occupied with making lines fast—then hearing a voice come from a few feet forward:

"Herr Schmidt, may I assist you?" The voice belonged to the French officer DeJordy. Having spent the night in the passengers' lounge, he was ready for an early departure as well.

"Yes, that would be kind," said Grey. "Allow me to introduce my father, Herr Schmidt, and my sister, Frau Gutenberg. Captain DeJordy."

Leclerc mumbled something, and Geneviève curtsied. DeJordy took Leclerc's right arm; Grey had his left, and together they lifted him carefully onto the dock.

"*Danke schön*," said Leclerc, in a low, hoarse voice.

"Where are you headed to, friends?" said DeJordy. "Perhaps I can be of some assistance."

"Over to the sea docks," said Grey. "But you are much too kind— we will be quite able to manage from here."

"Nonsense—it will be my pleasure," said DeJordy. "In a situation like this, an extra set of hands is always useful. May I?" He was extending his hands to take Geneviève's parcels from her. Geneviève looked at Grey.

"Should you leave your own luggage behind, Captain?" said Grey.

"My luggage went ahead of me—it was more prompt than I, and made it to the barge I'd intended to take. I imagine it spent its trip comfortable in the private cabin I had booked, ha ha!"

Grey nodded to Geneviève, who let DeJordy take her things.

"You are a gentleman, sir," said Grey, helping position the crutch back under Leclerc's arm and replacing the other arm over his shoulders. "Let us go."

At the speed of Leclerc's crutch, the foursome made its way through the dockyard, weaving through crates and bales of this and that. A rank of brick warehouses, with one end open to the river docks and the other to the sea, loomed up ahead of them. Grey steered the group up an alley between a pair that appeared to be a chinaware-house, on the left, and a giant store of furriers' pelts on the right. A hundred yards ahead, he could see . . . not the North Sea, but ships riding slowly up and down atop it. And he could smell it, and hear the gulls calling.

The path ahead of them was empty—probably because it had been overused and rutted, and muddied by the sea air. The going became slower, with DeJordy holding onto Leclerc's right elbow as he tried to find dry spots to place the end of his crutch. The crutch slipped and sank an inch into the mud; Leclerc lost his balance and tipped forward; Grey and DeJordy caught him before he fell, but not before the scarf slipped off his face and onto the ground.

DeJordy bent down to retrieve it, stood up to return it, and looked Leclerc square in the face. His look of surprise left no doubt that he knew just who Leclerc was.

Grey pulled the empty pistol out of his trousers, cocked it loudly, and pointed it at DeJordy. DeJordy—still shocked—put his hands up, more out of reflex than compliance. A few yards down the alley was a wooden door, into the furriers' warehouse. Grey pointed to it with the pistol's muzzle.

"In there," he said to DeJordy. To the Leclercs: "Don't wait for me."

DeJordy backed away from Grey, then turned to the door. "I'll have to lower my hands," he said.

"Just your left hand," said Grey. "That should be enough."

DeJordy lowered his left hand, pushed on the door, then pulled on the frayed string latch-loop. "It's locked," he said.

"Take two paces towards the sea," said Grey. DeJordy did as he was told, and Grey stepped up to the door, made sure of his footing, then kicked the door open. "Inside," he said to DeJordy, backing away.

With the pistol, he waved DeJordy into the warehouse, followed him in, and closed the door behind them. It was a gigantic, musty room of narrow aisles running between gigantic bundles of pelts. Grey pointed the pistol at DeJordy's face and put a finger up to his own lips. For a moment the two men listened in silence. Then, satisfied they were alone—that the warehouse was empty—Grey lowered the pistol to a less threatening attitude. Pointed it somewhere around DeJordy's belly.

"It gives me no pleasure putting you in this position," said Grey. "You've been a thoroughly decent fellow. But I'm going to have to tie you up." With his free hand, Grey unkotted a rope binding a bundle of skins and pulled the rope out. "I'll make sure someone comes by in a few hours to cut you loose."

"Can Joseph Leclerc really be a traitor? Or are you kidnapping him?"

Grey ignored the question. "Turn around and put your hands behind your back."

"Very well," said DeJordy. Slowly he began to turn. When he'd gone ninety degrees, he dashed forward, leapt, and grabbed hold of a ladder. He began to climb it, up towards catwalks that were balanced precariously atop the pelts. Grey was ready for this—had seen the Frenchman glance at the ladder several times before his leap. He grabbed DeJordy by one leg and wrenched him down onto the floor. DeJordy landed on his back. The air was knocked out of him—but he wasn't stunned; still gasping for air, he kicked wildly at Grey's pistol. Another reflex; no doubt he thought he was a split second from being shot. The kick connected and sent the pistol flying, then skittering, down one of the pelt aisles. And DeJordy was rolling, springing back to his feet. He reached into one of his boots and produced a bayonet.

"Do you feel naked without your pistol?" said DeJordy, haughtily.

"Not really," said Grey, pulling a long knife out of his trouser pocket. "It wasn't loaded."

DeJordy said nothing, but crouched defensively and began to circle Grey.

"Captain," said Grey, "as I said before, you have acted honorably in this, from start to finish. Let me bind your hands, and in three or four hours you can go your way, none the worse for wear. Otherwise, I'll be obliged to kill you."

"Do your worst, bastard," said DeJordy. Still circling.

"I beg you to take my word, sir, that I am better at this than you." Grey deftly flipped the knife over in his hand.

"On your guard," said DeJordy, and lunged.

Despite certain objective similarities between knives and swords, knife fighting is a good deal more like boxing than it is fencing. And as much time as Grey had spent with a sword, he'd spent ten times as much time having his stuffing beaten out, and beating out the stuffing of his fellow marines. Toeing the line is how a soldier keeps in fighting trim at sea. And a belaying pin makes a good approximation of a bayonet.

Even so—for all Grey knew, DeJordy was a tried and valiant soldier. And he was lunging.

With his empty hand, Grey chopped at DeJordy's lunge, pushing it wide. At the same time, he swiped his own knife tip across DeJordy's chest, hoping a deep, but not mortal, gash might serve his purpose.

Instead, as Grey brought his cut across DeJordy's front, DeJordy grabbed Grey's wrist and pulled it in the direction of Grey's movement, throwing him off-balance. With his right leg, DeJordy kicked Grey hard in the left shin, sweeping Grey off his feet.

Grey landed on his back. He had heard of savate—shoe fighting— the so-called *jeu marseillais* where French sailors beat each other senseless with kicks and open hands. In Marseille, a closed fist was, legally, a deadly weapon. He'd never encountered savate in nature, and had a rather low opinion of it—any Englishman worth his salt knows that no gentleman kicks in a fight. He might as well bite or scratch. These were all maneuvers reserved for women.

But that was an academic rather than a practical view. At the moment, Grey was flat on his back, and DeJordy's heel was plummeting towards his face. Grey rolled to his right, did one and a half revolutions, and sprang back to his feet, just in time to avoid an upward kick from DeJordy's other foot, and to knock away a backhand slice aimed at Grey's belly.

Grey stabbed at DeJordy's chest. DeJordy knocked the jab away with his elbow and sent a long, sweeping kick into Grey's midsection. Grey stumbled backward, crashing into the wooden framing that held the great fur bales in place. DeJordy stabbed at Grey's ribs; Grey grabbed DeJordy's forearm and guided the bayonet into the pelts behind him, then sliced backhand with his own knife, at DeJordy's flank. DeJordy grabbed Grey's wrist, twisted it outward, and threw Grey to the left; sent him rolling across the floor. Grey got back to his feet just as DeJordy closed ground and sent another long, circling kick at Grey's midsection.

This time the kick was less unexpected; Grey leaned into it, grabbed DeJordy by the calf and knee, and threw him into the wood framing, which crumpled inward, sending an enormous bale of pelts tumbling off the top. Grey stepped back to avoid being walloped by it. The bail slapped onto the ground, skin side down, sounding like a giant palm on a giant drum. DeJordy put a foot on it and shoved it across the floor at Grey's knees. Grey stepped to the side, and DeJordy was on him again, slicing rapidly back and forth, while Grey danced backward, waiting, then landing a blow with his empty hand on DeJordy's stabbing arm as a slice went past, staggering DeJordy and giving Grey an opening for a stab of his own, straight into DeJordy's unprotected liver.

Before Grey's blow could land, DeJordy had released his bayonet and shot both hands back at Grey's right arm, grabbing it, stopping it, bending it at the elbow, and stepping forward, so that the men were facing each other, inches apart, and Grey's knife hand was pinned to his own chest.

DeJordy began to twist Grey's wrist, pointing the knife inward, pushing Grey's hand to drive his knife into his own lungs.

Grey's left hand tried to pry DeJordy's off, to no effect. So Grey opened his right hand, letting the knife fall. He caught it with his left, at the height of DeJordy's hips, and stabbed up-and-in, into DeJordy's gut.

DeJordy gasped, stumbled backward, clutched at the wound, and fell. Shock took him in a matter of seconds, and in less than a minute he was dead.

Grey couldn't claim he was altogether sorry DeJordy was dead. He wasn't overjoyed either. He was just tired. It had been a very long week.

Grey dragged the dead officer down one of the aisles, into a darker recess of the warehouse, and tucked him into a bundle of Louisiana skins bound for a market in some small German state. Then he tidied the battleground, and himself, as much as he could, and returned to the alley.

There was no sign of the Leclercs, but a pair of fresh wheel ruts suggested they'd chosen to trust a longshoreman to help them on their way. Grey followed the tracks towards the sea, trying not to break into a jog. The water's edge was paved with brick, and beyond the alley, after a few yards of muddy streaks, the tracks disappeared.

Grey went on in their direction, along a long line of merchant boats tied up on the quay, gently rocking as the North Sea lifted them up and down. Beyond them, in the harbor, were ships at anchor, and men coming and going by gig and jolly boat.

And beyond them, moving slowly, was a small merchantman just setting its sail and heading into open water. Grey was seized, suddenly, with the fatalistic certainty that the Leclercs were on it.

"Are you Mr. Caffery, sir?" said someone in Dutch. Grey turned. It was a fisherman. Judging by the smell.

"Yes," said Grey.

"The lady told me how you looked and paid me a gold florin to row you out to the *Stad Gouda* when you arrived. Told me she'd give me a second one upon delivery. Please to come along, sir."

The man waved impatiently for Grey to follow, and Grey did.

"Is *Stad Gouda* the ketch setting her sails there in the channel?" said Grey, still looking at the departing merchantman.

The fisherman squinted. "No," he said. "She's the hermaphrodite brig abaft her."

Grey shrugged. He'd been wrong before.

Grey followed the fisherman down a ladder and into a two-man gig. "You can row too, sir, if you're in a rush," said the fisherman, in a challenging voice. Grey lowered the second set of oars and pulled along, taking direction from the fisherman-cum-coxswain. Even with two men putting their backs into it, the going was slow. It took a long quarter hour to reach *Stad Gouda*. When they got to her, she was filled with a Dutch work song as her crew circled the capstan, raising the best bower.

"AHOY THE BRIG," called the fisherman. "THROW US A LINE, WILL YOU? A MAN TO COME ABOARD." He didn't wait for a response, but tapped Grey on the shoulder. "Hold her here," he said, and clapped hold of the accommodation ladder. The fisherman climbed aboard, and Grey caught the *Stad Gouda*'s line, seizing it to a cleat. A moment later the fisherman climbed back down. He patted his purse and said to Grey, "You can go up now."

"I'm obliged to you," said Grey.

"I haven't got all day, you know," said the fisherman.

Grey had an impulse to tip the man into the sea but resisted it, and pulled himself up the ladder; pulled himself over the gunwales to the notice of no one but Geneviève Leclerc, who was waiting for him at the rail.

"You cost me two gold florins," she said. "But let us call it even."

"Where's your father?"

"We've let the great cabin, such as it is. He's already set up in the captain's cot."

"Thank God," said Grey.

"You give yourself very little credit," said Geneviève.

"I could sleep for a month," said Grey.

"SHEET HOME, YOU SORRY B——ERS," called a boatswain. The *Stad Gouda* began to set her sails and was soon making steerageway.

As the Goudas hauled away, Grey enjoyed the sense of his mainspring loosening. He took a deep breath and enjoyed it. He and Geneviève had moved up to the quarterdeck to get out from underfoot, and now stood next to each other on the starboard rail, watching the sun rise. Behind them, the *Stad Gouda*'s captain was saying something to the helmsmen about the land breeze and his personal views on the best sailing points of gaff-rigged brigantines. Grey, who had a well-defined opinion on the subject, turned to express it. A moment later Geneviève interrupted:

"Gentlemen, if you please—what is that?"

Grey and the two others turned to see. A bright red rocket was shooting skyward, now peaking, now coasting back down to earth.

"It's a signal flare, ma'am," said the captain, raising his spotting glass; looking back towards the land. "Calling ships' attention to something onshore."

The helmsman retrieved a second glass from the binnacle and offered it to Geneviève. "If you care to look, madame?"

"Thank you," she said, raising it, following the captain's gaze.

"It's a signal for us," said the captain of the *Stad Gouda*. "Ordering us back to shore: an emergency."

Grey was already emptying his purse into his hand; counting its contents. "Sir, I will give you eighteen pounds English to have failed to see that rocket, along with my note of hand for fifty more when we reach Harwich."

The captain reached out his hand, palm up. "What rocket?" he said.

"Saints preserve us," said Geneviève, her voice cracking.

"What?" said Grey, turning to her. She was white as a sheet. "What is it?"

She lowered the spyglass from her eye. "A ghost," she said, quietly.

"DeJordy?" said Grey, astonished, taking the glass from her hand and looking back at the shore.

"No," said Geneviève. Grey pointed the spotting glass at the dockmaster's house, the source of the signals.

Standing on its roof, at the base of the telegraph pole, was a man in a uniform—his shoulders wrapped in a blanket—his face sunken and waxy, and far whiter than Geneviève's.

"Théodore," she said.

24

A T HARWICH, as the *Stad Gouda* warped up to a quay, Grey
spotted a young midshipman onshore, eating a biscuit and
looking lazy. Identifying himself as Captain Grey of the
Royal Marines, Grey bellowed an order to the boy to find four
marines and a litter and have them waiting on the quay by the time
Gouda was moored. The mid skipped off to obey, and when a plank
was laid for unloading, a marine sergeant and three of his men were
standing at attention, awaiting Grey's orders. They carried their
litter on board and carried Joseph Leclerc, awake and in awe of his
surroundings, off again. Grey went ahead, to draw funds from an
emergency purse kept at the port admiral's office, and then to find
the best-sprung coach to be had for ready money. As the marines
put Leclerc into it, gently as anyone could—there wasn't one of
them who hadn't experience with a litter, and most of it at sea—
Grey found a rider to carry word ahead to Sir Edward.

Grey told the coachman he'd hired to go have a smoke; and for
a half hour or so, Grey sat on the vacated driver's bench, encoding
letters to be carried back to the continent. They were to go, circu-
itously, to confidants of his who might be able to learn if Théodore
had taken Louis Antoine. He handed the letters, along with fifty
pounds owed and another ten to act as Grey's postman, to *Stad Gou-*

da's captain. After unloading his soft cheese and butter and reloading with hard cheese and coffee, the captain weighed and returned to Rotterdam that same day.

BEFORE ANY of the letters were answered—after the service had taken charge of the Leclercs and sent Grey off for the normal interrogation; after Grey had gone hoarse telling and retelling the story; after a week and a fraction had passed—Grey received a hastily written note that had passed from a Dutch fisherman to a British man-of-war on the blockade of Anvers, and then to a captain's cutter that carried it up the Thames to the Admiralty:

> *TG—Be aware that Théodore is alive. (As am I) —LA*

This was March 19th. Joseph Leclerc was recovering well at Harrington House, a town house just a few steps up Whitehall from the Old Admiralty Building. It was tucked at the end of a cul-de-sac called Craig's Court, and was kept by naval intelligence for matters requiring atypical discretion. For a week, officers of His Majesty's secret intelligence service had worn ruts in its floor, pacing and waiting for the permission of Leclerc's government doctors to speak to their patient. But in the ten-minute audiences granted once or twice a day, they had already gleaned a passel of the choicest secrets imaginable.

News of one, in particular, was conveyed to Grey by the chief of staff personally:

"Tom," said Aaron Willys, stepping into Grey's office as Grey deftly covered up the Rosetta rubbing he'd been working on—a treat to celebrate Louis's letter finally setting his mind at ease, "do you remember the cipher out of that frog boat *Marianne*'s dispatch bag—the one you plucked out of the Bay of Biscay?"

"I do," said Grey. "From Bonaparte's desk, didn't you tell me?"

"Indeed," said Willys, with the look of a father on Christmas morning. "Well, your man Leclerc's given us the key."

Grey grinned from ear to ear and slapped his desk hard. "Damned fine, Aaron," he said. "That'll wipe the Corsican's eye now, won't it?"

"It will," said Willys. "Care to read it?"

"You have it writ plain already?"

"I have," said Willys, stepping forward, laying the plain text on Grey's desk and seeing the Rosetta stone peeking out from under a heap of memoranda. "May I?" he said, picking the rubbing up and walking towards Grey's office window, which he slid open. Grey looked at him plaintively.

"Read it," said Willys, tearing strips off the rubbing and tossing them out into the rainy afternoon.

Grey shook his head, muttered something about a lifetime's service to king and country, and then turned to the decipher.

" 'Evidently addressed to Louis-André Pichon,' " said Grey, reading aloud, " 'French ambassador to Washington.' "

"Yes," said Willys, throwing out the last strip and shutting the window.

" 'To Pichon—Secure at once, by any means and without fail, a treaty to guarantee a monopoly on American lumber exports. Napoleon.' " Grey looked at Willys. "Tremendous."

"It is, in fact," said Willys. "Though I didn't expect a blunt instrument like yourself to get it in one. Leclerc tells us that the lumber yields from the south of the continent—from the south of France as well as Napoleon's fiefs in Italy—have been very disappointing."

"The French are out of wood?"

"Just so."

"I retract my sarcasm."

"As you should. HMS *Diana* will be leaving with a trade embassy to Washington in"—Willys looked at his watch—"less than four hours. So far as we know, Pichon remains ignorant of the fact that he's meant to be buying up the Americans' lumber. If we can beat him to the punch—keep America's trees out of the frogs' flippers— well, you talk about wiping Napoleon's eye."

"Indeed." Grey was nodding thoughtfully. Indeed. "I'd say this calls for a drink."

"It does," said Willys, "but I'm afraid you'll have to toss off the bumper without me; the old man shows no sign of desisting anytime in the foreseeable future."

Grey shook his head. "When was the last time you were home?"

"Saturday a week. Have you been out to Sheerness?"

Grey shook his head. "I'm staying at Buttle's."

"Well, take up my place and drink off a full glass," said Willys, rolling his shoulders and straightening his coat.

"I'll drink and be jolly and drown melancholy."

Willys was walking out into the corridor and called back, "And there's to the health of each good-hearted lass."

25

O N HIS WAY TO BUTTLE's, Grey looked in at Harrington House, intending to ask the men on duty for a précis of the Leclerc interviews. Grey answered the innocuous challenge of the butler, who Grey knew had a loaded pistol under his justaucorps (the term "butler" was used advisedly): "Good evening, sir"—"Surely, Potter, it's still the afternoon." Grey stepped inside, where he found Leclerc's doctors and Sir Edward's interrogators very nearly at swords drawn over when and for how long the latter could question the charge of the former.

"Gentlemen," said Grey, "perhaps I can be of some assistance: Could I offer you a coin to flip?"

"And who are you, sir?" snapped one of the doctors.

"A man you'd best mind your manners to, sir," snapped one of the intelligence men. "Or you'll get a cuff on the ear."

"I'm Grey," said Grey, extending his hand to the irritated doctor.

"Ah yes, Grey," said the doctor. "Our patient has been asking for you. Perhaps you would care to look in on him; it's the second door on the left. It might prove a calming influence after the incessant and I daresay *destructive* persistence of these men."

"You daresay, do you?" said the same intelligence man. "I'll dare do more than that, you halfpenny sawbones b——d."

Grey smiled to himself as he walked past and up the stairs; this particular gentleman of naval intelligence had spent several years before the mast, and after remarking on the doctor's lineage, the marital prospects of his mother, and the species of his wife, he was turning to the doctor's method of eating sausages when Grey knocked on the second door on the left, and was let in by a nurse.

"Mr. Grey!" said Leclerc, in evident high spirits. "Né Caffery. I'd been hoping you'd come by, to give me the opportunity of thanking you in a more suitable fashion than at our parting . . . I'm afraid I wasn't myself; could barely stay conscious, you understand."

"Of course, sir, and I'm sensible of the courtesy, but your thanks were more than adequate—I'm glad to see you looking so much better." Indeed, Leclerc was still quite pale, but at least now he had the pallor of a living man and not a piece of Dover sole.

"Thank you, Mr. Grey, thank you. Please, have a seat, won't you? I'm afraid the damned doctors—or I should not say damned, but rather, stern—the damnably stern doctors will turn you out any second, but do at least tell me how you've fared yourself since our arrival. You were more than a little scraped up over those long few days."

"You're kind to ask, sir," said Grey, sitting down. Even more than the change in complexion, there was a glaring change in Leclerc's temperament. A new life will do that to a man, of course. As will a brush with death. "I'm very well," Grey continued. "A sea voyage always puts me right, even so short a trip as a Dutch crossing."

"You're a thoroughgoing seaman then, aren't you? I know soldiers who are that way about getting on horseback. I don't happen to be one of them, but I could easily wish I were."

Grey nodded. "How is your daughter, sir?" Grey had of course assumed she would be here—had expected her, rather than an English nurse, to let him in.

"Oh, she is more like you, sir, a quick recovery. She has been taken to the bosom of our émigrés here; officers of the Condé have been most attentive. Most determined to persuade her of the value of the *petit* Paris that's been made here."

"Very good," said Grey. Well, that would spare him the trouble of showing her about. Just as well. Or in fact, better. He had so little time to himself. God bye her.

"Which reminds me," said Leclerc, "speaking of Condé, how is the duc Louis Antoine? I am told he stayed behind us."

"Yes," said Grey. "But I've had word from him that he is alive and, I gather, in good order."

"Splendid, splendid," said Leclerc. His voice was growing softer.

"I think I had better move on, sir," said Grey. "There's much to be done. But I'm glad of a chance to see you well."

"Thank you, Grey, thank you. Yes, do please come again. I know Geneviève will be sorry to have missed you."

"I will, sir. *À tout à l'heure.*"

As Grey passed back out through the foyer, Potter the butler—a man well over six feet—had interposed himself between the service men and the doctors, and seemed to be mediating over the subject of a tincture bottle thrown at someone's head.

THE WEATHER had improved from the midafternoon, and though it was still quite chilly, Grey walked from Whitehall to Buttle's, arriving there before night had quite fallen. Mathers informed him that Pater had asked for a word upon his arrival, and that he could be found in the dining room; a page would lead him there. Pater was, unusually, deep in his work, with half-glasses perched on his nose and before him a ledger, into which he was conveying figures circled in several newspaper leaves that were spread in a half circle, beyond the ledger, from his left elbow to his right.

"Ah, Tom, good—you'll join me for dinner, won't you? I'm damned sharp-set—Roman lions ain't in it—but I've just got to put some final touches to this program." He poked the ledger with his pen. "The market, you know. Your holdings are doing well, of course. Have a drink and I'll be with you in five minutes."

"Coffee, if it's reasonably fresh, and a dram of whiskey," said Grey to the page, whose name momentarily escaped him.

"Bring him the Old Bourbon whiskey," said Pater, without looking up from his work. "Club's getting it again now that the Americans have bought Louisiana."

Grey took an easy chair, lit a cheroot, and drank his coffee while working out a chess problem in the *Monthly Magazine*. He drank the dram of whiskey when he solved it. Before he could attempt another, Pater called the page to clear the table.

"Phillips, take all this up to my room, will you? There's a good chap. And send Oscars over."

"You wanted to speak to me," said Grey, lighting another cheroot.

"Yes—it's nothing important, just that your signature page is full, and the membership committee plans to sit on you sometime in the next week or two. Having nominated you, I'm implicated. And I suspect that this will be the last dinner I stand you as a guest."

"I appreciate that, Pater. Your putting me down for a place in the books. Not to mention your letting me abuse your own membership," said Grey.

"Nonsense," said Pater. "Don't think of it. Or rather, do, and repay me by playing my partner at a whist table this evening—there are a couple of fellows back from India who've shook out the pagoda tree and need a lesson in prudential finances. But let's eat first. Oscars—"

The steward had appeared between them, ready to take their dinner orders.

"Onion soup, veal collops; asparagus, turtle, and blancmange; black caps and a slice of that almond cheese cake I had earlier. Thomas?"

"Toast, tongue, peas, and Camembert."

"Very good, Mr. Grey, Mr. Pater," said Oscars. "Shall I call the wine waiter?"

Pater gestured deference to Grey.

"I shouldn't think so—just another of the bourbon, a blanc de blancs of your suggestion, Oscars, and coffee."

"Blanc de blancs?" said Pater.

"Yes," said Grey.

"You're a bold one, aren't you? Very well, Oscars, same for me, but tea to finish."

"Yes, sir. May I recommend the '97 Ruinart? We were able to procure several cases during the peace, but it is dwindling almost to nothing. And it shouldn't be missed."

"Thank you, Oscars," said Grey. "Bring it with the first course, will you?"

"Sir," said a page—Parslow—walking quite quickly up to the table and addressing Grey, "there is a man in the lobby from the Foreign Office who is most insistent that he speak with you."

"Almighty God," said Pater, rolling his eyes.

"I apologize, Pater—will you excuse me?"

"Of course, Tom. But I won't be made to answer for the eventual condition of your toast."

Grey followed Parslow to the lobby. A junior officer of naval intelligence was waiting there. Grey waved him into an alcove where they could speak privately.

"Sir Edward wonders if he might have a word, sir. Back at Admiralty House."

A CABRIOLET took Grey back to Whitehall; inside of a quarter hour he was stepping into Sir Edward Banks's outer office—finding Willys waiting there for him, and being waved by Willys into the inner office, where Banks had forgone his desk and was pacing by the map table.

"Grey: Come in. Something has happened."

To Geneviève? was Grey's first thought. Kidnapped back to France? Maybe to use as a pawn against her father?

Banks continued:

"We've received a letter from Bathilde d'Orléans—she used every means at her disposal to get it to us at all speed, but it's been three days, and given the urgency . . . I'm not sure, at this point, if I can in good conscience release you to act on it. I don't think it would make any difference."

Grey felt his sinews tightening; his muscles coiling up, so to speak; making him ready to spring into action. At the same time, he could almost have strangled Banks for taking so long to drop the final veil.

"Sir, if you would——"

"Yes——you'll excuse me for thinking aloud; this is the long and short of it: on the night of March the thirteenth, French dragoons crossed the Rhine near Strasbourg, made their way secretly to the house where *le duc* Louis Antoine was staying, and surrounded it. After Louis'd gone to it pell-mell——I don't know how many he knocked on the head——they dragged him back across the river to France. As of the fifteenth, he is being held in the dungeon of the Château de Vincennes. He has been tried, by military tribunal, and sentenced to death. The execution has been stayed pending an appeal to Napoleon, for clemency, arranged by Bathilde to be made by the Russian plenipotentiary in Paris. The appeal will not be granted. Bathilde is playing for time, for us——but I fear it is already too late to do anything."

Grey was calculating routes and tides. "I can be in France by dawn," he said. "And in Vincennes by tomorrow night."

"He may be dead by then," said Banks. "He may be dead already."

"I understand," said Grey.

Willys stepped forward. "As there's not a moment to lose, or to acquaint another officer with the situation, may I, Sir Edward, be allowed to accompany Grey?"

"You may not," said Banks.

"I'll move faster alone," said Grey. "But I thank you, Aaron." Willys shook his hand.

Banks was standing over his desk, writing. "These are orders requesting and requiring all naval personnel to take direction from you as regards your immediate transport to the coast of France. Our tender HMS *Yellowjacket* is docked on the river; she's American-built—a Baltimore clipper; extremely fast. Take her across. God speed you, Tom. And I'll add—take these as explicit verbal orders— if effecting a rescue of the duke proves obviously impossible, do not get yourself killed attempting one anyway."

Grey nodded and accepted the written orders Banks was holding out to him. "You'll excuse me, gentlemen," he said, and walked quickly out of the room.

26

THERE WAS, OF COURSE, no possibility of warning the British Channel fleet of *Yellowjacket*'s mission. And to have any chance of delivering Grey onto the Norman beach before sunup, there would be no time for *Yellowjacket* to haul her wind and make her number if challenged. There was a dimmish, waning moon—enough to be spotted by; not enough for semaphore to be read. So *Yellowjacket*'s captain—a young commander by the name of Boyle—agreed that they would make this a smuggling run. Boyle would fly them through the blockade at *Yellowjacket*'s best speed, put Grey ashore, and make his apologies on the way out. Provided his clipper hadn't first been shivered by an overzealous warning shot.

"It's a shame we didn't ship black sails, like that cove coming back from Crete. You know, the fellow who put an end to the bull-headed chap." Boyle was speaking softly; he and Grey were standing shoulder to shoulder on the quarterdeck, at the windward rail. Boyle had just had a reef shaken out of the mainsail. And the sail did seem awfully damned white in the dim moonlight.

"Theseus," said Grey.

"Yes," said Boyle, "that's the fellow." After a second, he continued: "And who was the other one, the bullish fellow trapped in the labyrinth, who ate the prettiest girls from Athens?"

"The Minotaur," said Grey.

"Just so," said Boyle. "Perhaps if they hadn't kept him in that s——ing maze, he would've been less beastly to them. Come a point to larboard." The last remark he directed at the helmsman.

"*On deck there!*" came a shouted whisper from the rigging. "*Two sail hull-up on the starboard beam!*"

"That'll be the fleet," said Boyle, squinting to his right. "Keith: another point to larboard."

"Aye aye, sir," said the helmsmen, making another small adjustment to the wheel, then resetting his hands on the spokes.

"*On deck there! Two sail hull-up on the larboard bow.*"

"Steady as you go, Keith." Then, to Grey: "That'll be the rest of the fleet. Keeping their stations well, aren't they?"

"Aren't they," said Grey. *Yellowjacket* was making fine speed, and—with the fleet in sight—it wouldn't be long till they'd see the French coast. Boyle had his own coxswain and boat crew waiting at the break of the quarterdeck, ready to lower the launch and pull Grey ashore. Grey was all in black: half-boots, tarpaulin trousers, and jacket buttoned at the collar. He had a small tarred bag—food and tools—slung on his back; the Girandoni, tarpaulin-wrapped, and his sword were slung beside it, and all was made fast with a belt tightened just under his ribs.

"*On deck there! Frigate, dead ahead!*"

In an instant Boyle had his glass up; was scanning the inky night forward. It took him a moment to spot the ship in question: a British fifth-rate moving west as part of the line of blockaders on patrol.

"Hard a-starboard, Keith," said Boyle calmly. "All hands to the windward rail, and warn 'em silence on deck." The order was passed forward—the boatswain refraining from the traditional bellow.

Morning was fast approaching, and the moonlight was beginning to be diffused into a landward mist hovering over the water. It wasn't much to hide in, but it was enough to keep the crew hopeful. More usefully, perhaps, Boyle was taking them windward of the nearest blockaders, to help lose the sails in a background of whitecaps.

"*Land! Larboard beam!*" A sort of shouted whisper.

"*Shut your f——g gob, you lubber c——,*" came a different voice from the rigging.

There was the sound of scuffling around the head of the foremast.

"*Shut those fools up,*" said Boyle, leaning over the quarterdeck rail and whispering to the boatswain, who jogged forward.

"*Silence!*" hissed the boatswain. "*Silence there at the foremast, you infernal b——s!*"

"Five points to larboard," whispered Boyle, calmly, to the helmsman Keith. The frigate that had been dead ahead was now within pistol shot on the larboard quarter aft, but *Yellowjacket* was putting distance between them. The two sail to windward, however, were closing in, on the starboard bow. If they weren't already within rifle shot, they soon would be.

Like Jason and his Argonauts—Grey shook his head: Boyle had got him thinking Greek—like the Argonauts racing between the Symplegades, trying not to get crushed between the clashing rocks at the mouth of the Bosporus—here they were amongst a line of blockading ships—of their own fleet, yet—who could, with the greatest ease, blow them to Hades. Cyanean Rocks. Scylla and Charybdis. A needle's eye and a Baltimore camel.

"Another five to larboard, Keith," whispered Boyle.

But they were through now, with the frigate astern leeward, the others windward, and the coast of France again dead ahead. Grey slowly exhaled. Well, there was that done. The least of the troubles he would encounter in the next twenty-four hours.

"If there's anything you need to do before we haul up and put the boat down—now's the time," whispered Boyle.

Grey nodded. "I thank you—I'm ready on your word."

Boyle nodded. Ahead and above them, the sound of scuffling resumed in the rigging.

"Damned press gang, filling *Yellowjacket* up with gaolbirds and idiots," said Boyle, quietly, and the boatswain hissed again for them to shut their fool mouths.

Then the quiet thud of a punch landing hard, and the scream of a man falling out of the rigging, and the much louder thud of him hitting the deck.

A pair of men ran off the starboard rail to check the fallen jack; see if he was dead. The rest of the boat seemed to hold its breath.

Then a loud crack of thunder, a distant flash of flame, and a nine-pound cannonball punching holes through the mainsail and foresail.

"Hard a-larboard," said Boyle, calmly. "All plain sail. Put the wind on our rear quarter, Mr. Keith."

"Ain't there s'posed to be a warning shot?" said a man on the rail.

"That was a warning shot," said another. "Blind sods."

"Captain Boyle," said Grey, "you're running towards Dieppe? Much further and I won't be able to land."

Another shot boomed out; it threw up a great billow of white water ten yards behind the taffrail.

"That's right, Mr. Grey. Once we've run clear of the squadron, we'll tack up again."

Grey narrowed his eyes and stepped closer to Boyle. He spoke very quietly, so as not to give the impression of argument to the crew.

"That will take ages, sir."

"It may, sir," said Boyle.

"I must land before dawn."

"It may not be possible."

"It is *imperative*."

Another cannon shot. Grey didn't see where it hit.

"Not so imperative as my ship staying afloat, I shouldn't think."

"How close can you run inshore, sir?" said Grey.

Boyle looked at him and shook his head. "You can't mean to swim, Mr. Grey."

"How close?"

"Perhaps two miles. A mile and a half. No closer."

"A mile and a half will do me fine, sir."

Boyle stared Grey down—wondering, no doubt, if he should introduce the subject of the sea's temperature.

"So be it," said Boyle. "Mr. Keith: two points landward." To Grey: "I could try hauling my wind and surrendering—but I wouldn't put down a boat until I was sure it wouldn't be fired upon."

"I understand, sir. I will swim. Can I still expect you at our rendezvous the night after tomorrow?"

"You may," said Boyle. "I believe once I inform the fleet of my orders they'll be less determined to sink me."

"Very good," said Grey. He took the bag off his back and quickly removed everything that could conceivably be left behind. He made a pile of most of the food, spare clothes . . . and, reluctantly, added to it his ammunition, the Girandoni's tools, and the Girandoni itself.

"May I entrust this to you, sir?" said Grey to Boyle. Boyle nodded and called for his steward. Meanwhile Grey resealed the bag and reslung it on his back. He made it fast, checked his sword was fast as well, then walked forward to the *Yellowjacket*'s waist.

Three minutes later, a ship's boy approached Grey. As he opened his mouth, there was another volley from the pursuing frigate's long-nine bow chasers. They hit either side of the *Yellowjacket*. Just yards from hitting home.

"We're at a mile and a half, sir." At the same time, the *Yellowjacket* began to heave to, signaling her surrender.

"Thank you," said Grey, opening the entry port.

"God bye you, sir," said the boy.

"Thank you," said Grey. He dove into the water, four or five feet below him. It was suffocatingly cold, but he came quickly to the surface and began to crawl hard towards the beach.

27

TARRED CLOTHING may keep out wind and spray, but it is just beside useless against submergence. When Grey pulled himself out of the surf, he was shivering so that he could barely use his hands, which were hard at work trying to unknot his bag and extract a flint striker. He gathered some dead sea grass lying at the beach's high-water mark and some chunks of driftwood, and made a fire. It might draw unwanted attention, but to hell with that—if he didn't warm up and dry off, the only thing that would stay hidden would be his corpse. In any case, the first daylight was already visible in the east, so the firelight wouldn't announce his presence as loudly as it would have an hour earlier.

It took an agonizing two minutes to get the fire going. Then, standing almost on top of it, Grey stripped off his clothes and began to dry himself, and them. This took perhaps a half an hour, after which he felt nearly human. He ate a few bites of damp cheddar and began the long walk inland.

The pebble beach gave way to scrub and then Norman bocage: fields and pastures separated by small stands of forest. Grey might have kept to the wending tree lines if time had been less pressing—instead he gambled on looking more like a vagabond wandering the fields than an Englishman on a commando. To look less like a villain, he turned his jacket tar-side in, so that it was a dirty cotton white instead of bandit black. Here and there, despite the early hour, pastures were already in use, and dotted with the white of sheep and the brown and white of Normande cows (according to Geneviève's brief lesson on French dairy farms, they were not Guernseys, nor Jerseys, nor Alderneys for butter, but they were good—and for meat, much better). Crossing through one hedge forest, he selected a stout walking stick, which he used once or twice to ward off sheep dogs. Though none of them seemed particularly desirous of a fight. Probably because even their grandfathers' grandfathers had never had to fight an actual wolf. French sheep dogs had gotten soft. Very soft, he observed, scratching one around the neck, and having it follow beside him a little while, before the distant whistle of an unseen shepherd called it back.

Over the next hill, Grey passed through a forest line and into a Calvados orchard. If Grey believed in signs, he would have taken this as a good one, he decided. His father had kept an orchard, and Grey had spent many happy hours among apple trees. Finding some in Normandy should not have surprised him; the north of France was lousy with cider orchards, but that was neither here nor there. He decided the trees would probably grow white winter Calvilles—the strange, lumpy apple that Normans prefer, and of which Grey had always been fond. Shame he was out of season. On the far side of the orchard he found, finally, a road, and began to pick up speed.

But even a decent road didn't give him anything like the speed he needed; it took him another hour of walking before he finally found what he was looking for—a stable, behind a public house. He walked back to it. There were half a dozen horses inside, but there was no groom. Either the groom was a late riser, or he was at work on something somewhere else—perhaps he was the house chef as well. Grey shook his head. He didn't care to wait, and after a quick inspection, selected the horse that looked most like it could manage a fast cross-country ride. Giving Paris a wide berth, it would be about a hundred miles to Vincennes, and Grey needed to be there by nightfall. A stout blond and brown Breton with a white nose stripe looked fit for the purpose. Maybe not the fastest horse or the brightest, but he had something to him that Grey liked. Sangfroid, perhaps, and just what the circumstance called for. Grey decided on a generous price— given the circumstances of the purchase—counted the silver out of his purse, left it on the horse's fodder, saddled up, and trotted back to the road. At the road, he kicked into a gallop.

He rode all day, staying on the main road until the furthest out-skirts of Paris, and then turning west into the forest and winding towards the Château de Vincennes. The *Yellowjacket*'s Captain Boyle had been good enough to calculate for Grey precise astronomical directions to the château. Navigating would be easier once the stars were out, but as long as Grey had a watch, the height and direction of the sun would serve almost as well.

Still, it seemed like no time at all before the stars appeared. With a half dozen stops—every twenty miles or so—to trade his horse for a fresh one, and though they all made good time, it was near fully night before the gray towers of Vincennes could be seen pok-ing above the tree line. Grey tied up the final horse (whom he had named Roland. For why? He didn't know the horse's given name, but you must call a horse *something*, and Grey had decided he looked Rolandish); tied him far enough away that no guard's dog would smell him out. Grey left him with a lump of sugar purchased along with lunch in the midafternoon. With the dusk dwindling, Grey turned his jacket back to black and removed everything from his bag that he didn't plan to use getting into Vincennes or getting back out again. Then he began to stalk towards the fortress.

It was called the Château de Vincennes, but it wasn't one of the great gracious houses the word "château" calls to mind: aristocrat-built in Renaissance or baroque styles. The earliest parts were built in the early twelfth century, during the Crusades. Contemporary to the Tower of London, and with something of that ambience. It was most famous for its dungeon tower, near two hundred feet tall—one of the tallest towers in Europe; one of the few of its height that wasn't part of a cathedral. It was a grim place, and a fateful one. Henry V— for Grey's money, England's greatest king—had died here. If he'd lived, Paris would be the most beautiful city in the United Kingdom. But what of that? Once more unto the breach.

The fortress in toto was enormous: a rectangle two hundred yards by four, surrounded by a dry moat fifty feet deep. Its bailey was filled with an odd collection of buildings—barracks beside cloisters and palatial apartments, and an exact double of the Île de la Cité's Sainte-Chapelle. But the part of the enclosure in which Grey was interested—the dungeon tower—was separated from the rest; it stood alone on the western edge, on a sort of stone island, surrounded by its own moat, also dry, sixty feet deep and ninety wide. The only entrance was a gate at the end of a high, narrow bridge, wide enough for one man only, extending from the separate bailey of the château proper. The island—the motte on which the tower and its enceinte stood—rose out of the moat at a forty-five-degree angle; smooth stone creating a base for the tower at ground level— that is, sixty feet above the moat's bottom. The sloped stone joined seamlessly with the island's peripheral wall; another fifty feet, crenellated, with a guard tower at each corner. And inside that stood the mammoth tower itself, looming over the countryside like the Colossus of Rhodes. But twice as tall. And, of course, unlike the Colossus, it wasn't shaped like a man. It was shaped like a rook. A titanic rook at the edge of a titanic chessboard. Grey had studied the dimensions during the crossing aboard *Yellowjacket*, but they hadn't done the thing justice. Its scale could only be grasped at first hand.

And yet—it wasn't the first fortress Grey had breached, and it wouldn't, he hoped, be the last. And after all, one citadel, ultimately, is very like another. There are walls to be scaled, doors to be got open, and men to hide from or disable. Only the details vary.

Between Sir Edward's office and Buttle's—from which Grey had retrieved his work clothes and the much-lamented Girandoni— Grey had stopped at the basement office of the quartermaster of naval intelligence. He'd requested the tarred duck bag and the things to fill it: the flint striker, a great deal of rope, several grapnel hooks, and so on. The quartermaster—a navy man in his youth who'd gone ashore to apprentice with William Watson and never returned to sea—had suggested the Girandoni's air mechanism might launch a hook and rope as well as it launched a bullet, but there had been no time to investigate. Just as well, as it turned out. Instead he had supplied Grey with a small crossbow that would do the trick. Grey removed it, along with the hook and rope, which he slung along diagonally across his back. With a last look at the things he was leaving behind—should he bother to bury them? It seemed like a waste of time—he couldn't bury the horse, after all—he set his jaw and approached the moat edge.

And there he waited. His hopes of getting inside depended on a slow climb. The slow climb depended on placing his grapnel. Placing the grapnel—and having it stay placed—would require no one knowing it was there. And for that, he needed to know where the prison guards were, and where they weren't. As it *was* a prison, and not the military fortress of its younger days, the guards' job was keeping men in, not keeping them out. That would make things easier. It helped too that instead of lighting the place with torches, the guards carried candles. Grey could see their lights moving slowly about, through crenels and archers' loops.

Grey waited. To shoot a hook and line across a ninety-foot gap requires enormous energy. It was lucky that the navy, for the purpose of passing ship-to-ship lines, had devised a crossbow that could do the job. It was a large pistol crossbow, handy for ships and small enough for Grey's tarpaulin bag. The difficulty was in the draw. To find enough force to throw the hook and rope, the wooden "bow" of the crossbow had been replaced with an iron cart-spring. It couldn't be drawn by hand, but required the use of a windlass ratchet; cocking took several minutes.

Grey waited the better part of an hour, until he was satisfied that the guards made quarter-hourly rounds, and otherwise confined themselves, probably, to a guardroom somewhere in the enceinte's interior. As soon as the candlelight disappeared with what he guessed was the ten o'clock patrol, Grey got to work.

His crossbow was cocked; a line was fast to a tree at one end and a grapnel hook at the other, and the hook was loaded into the drawn cart-spring. Grey knelt at the moat's edge, took aim at the space above the enceinte's crenellated top, said a prayer, and fired.

The crack of the spring releasing was almost loud as a gunshot, and the recoil nearly lost Grey his balance. The flight of the hook and line across the moat seemed to last a lifetime. But it made it—over the battlements. Grey heard, just barely, the clang of metal on rock, and could only hope that the guards were sufficiently far away, or inattentive, not to have noticed. He tugged on the line and felt it catch. He tugged—hard—to see if it was caught snugly. He took the slack out of the line by tightening it at the anchor tree. And then, there was no more excuse for delay. He lay on his back beneath the line, took hold of it, slung his feet up and over it—locking them, as best he could, at the ankles. He pulled himself up, to check the line could support his weight; gave it a few seconds to snap loose, if it was going to. And then he pulled himself, hand over hand and headfirst, over the edge.

In an instant, he was dangling sixty feet in the air, and reminding himself he'd done this in ships' rigging he knew not how often. And this time, there was no sea motion to worry about. Easy as kiss-your-hand.

Hand over hand, he pulled himself towards the fortress. There was a considerable incline in the rope, as the wall was fifty feet higher than the moat's edge, but this made the going surprisingly simpler, as it kept Grey's head above the rest of his body, and kept his disorientation to a minimum.

He was better than two-thirds of the way across when he heard voices below him. From some dry water channel that had once filled the moat, two men had emerged, and were walking, in no great hurry, across the moat's grassy bottom. They selected a suitable spot and lowered shovels from their shoulders, and began to dig a grave, and to talk about it loudly, over the sound of their work. Apparently, Paris soil was much easier to dig graves in than the Austrian sort, which was awfully rocky. They must have been with the army. Maybe they still were.

Grey could watch them upside for only a moment; the blood was rushing to his forehead. They wouldn't hear him above the sounds of their digging and jabbering. And Grey had a feeling in the pit of his stomach that he knew for whom the grave was being dug. He hoped only that it was being dug in advance of its being needed; the French army liked to show prisoners their graves before shooting them. It was an eccentricity.

Another five minutes had him to the wall's top; had him gripping the rough stone and pulling himself awkwardly over. And then he was on the battlements and looking left and right, with his hand over his shoulder on the hilt of his sword, in case a guard had decided to change his watch pattern. But there was no one, and Grey permitted himself a minute to catch his breath before walking to the battlements' inner edge.

He looked down at the courtyard. It was empty. He could hear voices, very faintly, on its far side, where the guards presumably stayed between their rounds. Probably in the gatehouse, where the one-man bridge passed through the enceinte's eastern wall and emerged, just as spindly, in its interior, about twenty feet above the courtyard's ground level. At least, that's what the Admiralty dossier described. Grey had no intention to look for himself. The colossus tower's west side—its rear—was unguarded, and that was enough.

First he spent five minutes recocking and reloading the crossbow. As he spun the windlass, ratcheted the spring back, he looked up at the tower's top. He had no way of knowing where Louis was being kept, but he presumed it would be in the "apartment" cells at the tower's top—fortunately, the Admiralty had exceptionally detailed plans of Vincennes, because the great English architect Sir John Vanbrugh—prior to his knighthood; prior to his designing Blenheim Palace—had lived briefly in Paris, evangelized for the Enlightenment, and managed to get himself arrested for (of all things) espionage. The French tossed him into the tower of Vincennes, but eventually details of the prison's inhumanity reached England, and the Sun King was persuaded to remove him to the apparently more pleasant Bastille. Vanbrugh's intelligence of the place was a hundred years old, but Grey suspected Vincennes wasn't much changed. The tower was five hundred years old, and though the exterior was scarred like the face of a pox patient, few fortresses could be said to have stood up better to half a millennium's bombardments and sieges. Indeed: the revolution had marched on Vincennes just as it had marched on the Bastille. The Bastille had been turned to rubble, but Vincennes's tower still stood.

Vanbrugh had testified that the more the French wanted a man isolated, the higher he was kept. This made sense to Grey, but he would have aimed to enter the tower at the top anyway, because Vanbrugh's plans showed no other way in, bar the impassible bridge. At the tower's top, however, were a series of turrets and catwalks, to be used for the repelling of assaults and the frightening of prisoners. That was Grey's target. He cranked every ounce of tension he could into the bow. The quartermaster had claimed it had a hook-and-rope range of a hundred yards, ship to ship. In theory, that would be enough. Grey may have had his doubts, but it was much, much too late to yield to them.

When the crossbow was finally cocked, and Grey was satisfied that the dark western half of the fortress bailey was empty, he slid down a ladder and walked slowly towards the tower's base. To be sure of the aim, he wanted to stand back as far as he could, to decrease as much as possible the angle of inclination. But the aim wouldn't matter if the distance were too great. So he needed too to stand as close as was practical. He was trying to settle on a perfect medium when the sound of footsteps crunching along the north side of the tower froze him. With gravel underfoot, Grey didn't dare run to the wall for cover, or drop to the ground. His best hope was to trust in the darkness and his black clothes.

A Frenchman—a prison guard, in a raggedy sort of a uniform— walked around the corner of the tower, about twenty yards to Grey's left. He was carrying a lantern and breathing heavily, staggering slightly, and looking generally the worse for a night of drinking. At first he continued to walk to the west, where Grey presumed a

latrine emptied into the moat. Grey wondered if the gravediggers
were clear of it. The drunk guard reached the bottom of the ladder
Grey had used to climb down from the enceinte wall. He contemplated its height, snorted contemptuously, and turned back towards
Grey. He slid the lantern's handle into the crook of his elbow and
began to unfasten his pants. The lazy son of a bitch was going to
relieve himself against the tower wall. Grey had seconds to act.

The man stopped. He'd caught a glimpse of Grey, the outline of
a shadow in the night. He held up the lantern. It lit up Grey's face.

"*Arrêtez-vous!*" the man started to shout, and Grey shot him in the
face with the crossbow. The sound was like a hammer coming down
on a pumpkin.

The man was dead; the lantern was on the ground and shattered.
Grey had no idea if the man's comrades had heard it shatter, or heard
the man's shout, or his death. But he was certain he didn't have minutes to rewind the crossbow.

His certainty was justified seconds later by the sound of voices
and feet. They didn't sound alarmed. Just curious. But the alarm
would come. Grey was in check, and the only move he had was one
he'd hoped very much to avoid.

Quick as he could, he slipped off his boots and stockings and
threw them as far away from the tower, into the gloom, as he could.
The crossbow, cord, and bag followed. Everything but his sword. He
had time for no prayer longer than "God bye me" as he crossed the
last few yards to the tower's base and began to climb it, with only the
miserably dim moonlight to guide his hands and feet to safe purchase
in five hundred years of battle scars.

How many hours had he spent climbing up ratlines and through
rigging, in high seas, under enemy fire? This climb could be no
harder, he said to himself, without conviction. And up he went.

The going was slow. Left hand, left foot; right hand, right foot.
The best holds were the ones gouged out during the revolution. The
older ones—from the French religious wars, Grey presumed; the
Hundred Years' War, perhaps—were more weathered and smoother,
though the old bombardments had done good work knocking out

mortar, which made for an almost ladder-like climb in places, where the grout between the giant stones had been thicker than his fingers and was now gone.

He was already a good twenty feet off the ground when the dead guard's body was discovered. Twenty feet, about one-tenth of the way there. Of course he couldn't see what was happening below him, but there was a good deal of alarmed shouting and confusion. He wondered if his footsteps had left a trail in the gravel. Probably not, and in any case, the way the excitable guards below him seemed to be running about, they'd doubtless scattered it by now.

Forty feet, and his arms were beginning to burn. This was about the height of a frigate's maintop; he wasn't in the shape he ought to be. He wondered how many men were stationed in the fortress. No garrison was billeted here, so it might just be the prison guards. Or perhaps some of the dragoons were still about. That would be more worrying.

There was a slight ledge that ringed the tower a quarter of the way to the top. Grey could rarely remember being gladder at anything than the discovery that he could stand on it for a moment and rest. He took deep, smooth, quiet breaths; he could hear nothing below him for a moment as blood pounded in his ears. As the pounding subsided, he could hear the voices of the guards again, still beneath him, talking lower now, and sounding not so much confused as mystified.

Grey started to climb again. He could see another ledge above him, ringing the tower halfway to the top. He could also see that before he got there, he would cross a line from shadow into pale moonlight, unless the clouds closed ranks again. Would it make the climbing easier or harder? He would see the handholds more clearly, and perhaps the prison guards would be able to see him clearly too.

Sixty feet, and a ring of archers' loops let him climb a few yards using different muscles, a blessed relief. His face was red hot, and Grey stopped for a moment to push each cheek in turn against the cool stone. Stiffen the sinews; summon up the blood; on, on, you noblest English. He was nearly halfway to the top.

He was in the moonlight now, pressing slowly on, hand over hand, foot over foot. And now on the halfway landing, resting, trying not to cough for fear a convulsion would send him backward over the edge. Once more unto the breach. Ninety feet up. A hundred.

How long had he been climbing? Ten minutes? Twenty? An hour? God alone knew.

A hundred and twenty feet. Spots before his eyes. A hundred and forty, and he could start to sense the end above him. Someone had once told him that when he found himself in extremis, the best thing to do was recite poetry. Something from *Hamlet* had been circling round and round in his head: "He is in heaven, send thither to see. If your messenger find him not there, seek him i' the other place yourself."

But he needed something with a blunter rhythm to it. Hand over hand, foot over foot.

Farewell and adieu to you, fair Spanish ladies,
Farewell and adieu to you, ladies of Spain,
For we've received orders to sail back to England;
We hope in a short time to see you again.

Now let every man toss off a full bumper.
Now let every man drink off a full glass,
We'll drink and be jolly and drown melancholy,
And here's to the health of each good-hearted lass.

A chip of stone exploded above him, near his right hand. He pulled the hand away by reflex and almost lost his grip; almost fell. Below him there was shouting. He'd been seen. The guards were trying to shoot him down, and bellowing to each other for better powder; for a rifle; for the keys—the keys to the roof—get to the roof. Get to the roof, one was shouting.

How long does it take a man to run up two hundred feet of stairs?

How long does it take a man to climb thirty feet of sheer stone facing?

212 / J. H. GELERNTER

He was going to find out.

Faster now, faster. Put your back into it. Smartly, smartly. Pull, man—pull for home—pull for England—pull for your life.

Twenty feet left. Then ten. He couldn't feel his fingertips anymore, or his bare toes; all he could do was clamp them down tight and hope they wouldn't slip. Five feet. The crenels were just out of reach. He had a hand on them. Now two. He was pulling himself through the embrasure gap in the battlements. Elbows through. Torso. He tumbled forward onto the roof. Rolled onto his back. Heaved his chest up, trying to get a little breath into it.

Above his head, a key rattled in a lock, and a door flew open. Grey rolled his eyes back and watched, upside down, as a French guard lowered the barrel of his musket till it was in line with Grey's face.

Grey rolled onto his stomach.

"You're under arrest," said the Frenchman, in French.

In English, Grey said the most obscene thing he could think of, and began to climb to his feet.

"You're under arrest," said the Frenchman again; more emphatically this time.

"Your powder pan's open," said Grey. The Frenchman looked at his flintlock. He'd knocked open the frizzen running to the roof. The musket was useless.

He dropped it and grabbed for his sword. Grey's was already drawn, and at the man's neck.

"Where is the Duke of Enghien?" he asked.

"In—I believe in the interrogation cell."

"Where's that?"

"In the king's apartments."

"And where are they?"

"Just below us. Just one level below."

"Hold up your keys."

"I have no keys."

Grey's sword was still at the man's neck; he made a shallow cut in the man's jaw.

"I heard you unlock the door, Mr. Guard. You have two seconds—one—"

The man fumbled at his belt and held up his keys.

"Which one opens the door to the interrogation cell?"

"This," said the guard, selecting one key and holding it up.

"Thank you." Grey was glad he hadn't had to dangle the man over the edge to persuade him. There wasn't time. "Turn around," he said. The guard turned. Grey reached forward and took the ring from his hand. There wasn't time for tying men up either, so Grey crashed his sword hilt down on the back of the guard's neck. The guard crumpled. Grey hoped he was unconscious and not dead, but had neither the energy nor the inclination to check.

In any case: the man had left the door open, which saved Grey some difficulty. It opened from one of the corner turrets and led to a spiral staircase. Grey assumed the staircase led all the way to the ground, or at least the main floor. Either way, the guards who'd stayed at ground level shooting at him were now running up it. That's what it sounded like. The slap of boots on stone echoes a long way.

At the next landing was a heavy wooden door, carved oak and probably beautiful in its heyday. At least three kings had died behind it (Grey presumed; in any case, they'd died in the tower somewhere). Grey slipped the key into the lock and turned it as gently, as quietly as he could. The latch opened smoothly. Clearly this was one part of the fortress that was well looked after.

Grey nearly threw up at what he saw on the door's other side. Louis was hanging from his wrists, which were shackled on a long chain. The chain was strung over something like a meat hook that hung from the ceiling. Probably, long ago, it had taken the place of a chandelier. Louis's toes just scraped the floor; the rest of him had been beaten bloody. A man stood between Louis and the door, with his back to Grey and his fists wrapped in rawhide. He was pounding Louis like a butcher pounds a poor cut of meat.

Grey held down his bile and locked the door behind him, lowering the oak door brace for good measure.

"Ah, Mr. Caffery." Grey turned back from the door. It was Théodore, in riding boots, dragoon-green riding pants, and a collarless white undershirt soaked in Louis's blood. The blood gave some color to his otherwise ashen skin. His features were still sunken and waxy, the way they'd looked at Rotterdam. But clearly Théodore was a strong man who had already recovered much of his strength. It was still less than a month since Geneviève had shot him. Altogether, Faustian might have been the most suitable adjective.

Grey unclipped his over-the-shoulder sword belt, pulled out the sword, and let the belt fall to the floor. "The name's Grey, actually— Thomas Grey. I'm going to kill you now."

"I understand your impulse, Mr. Grey," said Théodore, "your whore having failed to dispatch me on your behalf. But surely you wouldn't kill an unarmed man."

There was a loud knock on the door and an out-of-breath call through it. "Major Théodore: We search for an intruder."

"Would I kill an unarmed man?" said Grey. "A man? No. But clearly you've never been a man."

"Tsk-tsk," clicked Théodore. "So superior. Very well. Here is my throat. Cut away."

Grey scowled at him. "Where is your sword?"

"There," said Théodore, nodding to his left, where a mahogany table had been pushed up against a wall and draped with a jacket, shirt, shako, and sword.

"Send the men outside away."

"I'll have the sword first," said Théodore.

"Have it then," said Grey.

"Your generosity staggers me, sir," said Théodore, sneering, walking over to the table, pulling a saber out of its hilt. He called towards the door:

"Your intruder is here." This in answer to the guards. "But the door is braced." Théodore turned to Grey now, smiling. *"En garde?"*

The men outside began to beat the door inward. Grey wasn't concerned. The brace beam would hold a good long time.

"You know," said Grey, "I don't believe I'm a bloodthirsty man, but I genuinely relish the thought of killing you."

"I'm touched to learn I've moved you so deeply," said Théodore. "To me, though, you will just be another in a long line, and soon forgotten."

With the word "forgotten," he lunged. Grey parried the blow to his left and sliced back to his right. Théodore parried that and cut upward at Grey's chin. Grey leaned back and had to retreat a few steps to regain his balance. Théodore seized the initiative and lunged forward again, thrust to one side, then the other, driving Grey back towards the wall. Finally Grey had to slap Théodore's blade away with the flat of his own and dance off to his left, to keep from being cornered. Théodore scoffed.

"Your swordplay, Mr. Grey, is too much like your chess play. Too aggressive and thoughtless; thinking one move ahead instead of five."

You should try me before I've climbed a sheer mountain, said Grey, in his head. He was too breathless to say it aloud. Théodore lunged a third time, saber before him like a fencing foil, making short cuts back and forth through the air just before Grey's chest. Grey parried cut for cut, and after a few steps giving ground, stood fast, and the two men had a wild, lightning exchange of stabs and slices, press-and-parries, before Théodore again got the upper hand, using a riposte to Grey's ribs to push him off-balance and force him to jump back in another retreat.

And Théodore was charging forward again. Grey lunged forward to meet him, and their two blades slid along each other's lengths, clinching at their hilts. The two men came together, shoulder to shoulder. Grey head-butted Théodore's nose, and broke it. Now it was Théodore retreating, and Grey chuckling.

Théodore sniffed away some blood and wiped his face on his upper arm. He looked over his shoulder at Louis, snorted at Grey, and used his saber to cut a slice in Louis's thigh. Louis, who had seemed to be unconscious—snapped awake and hissed out a moan through clenched teeth.

"A touch, a touch, I do confess," said Théodore, in English, in a mocking theatrical voice.

Grey scowled and attacked, concentrating his anger and disgust in a flurry of advancing stabs; Théodore gave ground, stepped to the side, let Grey lunge past him. Grey half turned and left himself open to riposte from Théodore. Théodore followed the turn and made a cut deep in Grey's shoulder. Grey winced.

"Yes," said Théodore, "your play is weak, and your endgame amateurish." He spit red onto the floor.

"You *severely* overestimate, sir, the offense I'm likely to take at insults to my abilities in chess." Théodore spit blood at him. Grey continued, "At the same time, I would say you underestimate the value of an unexpected attack to throw an opponent off-balance."

Louis had shimmied the chain that bound his hands off the meat hook he'd dangled from, and stalked up behind Théodore. He crossed his hands, looped the chain over Théodore's neck, and throttled him. Théodore gasped for air and thrashed about. Grey could have put him out of his misery, but he felt no sympathy for the man—none at all—and didn't want to rob Louis of his well-earned revenge. It took about two minutes for Théodore to die. Grey used the time to find the keys for Louis's shackles. They were on the table with Théodore's overclothes.

He knelt to unlock the bolts at Louis's wrists.

"How good to see you again, Thomas," said Louis. "You appeared at an advantageous moment."

"I can say the same to you." Grey stood and helped Louis to his feet.

"There seem to be some of my countrymen banging at the door."

Grey had almost put the pounding on the door out of his mind. The heavy oak brace was still in fine fettle, but the two metal fixtures that held it up were starting to bend.

"Yes," said Grey. He took a deep breath and let it out slowly. "Well, give me a few moments' rest first."

"I mean to say, Grey, that there's another way out."

"Ey?"

"The king's apartments always have an escape route."

"Do you speculate, or do you know that?"

"I used to play here as a child. You forget that I'm a prince of the blood."

"You used to play in a prison?"

"Well, not when it was occupied. But we often heard mass at the Sainte-Chapelle."

Grey nodded. "Well, thank God for that. Shall we go?"

"Give me a moment. And I need shoes."

"Yes, so do I, actually," said Grey, looking at his bare feet. "Shall we shoot odds and evens for Théodore's?"

"It's all right, I believe my boots are here somewhere . . . with the rest of my things . . . Ah: yes." Louis opened up a chest, extracted a pair of riding boots from it, along with a coat. "I didn't have much time to dress in Strasbourg. Or I would have brought something more practical." With difficulty he pulled on the boots. Their relative cleanliness stood in stark contrast to his bloodied breeches and cotton shirt. Grey grimaced and pulled off the dead Théodore's boots while Louis pulled on his jacket.

"You know," he said, "your King James the First had a sally tunnel like this one. But when the assassins came for him, it did him no good. Do you know why?"

"James the First died of a stroke, did he not?"

"Ah yes, I mean James the First of Scotland."

"And why didn't his tunnel work?"

"Because it passed through a cellar that he'd had—just weeks earlier—turned into a handball court. His men bricked up the passage to keep balls from rolling down it."

Grey looked at him. "*Come* now."

"On my honor," said Louis.

"Handball," said Grey, shaking his head. "A dangerous game."

Louis smiled, then groaned. He'd just fastened on his sword, and had his hand in a jacket pocket.

"Those bastards," he said, "have broken my pipe. Again!" He held a few pieces of clay on his open palm.

"For the love of God, Louis," said Grey.

"Yes," said Louis. "Come."

He waved Grey towards the bedroom. It was barren; just a bed and a pot. Whatever royal appointments it may once have had had been excised entirely. Grey was not convinced the prison guards would breach the apartment door anytime soon, but to be safe, he closed, locked, and braced the bedroom door as a second line of defense.

"Here," said Louis, pointing to a blind window. "Push."

"Why haven't you used this before now?"

"This is the first time since they took me that I've been unwatched. You see, I have a death sentence, and that seemed to put considerable pressure on Théodore to work quickly. Wanted the names of my men still in France. In fact, the only occasions on which I was out of his company were when Josephine tried to persuade me to come over to the Corsican's side."

"Josephine? Napoleon's Josephine?"

"The same. I've known her since we were children. Our mothers were close. Push! Push!" The two men were giving all they had trying to shift a wall that seemed to Grey utterly solid.

Grey turned and put his back into it. Théodore's boots were big for him, and he wasn't getting the purchase he wanted—

And the wall started to slide. Straight back; not on a hinge. Once it was moving, keeping it moving was less difficult. It came to a decisive stop after a slide of just over two feet. Now, to its right, a passage cut into the thickness of the tower wall was visible.

"Hand me that," said Louis, pointing to a torch in a sconce, then taking a moment to double over and cough blood. Grey retrieved a torch for each of them.

"You better let me go first," said Grey. Louis didn't look as if he would be able to stand under his own power for much longer, and the passage was too narrow for Grey to help him along. If he went first, at least Louis could lean on him.

Louis nodded yes and Grey stepped past him and into the wall passage. It was very steep: a descending stairway that was just wide enough for Grey's shoulders. *Just* wide enough. You could barely have fit a playing card between them and the walls, on either side. "Careful," said Louis, "there's a drop at the end." Grey held the torch forward to try to see what he meant. Ten or so feet ahead, the tunnel ended against a wall, above a hole. Grey walked towards the hole and looked down. There was a drop of about five feet, with a stone step protruding from the far wall halfway to the bottom. Of course, Grey realized, there's no room for a turn—the passage doubles back on itself. Grey stepped down through the opening, then reached up to help Louis down. Ducking under the last step of the level above, Grey continued down the very narrow stairway, feeling something like a ball rolling down a bagatelle timer. There was another drop at the far end, and the process was reversed. Back and forth, back and forth, through clammy, fetid air that threatened to suffocate the torches. The descent seemed endless. And seemed to take them far deeper than the tower's close. Grey supposed they must be heading down through the foundations, through the stone island. In fact, the walls had changed—the stones were larger and rougher-hewn. And still the passage went on, deeper and deeper.

"Where does this come out?" said Grey, as he helped Louis down another level. It's hard to judge colors in torchlight, but Louis looked positively deathly. A weird echo of Théodore on the Rotterdam docks.

"In the forest," said Louis. His voice scratched; Grey wondered when he'd last had a drink. "To the west."

"Good," said Grey. "I left some things there. Water, food. A horse."

"Good," said Louis.

Another two levels down, and then, where Grey expected another drop, the stair stopped at a landing and took a sharp turn to the right. Grey followed the turn and stepped into a tiny room, very rough-hewn, cut not out of masonry, but from bedrock. A shallow bench—no deeper than a misericord—had been carved into the wall on either side.

"Let's rest a minute," said Grey, sitting on the left. Louis sat opposite him.

For a moment they looked at each other silently.

"For the love of God, man, stop looking at me like a mother hen. I'm fine."

Grey nodded.

"Under the circumstances, you should be looking at me with an expression that says, 'How marvelously well he's holding up; I am deeply impressed.'"

Grey snorted. "My face is not that articulate."

"No, of course not," said Louis. "You're English. It's a marvel you can manage any expression at all. Let us go." He waved for Grey to stand, but didn't seem to have the energy yet to stand himself.

"Perhaps you'd better go first, from here forward. I assume we'll be going up now, and I may have to catch you in case you crumble like the crust of a burned cream."

"You'll have to go first, to release the hatch at the far end. God knows how many years of soil will have built up atop it—I haven't passed through for at least twenty, and I can't imagine who else would have. Not since Louis Joseph's death, Louis Charles's growing up."

"Let's hope it's not too much to lift," said Grey, whose every fiber ached.

"No, the hatch opens down, so the earth falls inward."

"Well thought out," said Grey.

"Yes," said Louis.

"Very good," said Grey. "Shall we go?"

"One moment more," said Louis. "The fact is, I don't know how much further I'll make it."

"Nonsense," said Grey. Louis waved for him to be quiet.

"I've learned something that must get back to London, with or without me. When Josephine visited, she offered me a novel dukedom, in a new French aristocracy. I'm a prince of the blood, you see, a Bourbon, and it would wed the old and the new together. Legitimacy for the court of Boney."

"We've heard murmurs of this. That the Republic is to become an empire."

Louis nodded. "I refused her, of course. But the offer, you see, the offer was rather extensive. In the new empire, I will be Duke of Enghien, Courland, Livonia, Estonia. Duke of the Baltic."

Grey leaned forward. "The Baltic? You mean . . ." His mind was racing.

"Napoleon plans to move east," said Louis.

"It's the lumber," said Grey. "Bonaparte needs Russian lumber. We intercepted a message to that effect . . . Leclerc decoded it. He says the Mediterranean forests aren't producing what Paris expected."

"Alexander needs to know. My dear cousin the czar."

"I can't imagine he'll believe it if it's not in your own hand," said Grey.

Louis shook his head. "When you give him the message, tell him I asked that he look after Charlotte."

"Charlotte?"

"My wife."

Grey exhaled slowly.

"Louis," said Grey, "I had no idea . . . I was certain—I mean to say, I was told you were a bachelor."

"Yes," said Louis. "No one knows, excepting Alexander, and the priest who married us. No one. Charlotte is the niece of the Cardinal de Rohan. She has put on a religious disposition, living, to the eyes of Alexander's court, a monastic life at the Winter Palace. You see, if I produce an heir . . . Well, it is better that Napoleon not know. Tell Alexander that her name is my wax and password. Duchesse Charlotte Louise Dorothée d'Enghien, *natale de* Rohan."

Grey nodded.

"Very well, Louis. But you will tell him yourself."

"I hope I will," said Louis. "But let us go." He lifted himself to his feet. "After you."

Grey nodded again, stood, and started off down the tunnel. No more stairs; just a gradual incline carrying them up towards ground level.

They walked on a long way. Grey hadn't bothered to count his steps, but he felt they must have passed half a mile. The torches had little air to keep them burning, and were growing dimmer. They cast very little light ahead, so the end of the tunnel arrived abruptly.

"Here," said Grey, passing his torch back for Louis to hold. Grey looked at the trapdoor in the ceiling. It was held up by a half dozen crossbeams that had bowed over years of holding up the earth above. They would be under a great deal of tension, but they were meant to be knocked away, like the posts used to hold a ship up in the yard, which made the prospect of getting them out less daunting. Grey just hoped they weren't holding back an avalanche.

Using the hilt of his sword, he went to work banging the first brace out. The wood was soft and partly rotten at each end, where it was slotted into the tops of the stone walls. It gave way easily enough. Grey moved from the first beam to the last, to work inward from the edges. Two knocked out. Three. Four. The middle beams were bowing a great deal now. Grey knocked the fifth out, and the sixth snapped. Grey jumped back, the door flew open, and a single giant clod of dirt hung halfway through the opening. Grey stood at sword's length and gave it a start; down it came, and a flood of fresh air after it.

"Well done," said Louis, as each man filled his lungs. Grey slid his sword back into the scabbard on his back, stepped onto the dirt, and looked up. He could see tree limbs overhead, waving slowly against a background of stars.

"Come on," said Grey, putting his back to the wall and offering Louis his interlocked fingers. He boosted Louis out and climbed after him. On solid ground again—rather than above or below it—he gave himself one long moment, on his haunches, to enjoy the tidings of deliverance. A few deep breaths and he was up, leaning on a tree and getting his bearings. They were several hundred yards outside the moat—about as far away as he'd been when he'd emptied the bag and tied up the horse, but perhaps a quarter mile further south.

"That way," he said, making his best guess and pointing. The two men went quietly, not talking, not knowing if they had gotten away cleanly or were being pursued. At least Grey could say that if they'd been followed down the tunnel, their pursuers were far enough behind that he'd heard no hint of them. If, however, they'd followed Grey's trail back across the moat to his point of departure . . .

Louis put a hand out and stopped Grey, and pointed to their left. Just four or five paces away, two dragoons were prodding at the pile of things Grey had disgorged from his bag. As Louis saw them, one of the horses—either the dragoons' or Grey's—saw him, and Grey, and whinnied.

There was a clatter as all four men drew their swords and laid into each other. And just as quickly, they were inside the useful range of swords, and bashing with hilts, locking arms, kicking legs, wrestling one another to the ground. Two pair of men locked in a life-and-death struggle rolled for a few moments around the roots and leaves of the forest of Vincennes. Grey's forearm took a blow meant for his skull and followed it with a hook across the dragoon's face; he rolled the man onto his back and then bludgeoned him to death with his sword pommel.

A foot away, Louis was underneath the other dragoon—got leverage with a foot and threw the man backward over his head. The dragoon, Louis, and Grey were all up again at the same moment. Instead of reentering the fray, the dragoon retreated two steps, feeling along his belt, finding a pistol, and firing it into Louis's stomach. Louis staggered backward and fell; Grey ran the dragoon through, made sure of him, and was at Louis's side, trying to stop the bleeding.

"Grey," said Louis indulgently. "Grey, stop it, stop it. It's no good. That was the final blow."

"It looks like a flesh wound, you'll be fine."

Louis laughed. "It is not a flesh wound, I'm afraid." He was right. Grey could smell bile. "There's something more at stake, Thomas. They'll have heard the shot. There's no time. Get my message to Alexander; tell him Bonaparte's eye is on Russia. Tell him to look after Charlotte."

"I will," said Grey. He had a hand on Louis's shoulder. It was very cold.

"And, if you would, let my mother know . . . Well, tell her that I died well and without regrets. Take this." He pressed the broken pieces of his clay pipe into Grey's hand. "Now bring me these bastards' carbines. They'll have heard the shot. I'll keep their attention while you get away."

Grey hesitated. Louis snapped at him.

"*Now*, damn you, simpering idiot, or do you want this . . ." He drew in breath through gritted teeth. "All this fun to be wasted." He snorted, and Grey did as he asked, placing the dragoons' rifles, powder, and shot at Louis's elbow. Louis held a hand out for Grey to shake. "Here we are again," he said. "We won't be meeting in Paris, I'm afraid. But we'll meet at Philippi."

Grey took Louis's hand. "Ay, at Philippi."

"You remember her name?"

"Charlotte Louise Dorothée d'Enghien. De Rohan."

"Good. Now go." Grey nodded and turned. The horse he'd purloined—Roland—was tied up close at hand. As Grey climbed into the saddle, he heard Louis cocking flintlocks.

As he rode away, he heard the first of them fire.

28

Cher Thomas,

I am deeply sensible of the gratitude I owe you for your service and friendship to my son, to my dearest Louis, even if I can't now express it as it should be expressed, while my heart is still so full—so heavy. It was kind of you to write to me, to tell me of the quality of his final days and hours. When I can be comforted, it will be a comfort to know that I was with him then, in his thoughts, and that you were with him, in yourself. You say that he will not have died in vain, and I pray that you are right.

> *Come and find me in happier times,*
> *Until then, your*
> *Bathilde*

IN LONDON, the last piece to a puzzle laid out half a year earlier, by the bizarre perfidy of a blockade-runner, was finally fitted into place. A Baltic duchy; Baltic timber; Napoleon's navy, his army, and his plans for empire. The examinations of Grey were extensive, and conducted— once Sir Edward was satisfied—by the Admiralty Board, then the army at the Horse Guards, and finally the staffs of several concerned ministers, all of whom were careful to emphasize the extent of Grey's failure in not delivering the Duke of Enghien alive. Of Louis Antoine's wife, Grey told only Sir Edward and Willys, entrusting to them the responsibility of delivering Louis's complete message, and its key, to Czar Alexander. Grey had requested he be allowed to deliver the message himself, out of respect for Louis; this would allow him also to check personally on Charlotte. Sir Edward agreed this would be best, but was told firmly by the various responsible ministers and diplomats that it was out of the question. It was only when Grey threatened to make a private trip to the Winter Palace that he was allowed even to include a private letter to Charlotte, telling her in the fullest detail of Louis's efforts to protect her, and Grey's own sense of responsibility in that regard; putting himself at her disposal, and apologizing for his inability to see Louis safely through.

Through Sir Edward, Grey had the word of the ambassador, Lord Granville Leveson-Gower, that the letter would be delivered. Grey knew Lord Granville (as he was styled, for reasons not altogether clear to Grey). He knew Granville well enough to dislike him, considerably—to the full extent he would dislike any man whose singular achievement was being simultaneously a rake and a bore. He would have preferred the word of a better man, but as most dandies of the diplomatic corps maintained an instinctual fear of Sir Edward, Grey was reasonably confident the letter would reach its object.

Grey was accustomed to being excluded from the final stages of his work—the point at which it reached the level of politics. He didn't mind especially, as a rule, but on this occasion it left him with a strange, hollow feeling. As if he'd left his work undone in France and undone in England as well. Willys had detected this in him, and bucked him up once or twice, to the effect that Grey's discovery of the French need for timber and their designs on the Baltic would probably prove to be the most important work of his life. Where Britain had stood alone facing invasion, a new coalition would be formed against Bonaparte, to put a decisive, emphatic end to a decade of French wars. No treaty had yet been signed, but already the young czar had made clear to the British and to the continent that the murder of the Duke of Enghien would not go unanswered. The Holy Roman Emperor was expected to do as the czar did, and public sentiment was much on their side, despite the public possessing few of the facts. Stories of Louis Antoine's death had spread like rabbits across Europe, and had acquired certain touches of imagination. The most popular version had Louis and Napoleon in love with the same woman; had Napoleon, while courting her, fall into an epileptic fit and faint dead away; had Louis arrive at this moment to attempt his own seduction, and finding the tyrant of France defenseless, had Louis refusing to deliver a killing blow, as his honor would not permit it. Napoleon, emasculated by this, had kidnapped Louis as revenge.

The story's end, though, was quite accurate, as far as Grey had been able to confirm it. Louis had survived long enough to be dragged back to the moat of the Vincennes fortress, where he'd been stood next to the fresh grave and shot. His final sentiments (which seemed not to fit perfectly with the popular seduction-epilepsy story) were that he freely, proudly admitted fighting with the British, and against the revolutionary government. He expressed no regrets, but observed that his time in German exile had sated his love of sport: the shooting in particular had been superb.

It had taken no time at all for him to become a popular hero. Now rumor had it that Sweden's King Gustav IV had adopted Louis's dog. Even Geneviève Leclerc had been swayed. She now freely admitted that Napoleon was an enemy of liberalism who must be defeated if the revolution were ever to succeed.

What mattered, though, was this: The czar—perhaps the Holy Roman Kaiser too, and Sweden's Gustav—was convinced that Napoleon had no intention of respecting the peace. After a year of waiting every day for a French fleet to make a beachhead at Dover, Napoleon's invasion force—his "Army of England"—would be turned east, as the east began to assemble an Army of France. Britain's neck was off the chopping block. And in no small part, this had been effected by Thomas Grey. This is what Willys told him, anyhow. But Grey couldn't permit himself to agree.

They were standing in the courtyard of the Old Admiralty Building. Willys was waiting for Sir Edward, and Grey was just waiting. He had an appointment he wasn't anxious to get to, and wasn't certain he would keep.

"Any progress on the stone?" said Willys, after a long silence.

"Which stone?" said Grey.

"The Rosetta stone," said Willys. Grey looked at him acidly.

"Do you know the Forest of Tronçais?" asked Sir Edward Banks, who had emerged from Admiralty House and was walking towards his carriage. When hurried, which he was generally, Banks preferred to walk to the carriage in its stable stall rather than wait while it was retrieved. Grey and Willys fell into step beside him. "I'm asking you, Grey," he said.

"The Forest of Tronçais? It's in the Auvergne, I believe. Quite large. And quite high, on a plateau of the Central Massif."

"Yes," said Banks. "But it's not a natural forest, Grey—it was planned and planted. By Jean-Baptiste Colbert, one of the Sun King's ministers. His idea was that it would guarantee great oaks for the French navy, forever. This was in 1670. Colbert had thousands of oaks sown, carefully spaced and interspersed with minor flora in a most scientific manner, to ensure the oaks would grow up straight and true."

Banks's carriage had rolled out to meet him halfway; he was climbing aboard, and Willys with him.

Grey asked the obvious question. "And what happened to them, sir? This surfeit of good French trees."

"They're still there," said Banks. "I've just had a letter from a botanist at the Royal Society. He estimates they should be mature and ready for harvesting in no less than forty years. So let's each of us do his utmost to have the war won by then."

Banks was sitting in the carriage but hadn't closed his door. He looked down at Grey.

"You took us a long way in that direction, Tom—towards victory—in these last few months. No man could have done more. And I am in your debt." This rare moment of sentiment was ended quickly by Banks knocking on the carriage roof with his stick (not a cane; he never used it to walk, but Grey suspected it occasionally served as a bludgeon), and away the carriage rolled.

Grey continued on to the stables, where his horse Casca was waiting. He was expected, before long, at the new London estate of Joseph Leclerc—Leclerc now continuing his slow but encouraging recovery in more comfortable surroundings. The hostess, of course, would be Mademoiselle Leclerc, who wished to thank all those concerned with her father's delivery. Sir Edward and Willys were to be guests as well; as were a number of government functionaries with whom Grey was slightly acquainted. Perhaps it was the prospect of this *soirée intime* that had Grey out of sorts. Maybe it was dwelling on the Leclercs' escape from France: in its way, a succession of failures. Maybe it was an inevitable discussion of Louis that Grey was not prepared to endure. Possibly Grey was out of sorts because of an ambivalence towards Geneviève. Or because of the ambivalence he felt in her towards him, now that she was the newest bauble of London society, coveted by every host and hostess. Of course, she owed him nothing (he kept telling himself).

Grey had planned to ride to Buttle's for a drink, a bath, and suitable attire before going on to Petty Versailles, or Frog House, or whatever the Leclercs were calling their home. But he found himself riding past Buttle's, continuing past the Leclercs', out of town and into the countryside, east, towards Sheerness, on the road to Canterbury. Towards his own home.

He watered Casca—not because the horse needed to stop, but because Grey did—at a stable perhaps two-thirds of the way from London to Marsh Downs. He gave the groom a tanner to give Casca dinner, and then walked up the road to a public house called The Try Pot.

Inside were a dozen or so sailors and whalers—not a packing, but a good house, and all in good voice with the owner, Mr. Hubble, as he led them in "Roast Beef of Old England." His daughter, the young widow Mrs. Boothe, was behind the bar, making four-water grog and looking as self-possessed but unprepossessing as Grey remembered. He leaned on her counter and she came over to him, recognizing him at once.

"Why, Mr. Grey, sir, what can I do for you?"

"Grog, I think," he said, pointing to her work. She smiled and ladled him a cup. He put money on the bar but she waved him away.

"Oh, by no means, Mr. Grey; no charge."

Grey smiled and nodded, and drank. He finished the cup and asked for another. Mrs. Boothe brought it, the seamen struck up a thumping "Spanish Ladies," and Grey had almost to shout to make himself heard.

"How are your children, Mrs. Boothe?" he said, taking a sip of his second rum and water.

"Very well, thank you, Mr. Grey. Upstairs now, in fact, and sleeping—if they haven't chosen tonight to mutiny."

"I'm surprised they can sleep through this," said Grey, over the bellowed song, thinking of nights at sea when everyone before the mast had sung and stamped into the early morning. It had never kept him up, of course, but he was to the manner born.

"Oh no, sir," said Mrs. Boothe, "they can sleep through anything. They're good girls."

Grey nodded and sipped his rum. After a few sips more, he caught Angela Boothe's eye. She refilled his cup, and he asked her:

"Mrs. Boothe, do you play chess?"

The End

Historical Note

THERE'S A FAMOUS ANECDOTE about Benjamin Franklin—that during his time as ambassador to Paris, during the American Revolution but before the French, he played a game with a Frenchman, and instead of checkmating the Frenchman's king, he captured it. The French-man said, "In France, we do not take kings so," and Franklin said, "We do in America." The interesting thing is, this is not just a story; it happened, and was recorded in Thomas Jefferson's diary. What's more interesting is that the Frenchman in the story was none other than Bathilde d'Orléans, Countess of Bourbon and mother of Louis Antoine. And the story has a coda—Bathilde asked a chess kibitzer who "was overlooking the game, in silence," why he had nothing to say to Franklin's witticism. The explanation of the kibitzer, a Count Falkenstein, was that he was "a king by trade": in fact, explains Jefferson, this was "the emperor Joseph II then at Paris, incognito." This is the same Holy Roman Emperor Joseph referred to in the early chapters of this book: the uncle and predecessor of the chess tournament's host, Emperor Francis II. Sometimes, when there's really good chess to be seen, an emperor has to dust off his spectator disguise.

It should be noted that Franklin was a very good chess player, and that Jefferson said, of Bathilde, that "being a chess player of about his force, they very generally played together." The stuff about her beauty is factual too.

I'm afraid the Frankfurt chess tournament, though, is fictional. But Philidor's total dominance of chess and the vacuum he left in dying, his games with George Atwood at Parsloe's, and Johann Baptist Allgaier's emergence as his eventual successor are all factual. Allgaier would go on to teach chess to Emperor Francis's children, and it's considered likely that it was Allgaier who was hidden inside the "Mechanical Turk," controlling it, when it beat Napoleon in 1809. The calculations referred to by Atwood, of the number of possible chess games after X moves, were done by American mathematician George Shannon, who lived in the twentieth century rather than the nineteenth.

The importance of timber to the French, the English, and to everyone else involved in the Napoleonic Wars is quite factual, as is the question of American versus Baltic timber. Shortly after the events of the novel, Parliament would put a 275 percent tariff on Baltic wood imports, to try to wean British shipbuilders off it and get them to buy North American instead. But the specific plot events related to controlling the trade are fictional. Other than the planting of the Forest of Tronçais, whose trees finally matured as the age of sail died; the historian Fernand Braudel said that in planting it, "Colbert had thought of everything except the steamship." As for the Baltic duchy, it's fictional as well, but the fact is, Napoleon loved creating new duchies and bribing people with them. The imagined Duchy of Livonia et al. would have abutted the northern border of the real Duchy of Warsaw, which Napoleon would establish in 1809.

The false surrender at the story's opening is not based on any specific incident, but is culled from cases of French ships hauling down their colors and then, when the wind changed, literally or metaphorically, raising them again, as well as cases of surrendered French sailors murdering prize crews and retaking their ships. However, this sort of behavior was very rare, and as ubiquitously condemned by French mariners as by English. I don't want to give the impression that the Napoleonic French were, like some belligerents, prone to perfidy. They were not.

A few other details that I think are worth mentioning. The style of fighting known as savate, or the Marseille game, was real. In fact it's still real; it's not one of the more popular martial arts, but there are occasional tournaments. Sock Spiller, the head waiter of the real-life chess den Old Slaughter's Coffee House, was its real head waiter, famous for his dry wit, and for occasionally spilling drinks on people, leading eventually to the nickname "Punch Spiller." The Palais Thurn und Taxis is a real place; it was destroyed during the Second World War, but rebuilt using (I believe) the original designs. The family Thurn und Taxis really were the hereditary postmasters of the Holy Roman Empire. The Château de Vincennes is a real place and still there in the original; the description of its various fortifications is accurate, and most of them are still there, though the Nazis did their best to blow them up on their way out of Paris. The escape tunnel doesn't—so far as I know—actually exist, though it's based on any number of real-life counterparts. And the story of the handball-related death of Scotland's King James I is factual. As is the adoption by King Gustav of Louis Antoine's dog. The Captain Austen mentioned towards the beginning of the book, in charge of the anti-invasion defense of part of the coast of Kent, is a real man: Captain Francis Austen, who—by happy coincidence—was an older brother of Jane Austen. Who, of course, is the progenitor, broadly speaking, of all modern novels, and narrowly speaking, of all novels about English life circa 1800, and even more narrowly speaking, ultimately, of this novel.

Finally—that Louis Antoine was working with the British secret service; his being kidnapped at his home in the German states by Napoleon's dragoons; his summary conviction for treason, for covertly bearing arms against revolutionary France, for assisting and being assisted by Great Britain; his refusal to deny it and his execution beside his open grave in the moat of the Château de Vincennes are all factual. The part of the story involving the Leclercs and Grey is not, but Louis Antoine's death really was the catalyst for the War of the Third Coalition. Word of his murder, on Napoleon's orders, made him a popular hero throughout Europe, and caused the scales to fall from the eyes of many Bonapartists. Louis Antoine's death is the subject of discussion in the first scene of *War and Peace*, at Anna Pavlovna Scherer's party. In Constance Garnett's translation ("his" supporters being Napoleon's):

> "Since the murder of the duc d'Enghien, even his warmest partisans have ceased to regard him as a hero. If indeed some people made a hero of him," said the vicomte addressing Anna Pavlovna, "since the duc's assassination there has been a martyr more in heaven, and a hero less on earth."
>
> Anna Pavlovna and the rest of the company hardly had time to smile their appreciation of the vicomte's words, when Pierre again broke into the conversation, and though Anna Pavlovna had a foreboding he would say something inappropriate, this time she was unable to stop him.
>
> "The execution of the duc d'Enghien," said Monsieur Pierre, "was a political necessity, and I consider it a proof of greatness of soul that Napoleon did not hesitate to take the whole responsibility of it upon himself."
>
> "*Dieu! Mon Dieu!*" moaned Anna Pavlovna, in a terrified whisper.
>
> "What, Monsieur Pierre! You think assassination is greatness of soul?"

The famous quote, attributed to Talleyrand, summed up Louis Antoine's execution this way: "It was worse than a crime—it was a blunder."

Chess Note

ALL THE CHESS GAMES described in the book are real games of note. Grey's game against Sir Arnold was actually played by Karl Mayet (white) against Adolf Anderssen, in 1851. The one game between Grey and Atwood that's given in detail was played in 1911; Muhlock (white; no first name) vs. Borislav Kostic. The game between Grey and the chess shark was played in 1950 by Heinrich Lohmann and Rudolf Teschner. Grey's game against the Pomeranian was played in 1895: Andrey Dadian vs. Doubrava. Grey's very long game with Théodore was played in 1905, by Alfred Ernhardt Post and Aron Nimzowitsch. His game against Philo Parker was played by V. M. Manko and Jankowitz.

The championship game is the legendary Fischer–Spassky game 6.

Hymn Note

T HE TEXT OF "Jesu, Joy of Man's Desiring" isn't strictly
authentic, because there were no standard English lyrics for
Bach's "Herz und Mund und Tat und Leben" until the British poet laureate Robert Bridges wrote his around 1904. Instead I
(mostly) used parts of real eighteenth-century hymns, written by
Charles Wesley, adjusted and augmented to fit the music.

Acknowledgments

THERE ARE about ten thousand things that have to be done between a writer writing a book and that book appearing in stores. A lot of those things happen after the complete text, including the acknowledgments, have been finalized, which means I'm writing this partly blind, unable to thank by name a lot of people whom I'll want to thank when, a long time after I write this, the book is actually published. ("How long?" you might ask; *Captain Grey's Gambit* is a sequel to my first book, *Hold Fast*; I'm writing this exactly one week before *Hold Fast* is published.) So in addition to the specific thank-yous below, I want to say thanks to everyone at W. W. Norton and Norton's partners who got (will get) this book into its final form.

Now, specifically, I'd like to thank everyone at Norton who decided to publish this book. Even for better writers than I am, there's no way to fully express the gratitude you feel to the people who make you a real-life novelist.

Even more specifically, I want to thank my editor Starling Lawrence, who is quite simply the best editor in publishing, and the doughtiest champion an unknown writer could ever have.

Thanks to my magnificent agent, Warren Frazier, without whom I wouldn't be thanking anyone, because I'd still be looking for an agent, and probably trying to sell a kidney or my bone marrow.

Thanks to the invaluable Nneoma Amadi-Obi, who was my direct contact with Norton, and who held my hand through the publishing process from start to finish.

Thanks to the splendid team of project editors Rebecca Homiski and Don Rifkin and copy editor Amy Robbins, who not only made the book better, but never once made fun of my extremely high typo propensity.

And thanks to the splendid production team, who will have taken the book's text over the sellable-novel finish line: production manager Anna Oler; Elisabeth Kerr, who's working on the audiobook; Kyle Radler and Meredith McGinnis, who I think will be working on publicity and marketing—anyway, they worked on it for *Hold Fast*, so at the very least, thanks to both of them for that!

Thanks to all of my friends, who provided advice and moral support, and particular thanks to the ones I made play hours and hours of chess with me. Even more particular thanks to the ones who let me win.

And thanks to my mother and father, both for having been splendid parents and for reading and proofreading *CGG* before I sent it to my agent. Can't imagine where I'd be without them.

Last, I'd like to thank my brother, who was the first person to read and mark up the book, who provided invaluable advice on it, and whom I'm thanking last because I thanked him first last time, and I don't want the literally several people who read these acknowledgments to think they're too derivative of my earlier work.